THE ANCIENT FIRE

THE TRIPLE GODDESS

BOOK ONE

ELLEN READ

Serenade Publishing

Serenade Publishing

www.serenadepublishing.com

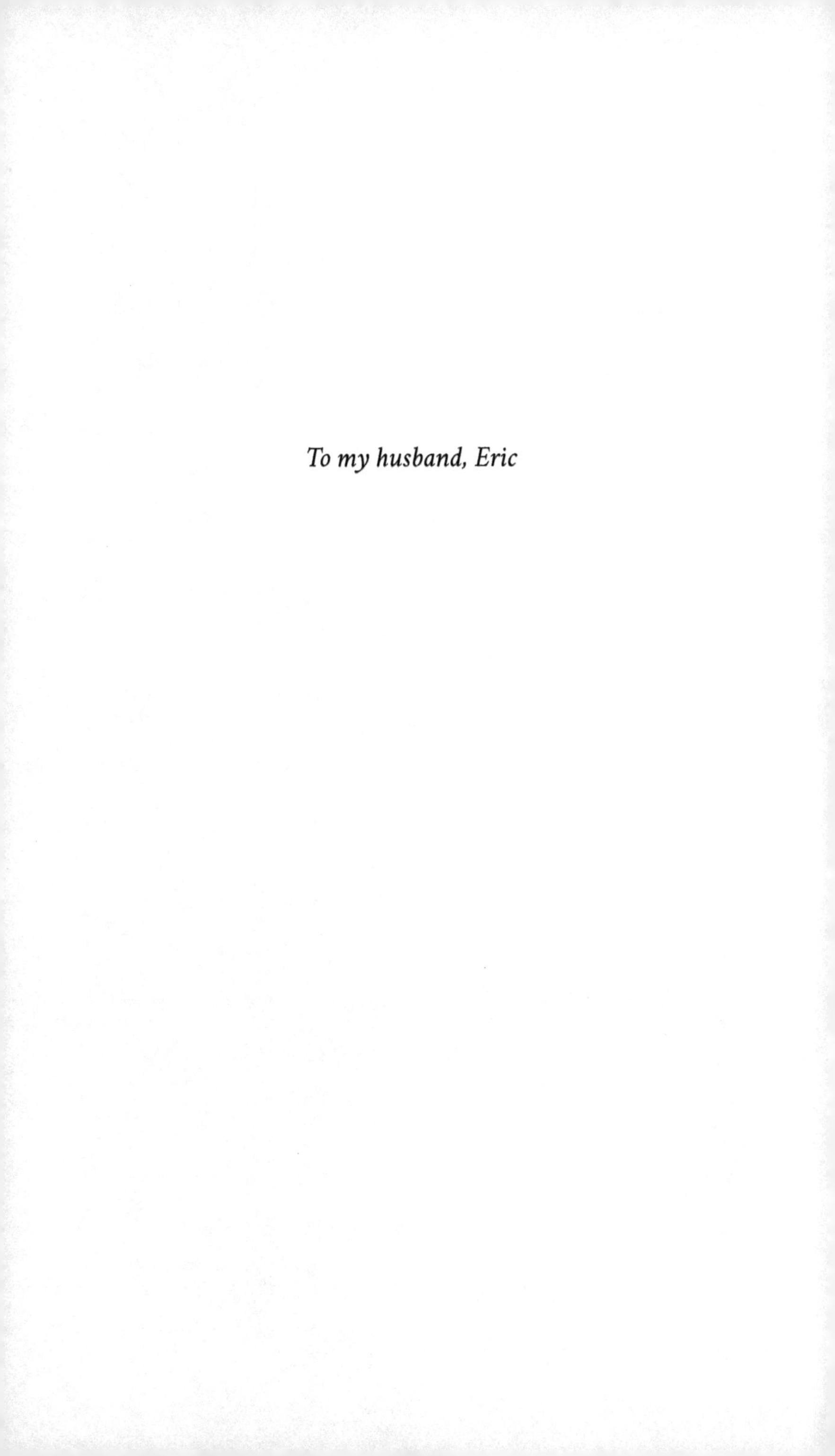

To my husband, Eric

Chapter One

THE ENCHANTMENT PROTECTED her and imprisoned her.

Bree accepted her life… to some extent. Áine, her aunt, told her they must endure their quiet existence in their cave home. They had each other. They had their books to read and study. Bree really only lived when she had her head buried in a book. She enjoyed learning of legends and myths of the Tuatha Dé Danann, the ancient race from whom she and Áine were descended. Her favourite books recounted their stories, their tales of heroism, how they came to this land from places far away in worlds that no longer existed.

'The Tuatha Dé Danann are a proud race,' Áine told her.

'Why did they leave their world?' Bree remembered asking when she was quite young.

'The Tuatha Dé Danann had to leave. Our civilisation was imploding. We couldn't grow any more. Our lands couldn't sustain our numbers. Tuatha Dé Danann are immortal. Hence the population was forever expanding.'

'So they came to this land?'

'Three groups of Tuatha Dé Danann set out to find new realms. We came here. Another group went to a Gaelic land on Earth, while a third group…'

Bree took her aunt's hands, sensing that all hadn't gone well.

Áine continued, 'We've received no word from the third group.'

'Did they go to Earth?'

'No, that was the purpose of the three groups. We all went to different lands to start new lives.'

'How do you know these things when they went to faraway places? Have they sent messengers?'

Áine smiled and brushed Bree's red hair off her face. 'We use telepathy, so we can communicate.'

Bree thought for a moment and then asked, 'Can you read my mind?'

'No, macushla, my darling, we must use it only for special reasons or in dire situations.'

'Our group of Tuatha Dé Danann brought magic with them when they came to this realm, and fairies too, didn't they?' Bree asked, her voice rising. 'And centaurs and other magical beings.'

Áine laughed at her niece's enthusiasm. 'Yes, but remember, not all creatures that inhabit this land are friendly or… good.'

When Áine's tone dropped, Bree stared at her aunt, and asked, 'Have we been bad?'

Áine smiled. 'No, we haven't been bad.'

'Why must we stay here? Locked in this house, this

cave? I want to see the creatures I've read about. I want to see our people.'

'One day,' Áine told her.

Áine always said *one day* but *one day* never came. Bree had been waiting for eighteen years and the day had never arrived. She wanted to see all the things she'd read about and that Áine had taught her. Áine drew them at times. Bree could never have imagined them without Áine's stories and sketches breathing life into them. Centaurs, oak trees, fairies, other young women, even men of her age. Sometimes she wondered about the men even more than she did about magic.

'Men seemed to be a strange breed,' Bree said. 'In the stories they are always boasting and going around fighting or killing foes.' They piqued her interest, especially one or two of the heroes depicted in her books, as they stood tall and broad shouldered.

'Some illustrations showed men fighting giants. Giants, of all things! And they won. How could that be? Men must be very strong,' Bree said.

'They are indeed.'

'Would I be strong enough to fight giants?' Her muscles were practically non-existent.

'I don't think you could fight a giant, macushla.'

'How does a bird fly?' Bree was fascinated by birds. How could they spread their wings and fly through the air? 'Why don't they fall to the ground?'

Every time Bree asked questions, Áine would stop the stories. Shut them down and pack them away. Why didn't her aunt want her to know more? Bree didn't believe that they'd ever leave this cave.

Bree longed to see the sun, to feel its warmth on her skin. She wanted to see the moon's silvery beams. The stars. The sky, sometimes blue, sometimes black. All she saw of them existed in her books. Just as she existed in her books. She had no other life than wondrous stories and illustrations depicted on parchment, and her small life, confined to the earthen walls of the cave she shared with her aunt.

She thought of the day that Áine told her of the enchantment.

They were sitting in their small living room. All of the cave's rooms were small, all with earthen walls, russet in colour, similar to her hair. From the parlour, Bree could see their kitchen—the largest of their small rooms—where they sat at a table with two chairs to eat their meals. All of their food came from a large caldron. When younger, Bree thought the cauldron magical… and it was, because how could Áine extract bread and cow's milk from the same bowl, and then later in the day, take roast chicken and potatoes from it to lay on the table. The bowl was never empty, nor was it ever full.

Bree realised that, although her mind was always looking for answers, she had grown up to accept her life and the manner in which she lived it. She always remembered that she was only seven years old when Áine explained why they lived as they did.

That day, her aunt sat down next to her. Áine had pushed back her red hair from her shoulders. Bree always wore her long, thick hair in braids, but strands escaped, to Áine's endless frustration. 'It's time I explain why we live here together, macushla.'

Bree widened her eyes to stare at her aunt.

Áine took her hand. 'We have been entrusted with an important task and because of this, an enchantment has been placed on us.'

'An enchantment?' Bree clapped her hands. This sounded like a good story.

'We must take care of the ancient flame. It came to this land with our ancestors, the Tuatha Dé Danann. It is our duty to protect it.'

'You mean the flame in the small cauldron?' Bree asked. 'Why?'

'It's a sacred duty.'

Bree crinkled her nose. 'Are we the only Tuatha Dé Danann left?'

Áine squeezed her hand. 'No, macushla.'

Bree saw the tears in her aunt's eyes. She jumped down from her chair and climbed up on Áine's lap. 'Then why? Why can't the other Tuatha Dé Danann take care of it?'

'Because it's special and safer here with us.'

'Is that why we live in this cave, without any windows?' Áine had explained that windows were openings in walls to allow light in. Apparently, one could see out to the surroundings countryside, too. It was difficult for Bree to imagine.

'It is, macushla.'

Bree fidgeted. 'Why do we have an enchantment on us?'

'To keep us safe… and to keep the flame safe.'

'How long do we have to stay here?'

Áine sighed. 'I'm not certain.'

'How long must we stay here?' Bree asked her aunt. She was eighteen and she'd never left the cave. Sometimes, she felt a restlessness quiver through her body. She wanted to ride and hunt and throw a spear, to be like one of the heroes in her books… although they all seemed to be men.

'Why aren't the women heroes?' Bree asked.

'Some women are heroes,' Áine said.

'Do women ride and hunt?'

'Yes, my darling.'

Bree knew her aunt tired of her endless questions. She sighed and went into the small room where the fire burned in a small cauldron that rested on a pedestal. Every day, she made certain the fire burned. She cleaned the outside of the cauldron and watched the flames flare. They fascinated her as they sparked and jumped. She'd never had to restart the fire. It never burned down.

'It must always stay alight,' Áine sometimes told her, her eyes wide, as if she saw something terrifying that Bree could never see. 'We must protect the flame.'

One day, Áine had grasped her hands. 'If anything happens, no matter what… remember to protect the ancient fire.'

'I will,' Bree promised. Although she wasn't certain what she'd promised. What could happen? How could she protect it?

On many occasions she wondered why the ancient fire had to be protected. After all, if it remained precious to the Tuatha Dé Danann, why did they hide it? If they needed it for warmth or food, it wouldn't do them any good hidden away with an eighteen-year-old and her aunt. Yet they, along with the fire, had an enchantment placed on them, keeping them safe. From what? That's what Bree wanted to know. From what? Nothing had ever happened to threaten them. If anyone did attack the cave, she would protect the flame, but she would also chase them away. She'd fight them. They had knives and she could always hit them over the head with a basin.

Her fantasy remained dancing before her eyes as she helped her aunt prepare their evening meal and wash their dishes. Once, when she spun around with a knife in her hands, her aunt looked at her with a strange expression on her face.

'What are you doing, macushla ?'

'Nothing.' Bree shrugged.

Later, when she lay back on her cot, the story continued. As the great hero of her people, she was welcomed and applauded throughout the land. She banished the giants and promoted a few young men in their leather armour to be her personal bodyguard. Not that she needed a bodyguard. After all, she had vanquished their assailants, but the young men were pleasant to the eye, so she'd keep them.

The following evening, they sat in the parlour—normally a time they read their books. These were not the study books that Áine had Bree read of a day, books about the history of the Tuatha Dé Danann and their culture. During the evening, they read books about the quests various heroes had undertaken—men again, Bree thought.

'Are there any other women in the Tuatha Dé Danann?' Bree asked.

Áine lowered her book onto her lap. 'Of course, there are women.'

'Why aren't any of these stories about women?'

Áine's face held that guarded expression she often wore when Bree asked particular questions.

'Why aren't women heroes?'

'They are, macushla. Maybe they're just not in the books you have.'

Bree knew her aunt was holding something back. She changed tack. 'What's outside this cave?'

'We're quite safe, Bree. Don't worry.'

'I think you worry sometimes.'

'It's my job to worry. I'm your aunt.'

Bree fell silent. Áine became more and more secretive. Bree couldn't work it out. How could she? She had no experience of life outside the cave's walls. As she lay in her cot that night, the first seed of a plan sprouted. Somehow, she was going to find a way to leave the cave, not to abandon Áine, but to venture outside to see the world for herself.

Bree's world roared.

She was reading in her bedroom when the ground beneath her shook and flung her to the floor. When she scrambled up, she lost her footing and slammed into the earthen wall. Dust poured down from the ceiling like dry rain, choking her, stinging her eyes. Her heart beat as it never had before.

The ground groaned even louder, once again throwing

her off her feet and onto her knees. Pieces of the earthen ceiling landed close by, one catching her on the shoulder. She cried out; the sound snatched away. Books fell from shelves where they had been stacked, landing across the floor, their bindings bending. Clothes fell out of cupboards and lay strewn on the floor.

Then, as abruptly as it had started, everything went quiet and the ground all around her became still.

What just happened? Áine had told her of earthquakes in faraway lands. It had to have been an earthquake.

Then Bree went cold. She remembered the flame! She must protect the flame. *Protect the flame.* The words had been bred into her, so much so, she didn't need to think of them. She breathed, her blood flowed in her veins, and she must protect the ancient fire. These things happened without conscious thought.

Bree ran into the room to the copper bowl that held the flames. It rested unshaken on its pedestal. She could hardly believe it hadn't toppled in the earthquake. To be certain, she put her hands on the small cauldron.

'If anything ever happens, you must first protect the ancient fire,' Áine had always insisted.

'What could happen?' Bree had asked her. They lived in a cave on their own. Nothing ever happened.

Again, the floor rumbled beneath Bree's feet. 'Áine,' she screamed, fearing for her aunt, who was in the parlour.

'Bree, are you all right?' Áine asked as she ran into the doorway of the flame room.

'I'm not hurt,' Bree assured her. She stared at her aunt. Her stomach tightened at the expression on Áine's face. Bree had never known fear, but she was sure that was what painted her aunt's features in hues of white and grey. She'd only ever known Áine to be cheerful and wise.

Bree felt the cauldron tremble beneath her fingers. 'What's happening?' she asked. 'Why is our home shaking? I heard the earth growl.'

'Something terrible has occurred in our world,' Áine said.

'An earthquake?'

'No, macushla.' Áine twisted her hands together. 'Although the earth quaked, I think we must prepare for the worst.'

'What do you mean by worst? What can be worse than an earthquake?'

Before Áine could reply, the ground roared once more. The fire in the cauldron flared. Bree felt the heat of it on her chest. The fire settled. Bree sighed, but too soon. The flames faltered, diminished and nearly extinguished.

'No,' Bree shouted. She plunged her hands into the bowl. What she hoped to achieve, she didn't know. Protect the flames! Every beat of her heart drummed, Save. The. Flames.

Áine hurried to the cauldron. Bree could see her aunt's shock at what happened next mingle with her own.

The near-dead flames slid onto Bree's palms and flared with renewed vigour. Bree cried out, but not in pain. The fire burned in her hands but didn't scorch her flesh. Energy coursed through her body. She felt at one with the red and orange dancing fire. Its power coursed through her. Her spirit soared and, for a moment, she gazed down at herself and her aunt as she floated above them. Then her body sucked her back down. She shook her head, her eyes wide, and stared at Áine. 'What's happening?' she implored.

'Bree,' Áine murmured, as she put her hand on her niece's arm. 'It's time.'

Bree turned her head. Áine had tears in her eyes.

'It's all right,' Áine said. 'Lower your hands and transfer the flames back to the cauldron.'

It astonished Bree that she could do it... and frightened her. She examined her palms. 'I'm not burned. Why isn't my skin blistered? Why didn't the fire burn me?'

'The flames are yours now, macushla.'

'I don't understand.' Bree lifted a hand and wiped tears from her aunt's cheek. 'Why are you crying?'

'I must tell you that your mother, my sister, is dead.'

Bree stepped back, rocked more by this news than the earth quaking beneath her feet. 'My mother? I know she's dead. You always told me that my mother died years ago when I was born. Why are you telling me this again?'

Bree had always wished she could have met her mother and now... now her aunt seemed to be saying her mother had only just died.

'It's the flames. They transferred to you. That could only happen if your mother had died.'

'No!' Bree exclaimed. 'Why did you keep me here, locked away, if my mother was alive?' She stepped away from her aunt until she felt the wall behind her, as if the earth that had hidden her for eighteen years could comfort her now. 'How could you keep her from me?'

'Macushla, I didn't want to keep you away from your mother. It was her decision. There was no way of predicting what would occur. Your mother knew of the uncertainty when she placed you, as a baby, in my arms and instructed me to care for you, to protect you. She knew she might never see you again.'

'But I've never seen her at all. I don't know her. Now she's gone.' Bree dashed her tears away. 'Why couldn't I live with her?'

'Bree, macushla.' Áine crossed the floor to take her niece's hands. 'Your mother wanted to keep you safe. You would have been dead years ago at the hands of your mother's enemies if you weren't here, hidden in this cave. I couldn't even contact your mother. The risk of someone sensing a disturbance in the ether was too great. She said someone would come for you, for us, when the time was right.'

'Someone?'

'Your mother knew it might not be her.'

'And my father? What of him?' Why had she never thought to ask before now?

'Your father was Bres, son of a goddess. He died many years ago.'

Pain constricted Bree's breathing. She'd never felt anything like it. Sadness overwhelmed her. When Bree saw tears running down her aunt's cheeks, she felt selfish for thinking only of her own anguish. She wrapped her arms about Áine. 'My mother and your sister,' Bree murmured into Áine's ear. 'You're grieving too. You knew your sister and loved her... but I will never know her now.'

Áine pushed back but still held her niece's arms. 'You are her. You became her the instant she breathed her last breath.'

'I don't understand. How can that be?'

'Her life force was in the ancient fire. When I fled with you, she gave me some of the flame.'

'That's why I've always had to protect it,' Bree murmured.

'So you see, there's always been something of her here with us,' Áine explained. 'Now her life has ended, her essence has transferred to you through the flame. You are her. You are Brigid, just as she was. You are the Triple Goddess.' Áine kissed her niece's cheek. 'I can't say more now. It's not safe.'

Triple Goddess? It was more than Bree could take in. This morning—not that they ever saw sunshine, but Áine had told her of its bright, golden rays—she was Bree who tended the flame, who cleaned their home's earthen floor, who learned her lessons, who read her books. Áine had taught her many things. She'd told her of their world—the sky, flowers, grass, birds and animals. But Áine had never told her about her mother, what sort of life she led, why she had sent her daughter away with her sister. Protect the flame! That was her main job. Now she learned that her mother's life force came to her through the flames. 'Triple goddess?' she reiterated. 'What is that supposed to mean, Áine?'

Áine swept her blonde hair up and twisted it into a bun at the nape of her neck. 'There's no time now, macushla. We must prepare to leave. Gather some clothes and books and come with me.'

Chapter Two

Bree followed her aunt into her bedchamber. It mirrored her own with earthen walls and floors, a narrow sleeping cot, a wooden chest for belongings, and books stacked high on a small table. Bree had never before wondered how they managed to have so many books. She asked her aunt now.

'I must confess I crept out on a few occasions,' Áine said with a shrug. 'Your mother left books from time to time in an oak tree close by.'

'In an oak tree?'

'It has a secret door and is guarded by the oak tree spirit.'

'My mother came to this oak tree with books?' A stab of pain plunged through Bree's chest. 'Then why couldn't she come here to us? It's not fair. Now I'll never see her.' Bree grabbed her aunt's wrist. 'Didn't she want to see me?'

Áine pulled her wrist free and lifted her hands to cup her niece's face. 'Macushla, my sweet girl, of course she wanted to see you, but it wasn't safe for her to come here.'

'Why not?' Bree pursed her lips.

'I'll explain everything soon, but now we must hurry. We have to protect the flame.'

Bree turned away. Protect the flame! She'd protected it all her life. Nothing had protected her mother. She should've been with her. Maybe if she'd been there, she could have saved her mother.

Everything felt hollow, as if her whole life had been for nothing. Bree swung back. 'I don't want to do it anymore. My mother is dead. Why bother now with the flame?'

Áine's blue eyes narrowed. Bree had never seen her aunt look so angry. 'Because you are your mother now. You will take her place. Because the flame is yours. Because she lives through the flame. She lives through you.'

Bree tossed her long red hair back from her shoulders. 'I'm pleased to know that… I am. I felt her presence in the flame but… It's all just so unfair! My mother is dead. She may be with me, in my heart, in spirit, but I'll never meet her, never get to know her. I've lived my whole life in this place for nothing.' Bree turned away. 'I'm going to my room.' She'd never argued with Áine, and she was sorry to do so now but…

'This is not just about you, Bree.' Áine's voice was stern. 'There are many people waiting for you. They depend upon you.'

Bree spun back. 'People waiting for me? I don't know these people. Why would they depend upon me?'

'They are your people. Please believe me for now. We must hurry.' Áine lifted the lid of her wooden chest. It was plain, without any decoration. She reached into it and extracted another much smaller chest. Ornate decorations covered this one. Áine crossed to Bree in the doorway and placed it in her niece's hands. 'This chest is made of *argat draiochta* to hold the ancient fire as we flee.'

The chest was cold in Bree's hands. She opened the lid. Inside was a miniature cauldron set into a base, which held it secure. 'It looks like silver,' Bree said. 'What did you call it?'

'*Argat draiochta*,' Áine replied. 'It is a magical metal smelted by your mother. She gave me the ancient fire in this chest. We must return it to its home the same way.'

'Home?' Bree questioned. 'I am home.' She kicked the floor. All she wanted was to curl up on her bed and forget everything.

'Transfer the fire to the chest,' Áine ordered. 'Then collect your belongings. We have to return to Tír na nÓg.'

'To where?' Bree frowned.

'To Tír na nÓg, the land of the Tuatha Dé Danann.'

Bree still couldn't grapple with the fact that so many people, unknown to her, could depend on her. For eighteen years, her life had mirrored the ancient fire, with its steady constant flames, but now it had been transformed into a raging fire. There was nothing for it but to do as Áine asked. Hadn't she always done as her aunt had bidden her? She couldn't begin to comprehend what the alternative might be.

'Very well,' Bree said. Her breathing had settled down. She'd never known her temper to flare before. She'd always been serene and composed.

Another tremor, this one milder, shook their home. Bree staggered and stared wide-eyed at her aunt.

'Hurry to the ancient fire. Transfer the flame.'

'What's happening?' Bree asked. The tremor seemed to have carried through to her voice.

'It's time, macushla. Someone's coming.' Áine hurried Bree before her.

'Someone. Who?'

'I don't know,' Áine said. 'Stay with the flame… at all costs.'

'What's that supposed to mean? Is it friend or foe coming for us?'

'At all costs, Bree,' Áine said and pushed her niece into the flame room.

Bree hurried to the ancient fire. The room was devoid of any furniture or decoration. Bree placed the *argat draiochta* chest on the floor. She stared at the flames. Could she place her hands among them again and not get burned? She'd done it before. What did Áine say? The flames were hers now. Her mother's essence was in the fire and had passed into her. She took a breath, hoping her mother was with her as she plunged her hands into the small blaze.

The flames slid onto her hands as if they had been waiting for her, jumping with glee and flaring with pleasure. Bree raised her hands close to her face. The orange flames held her mesmerised by their beauty. Their warmth was gentle on her cheeks. It was moments before she realised they were not burning her hands.

The room shuddered. Bree snapped out of her daze and bent down to the small chest. The flames jumped off her hands as if they knew what to do. She closed the lid, lifted the chest and held it close to her.

Something in the parlour vibrated and scraped, as if the earth itself was ripped open. Bree was frightened for Áine, who'd gone into the front room. From where Bree stood, she couldn't see her aunt.

What was happening now?

'By all the jumping fleas in Dagda's beard, how much magic is required to keep a child safe?'

The voice boomed out. The walls quivered. Bree jumped and sucked in her breath. The voice wasn't like any she'd heard. Given that she'd only heard Áine's and her own, the thought was insubstantial but… Who spoke in such a deep tone?

'Lu, thank Danu, it's you,' Áine said.

Neither of the names meant anything to Bree but Áine sounded relieved. That was enough for Bree. The booming voice belonged to a friend.

'Every second step I took I had to break an enchantment,' the stranger added.

An annoyed friend!

'It's true then?' Áine asked. 'Brigid is dead?'

'Murdered by Mór's hand.'

Bree pushed the *argat draiochta* coffer into her chest until it hurt.

Áine gasped. 'No! How could that happen? Why wasn't she protected?'

'It's far worse than you could know.' Lu's voice cut through the walls. 'Mór amassed a horde and bore down on the villages in the Outer Realm. Lady Brigid couldn't be convinced to stay at the palace. As you know, she rarely donned her armour, but this time nothing would stop her from riding out.'

'I know,' Áine said. 'My sister preferred enlisting her more gentle talents to help her people.'

'She left herself exposed,' Lu said. 'I was there, and I'd barely turned my back when Mór flew at her.'

Áine sobbed. Bree wanted to rush out to comfort her aunt and to ask this person to explain everything to her. Bree was more confused and distraught than ever. Protect the flame! Should she rush into the other room? Would she risk the flame's safety? Surely, Lu had to be a friend.

'Lady Brigid didn't stand a chance.'

'Did you have time to land a blow?' Áine asked.

'By Dagda's beard, I would've loved to have killed that witch a thousand times over.'

Bree had never heard words imbued with such ferocity.

'I looked into Mór's eyes,' Lu continued. 'Soulless eyes. Then she screeched—my ears still retain the horrible shriek—and she flew away, with her ravens swooping about her.'

Bree trembled, chilled by the stranger's words of Mór... her mother's killer.

'We're almost ready to go with you,' Áine said, after a pause that had swept about their home and held all of them suspended.

'Is the child ready?'

'She's not a child. She's eighteen.'

'Still so young.'

'And you are all of... what? Twenty-two?'

Lu frowned. 'Is she ready to take her mother's place?'

Áine paused. 'Lu, you have to remember that she's spent her life here.'

'You taught her well?'

'I have. She is learned but…'

'But?' Lu boomed.

Bree jumped. What did he expect? Of course, she was educated.

'I couldn't tell her who she was. I couldn't tell her everything.'

'By all that's holy at Lammas, why not?'

'Her mother forbade it. We dared not disturb the ether lest Mór find us.'

The air trembled. Bree could feel, even without seeing, Lu move around the front room. She had to go out to them.

'So we have an ignorant child to save us?' Lu's words found their way to Bree. Her anger stirred.

'She has her mother's sweetness and kindness.'

'By Dagda's beard, we don't want sweetness! We need strength and leadership. She'll be useless.'

Bree's anger boiled. She'd never felt rage burn within her before. She placed the ancient flame on the floor and strode into the parlour. 'I am neither useless nor ignorant!' she exclaimed, and then mentally quaked at the sight of the man before her—she wouldn't let him notice. Áine had told her men were like women but were usually taller. *Taller* was an inadequate description of this man. Bree was tall. She gazed over the top of Áine's head with ease. Not so with Lu. He was head and shoulders taller than Bree. Long blond hair was tied back from a strongly boned face. However, it was his breadth that astounded her… and he was half naked. In all the drawings she had seen, heroes were dressed in tunics and armour. This man's chest was bare, his muscles bulging and rippling beneath his skin as he moved. Armour capped his shoulders and he wore metal wrist guards. Leather straps crisscrossed his chest, no doubt securing weapons she noticed on his back. Bree stared at arms larger than she had ever thought possible.

'Aha,' Lu said, fastening his gaze on Bree. 'Nor too sweet, either, I'd say.'

There was an amused light in his blue eyes that irritated Bree.

'You know nothing of me,' she snapped at him.

'That's where you're wrong. I know more about you than you know of me.'

'Who are you?' Bree demanded. She was surprised by her tone of voice. It caused a smirk to hover over his lips.

He swept her a bow. It annoyed her even more.

'Allow me to introduce myself. I am Lu of the Tuatha Dé Danann, Lord of Lammas and the harvest festival of Lughnasa. God of the Sun, of Light and Fire, and god of warriors and battle,' he said, and raised his arm to reach behind his shoulders.

Bree controlled her surprise when, amidst a ringing of metal and a cry of what sounded like protest, he drew a mighty sword and held it in front of her. The most beautiful symbols Bree had ever seen decorated the blade and handle. She could have sworn the sword moved of its own accord.

'Cadeyrn likes to be released,' Lu said. 'He's itching for the next battle.'

Bree couldn't quite decide if Lu was teasing her. She wasn't taking his bait. She raised her chin. 'You call your sword Cadeyrn?'

'He insisted on the name. Cadeyrn, and my spear, Corraidhin, are always by my side.' Lu took a spear from where it leaned against the wall and struck it on the floor. A shaft of flame shot up from its tip. 'I don't want to get them excited yet. The battle is to come.'

'What battle?' Bree narrowed her eyes at him when he ignored her. 'Why do you bring your sword and spear into our home?'

'You may have missed me saying I'm the god of warriors and battle. Oh, and I do have my hound, Cunobelinus. I call him Kuon. He's waiting outside the door of your cave.'

'I missed nothing,' Bree said. She felt the fire course through her veins. Lu was arrogant and insolent. She was her mother's daughter. She was her mother, the Triple Goddess. She was Bree, Goddess of… everything.

'I asked you a question,' Bree said. 'What battle?'

All humour left Lu's eyes and lips. 'The battle to save our world, Tír na nÓg, the land of the Tuatha Dé Danann,' he murmured, although his words still held strength.

'Then we should make haste,' Bree said.

'Bree has the ancient fire ready,' Áine said. 'We'll grab some clothes—'

Lu cut her off. 'There's no room for clothes.'

'My books,' Bree said. 'I must bring some books with me.'

'By Dagda's beard!' Lu exclaimed, raising his voice. 'We can't take books! We can't take anything!'

Eyebrows raised, Bree stared at him. 'Why not?'

He huffed, then added in a lowered tone, 'My lady, we must travel light. We'll be lucky to reach the palace in safety as it is.'

Bree nodded. In this, she realised she must defer to him. 'Then we should leave the food bowl, Áine.'

'Food bowl?' Lu questioned.

'My sister made a small cauldron for us. She smelted it herself,' Áine explained. 'Its magic provided us with food and drink. It never emptied, nor was it ever full.'

'We can return later for these things,' Bree said. 'I'll collect the flame.' Bree flopped against the wall, her hand pressed to her chest as she inhaled, allowing her breath to slowly course through her body. Her legs and arms trembled. She'd acted nothing like herself. Yesterday... even this morning... she'd been sweet and shy. Where did this Bree come from? She knew the answer, of course. Her mother's spirit had awakened in her. She was her mother, and yet there was so much more she needed to learn. As much as Lu annoyed her, she would need to learn from him.

She lifted the *argat draiochta* chest, and then hurried into her room. She suspected that her long dress would be a nuisance but it would have to do. At least it was plain and simple. The mirror reflected a glimpse of green fabric; not something a goddess would wear. For a moment, she looked at herself. Green eyes she barely recognised stared back at her. Thick red hair floated around her small, pale face. She tied her hair back with a ribbon. A goddess? She would soon see.

Chapter Three

Patience was not Lu's strong point. While he waited for Áine and the girl to ready themselves, Mór's men could be working out ways to storm the Enchanted Veil. By Dagda's beard, he should have detailed Bearach to fetch the girl. His time would have been better spent with his Immortals, not playing nursemaid to a child. If not exactly a child, she wasn't much more. What good would she be as Triple Goddess with her naivety? The Tuatha Dé Danann needed a strong leader. And what did they have? A child.

Brigid should never hidden her baby away. Áine should have taught her more. Prepared her for what her task would be.

He conceded that the girl had gumption. She showed some promise. But they didn't have a year for her training, nor a month. They had days before Samhain when Mór and her men were bound to strike again.

Lu was about to call out, when they joined him. 'Are you ready?

Lu had sheathed his sword and held his spear, which every so often spat out a small flame. 'Let's go.'

Bree had used another dress to make a sling, so that the chest was slung over one shoulder. She was surprised when Áine produced a dagger and then a second one for Bree.

'I brought them with me all those years ago,' Áine explained.

The dagger was in a scabbard and Bree tied it at her side. She nodded at Lu, who seemed to be waiting for her command. He pushed open the door in the earthen wall, and they stepped outside.

A huge shaggy hound greeted Lu and prevented them from moving past him until he had sniffed Bree and Áine, inspecting them to ascertain if they were friend or foe. A deafening and resounding bark exclaimed they were friends. As the animal proceeded to lick Bree's hands, his long tail wagged, adding a further stamp of approval.

'Kuon. Here,' Lu commanded, and the giant hound, standing as tall as his master's hip, leaped obediently to Lu's side.

The movement nearly caused Bree to lose her footing. They stood on a timber walkway that was suspended over… endless nothingness. Bree's head spun.

'Don't look down,' Áine whispered.

Bree raised her gaze and sucked in her breath. She looked out over a sea of pastel colours. The air shimmered with a glimmering rose glow. She reached out, certain she'd be able to touch a mauve cloud that floated past her. She'd never seen anything as beautiful in her life. 'What is this place?'

'It's Annwfn,' her aunt explained. 'The Otherworld.'

'This has been just outside our cave all these years? Why couldn't we come here?'

'It would have disturbed the ether and if Mór had felt it…'

'Are we going to have a discussion or hurry on our way?' Lu demanded, stamping his spear on the walkway.

Bree narrowed her eyes at him. 'You are rude.' It was a shame he was so ill-mannered when he was so handsome. Her traitorous gaze fell to his chest.

'Pardon me,' Lu said in a mocking tone. 'Sit, Kuon. We're not in a hurry after all.'

'It's pardon me, my lady,' Bree said, raising her chin.

'My lady.' Lu made an extravagant bow.

'We should go,' Áine murmured and took Bree's hand.

Lu shook his head, as if exasperated, and walked on.

Kuon led them, running across palings of the walkway that looked none too secure. It made for a hazardous crossing on a bridge that swung from side to side. The boardwalk led to a small, grassy island that floated in the wondrous ether.

Bree paused when they reached the island, as much to steady her equilibrium as to gaze back at her home. After seeing the island they now stood on, she wasn't surprised to see that they'd come from another island suspended in the luminous air. The difference was that their home had an enormous oak tree growing on top of it. The island looked as if a giant hand had ripped it from the earth, taking a sizeable chunk of ground with it.

'I know there has to be a door in the tree trunk,' Bree said, 'but I can't see it. Where did we live? In the tree?' she asked her aunt.

'In the earth beneath,' Áine explained.

'My lady, we must go,' Lu urged, a barb of annoyance in his tone but no sarcasm this time. 'There will be time enough to ask questions.'

But would there be? Nevertheless, Bree nodded. Kuon led them across another walkway. Timbers were missing here and there. Bree was pleased to reach the solid ground of yet another suspended island, where another tree grew. Lu pushed past his hound and placed his hand on the tree's trunk.

'From this point onwards, we must be as silent as possible,' he warned. 'We'll enter this oak and step out into darkness. I'll use Corraidhin to provide some light but only when I think it's safe. The moon will be high and almost full as we approach Samhain.'

Bree had learned about Samhain and the other festivals that marked the passing of the year. Samhain was when the ghosts of the dead returned to the land of the living. It marked the end of the harvest season and the beginning of the darker half of the year.

'We will be heading straight to the palace,' Lu explained.

'Palace?' Bree asked, and then nodded when no answer proved to be forthcoming. From this point on, she had to trust in him.

'It will be dangerous until we reach the Enchanted Veil. Once we've passed through it, we'll be safe.'

'The Enchanted Veil is a magic wall that protects the palace and all in the Inner Realm,' Áine explained.

'Ready?' Lu asked, as he pushed on the tree. A door opened without protest. 'Kuon, heel,' Lu added, and took over the lead from his hound. He struck Corraidhin on the ground and the spear coughed out a small flame that briefly lit the interior cavity of the tree.

The space was still dark. The tree trunk looked like solid ground and didn't allow any natural light in.

Lu pushed on the other side of the tree and a section opened. They stepped out onto spongy grass.

There was enough moonlight to illuminate the area around them. Bree took a small tottering step backwards. She'd never seen so much open space. The glimmering clouds that surrounded her floating island home weren't confronting, but here, with open ground and trees looming out of the darkness, she felt afraid. She looked up and found the moon and the stars glinting on the black velvet of the heavens. There were clouds too, dark and ominous. Áine had told her of all these things but she could never have imagined the reality of their beauty. The darkness that hovered around the trees was blacker than anything she'd known. When she and Áine had blown out the candles in their home, there had always been the ancient fire, which cast a comforting glow throughout their rooms.

'Come,' Lu whispered, and then he sprinted across the open space.

Bree hesitated. Her feet felt as if they had taken root in

the grass, and she couldn't move. The openness terrified her. Also, she wondered who might be waiting, unseen in the trees, for them.

Áine squeezed her hand. 'It's all right, macushla. Run with me.'

Nothing happened as Bree and Áine crossed the open ground. Lu led them into a forest that smelled damp and musty, with the addition of other smells Bree couldn't identify. Her stomach tightened as she stepped into the darkness. It swallowed her whole. She looked behind and could barely see Áine.

'I'm with you, macushla,' Áine whispered.

Bree nodded and stumbled, tripping over a protruding tree root. Lu glanced behind and Bree felt his glare. She felt stupid for not watching where she was going, but she could not see the ground in the darkness. Fear stabbed through her. The blackness frightened her. Áine had never told her that nightfall could obscure everything else. Was this what Mór wanted to bring to their entire world? Complete darkness?

Bree touched the chest in its sling, making certain it was still there. It made her feel safe.

A noise startled her. She stopped so abruptly that Áine ran into her.

'It's an owl,' Áine reassured her.

'Come on,' Lu said. His anger urged them forward.

The trees thinned out and moonlight filtered in.

'Keep close,' Lu instructed. He halted, then bent over and ran across an exposed area of ground.

Bree and Áine ran side by side, following Kuon. Some of Bree's anxieties fell away, as they came to a stream, really nothing more than a tinkling brook. To her surprise, Lu stepped into the stream and proceeded to follow it. Kuon stopped to drink, and then bounded after his master. Bree and Áine lifted their skirts and stepped into the water.

'Why do we have to walk in the water?' Bree whispered. 'Is Lu mad?'

'It will muffle our scents and not leave any tracks,' Áine explained.

It wasn't long before the stream narrowed, and then narrowed again, until only a small spring gurgled out of the ground.

Lu struck Corraidhin on the ground and the spear sparked into life, its light enough to show they stood at the foot of a staircase cut into the side of a small hill. 'This way,' he said.

As they climbed the moss-covered steps, the spear remained alight to assist their ascent, but dimmed as soon as they reached the top.

The darkness was thick. Bree had difficulty discerning the landscape. Tall trees loomed in front of them, but to their right, the ground appeared to be open.

'We cross here,' Lu said. 'We're nearly at the Enchanted Veil.'

'What are those odd shapes all over the ground?' Bree asked.

Lu turned to her. It was a moment before he replied. 'This used to be a village of happy people. Yesterday, Mór's creatures descended on it and all but erased it. What you see are the remains of homes.'

The horror of Lu's words cut through Bree like a sharp

knife plunging into her heart. 'What about the people?' Bree was almost afraid to ask.

'Dead,' Lu said, his voice heavy. 'Every man, woman and child. Every animal. Wiped out.'

The sob unwittingly escaped Bree's mouth, wrenched from her as harshly as life had been taken from these people… her mother's people. Her people.

Lu bent to make his shape less visible and ran across the ground. Bree and Áine followed suit. Bree faltered as they hurried through the burnt timbers of the village. It wasn't fair that the acrid smell revived her, as it could not resuscitate its lost inhabitants. She felt tears trace their way down her cheeks.

Bree cried out as the last shapes they passed came to life and sprang up all round them. She stared in disbelief at the silhouettes outlined by moonlight. For a moment, she thought the dead populace had come to life. Then, as three men with swords lunged at Lu, she realised these figures were foe.

Corraidhin flared into life without any coaxing. Lu lunged at them with the spear, but the assailants jumped back to avoid the flames. In the moment's grace it gave him, Lu tossed his spear into his left hand, and reaching behind his shoulders, drew his sword. Cadeyrn hummed when he was released. Lu lunged with both spear and sword.

Kuon took one spectre on, growling and knocking him to the ground where the hound pinned him down.

Bree had no more time to notice what Lu or Kuon did. She had her own fight. One huge black silhouette towered over her. Even at close range, she couldn't see a face, just an arm raised high to cut her down. She drew the dagger from its scabbard, ducked under her attacker's arm and plunged the knife into his side. His body twitched but remained standing. She feared she hadn't done much damage.

A dance Áine had taught her, a jig, pushed itself to the forefront of her thoughts. Why she thought of it now, she didn't know. She loved to sing and dance but now wasn't the time. Or was it? She jumped back from her assailant as he grabbed his side. It was all the time she needed. She did two little steps and then kicked her leg high. She'd never been able to get enough swing up in the small rooms, but here, immersed in so much space, she sprang high and kicked the silhouette in the face. He fell backwards and she followed through by landing next to him. She slashed her knife across his leg.

'You won't be running too far tonight,' she said.

Her fallen foe wailed like a child.

When Bree rose, she saw that four bodies lay at Lu's feet. Áine had also had success with her dagger.

Lu shook his head when he looked at the assailant at Bree's feet. He walked over to her and plunged his sword into the man's chest. 'We can't have him alerting Mór.' He stared up at Bree. 'Dancing aside, you did well.'

Bree inclined her head, but knew he was mocking her. Even in the moonlight she saw a smirk on his lips.

'Are you all right?' Áine asked.

'I am,' Bree replied. In truth, she was shaken to see the dead bodies. She'd never encountered death other than in the stories she'd read and to have a man dead at her feet was unsettling and upsetting. 'Who are these men?' she added. 'Are they men? I can't see their faces.'

'Their faces are blackened,' Lu said, and bent over one of them. He wrenched something from the man's head, and then showed it to them. 'It's a hat of sorts, with a raven's beak placed so it will sit on the forehead. It stamps them as Mór's men.'

Bree went to touch it, but Lu threw it away. 'We must hurry,' he said. 'She'll soon know we're here.'

'How?' Bree asked.

'She has ravens everywhere. They'll fly to her.'

Bree touched the chest slung to her body, satisfied it was safe, then followed Lu as they left the burned village and the dead bodies behind them. Once they were on the other side of the clearing, Lu halted. Bree could see a stone bridge ahead.

'We must approach with care,' Lu explained.

The bridge was old, the sides dark with lichen.

Bree hesitated. 'I don't think it is safe to cross. I can't do it.'

'We must keep moving, macushla. Trust Lu to guide us to safety,' Áine said.

'I don't know him. How can I trust him?'

'Trust me,' her aunt said. 'Now come, we must go.'

They were more than halfway across it when three gigantic shapes loomed out of the trees on the other side.

Bree sucked in her breath. She couldn't move, her feet froze her to the spot. 'What are they?' she whispered to Áine.

Chapter Four

'Trolls,' Áine replied.

Lu stepped forward. Corraidhin's flames shot out and Lu waved his spear in front of the trolls. 'Out of our way.' Lu's voice boomed.

Three huge mouths in immense chunky heads sneered, showing blackened teeth. They didn't reply to Lu, but their large, lumpy shoulders shook with what could have been laughter.

'They're so ugly,' Bree whispered again. 'They look like something made of stone.' She stepped forward to better inspect them. Their chests were naked above dark trousers and bare feet. At first, they didn't appear to have weapons but as one of them moved an arm, Bree noticed a spear in his hand.

'They're most likely bridge trolls,' Áine told her.

'What do they want?' Bree called to Lu.

'To stop us. What do you think they want? They're not a welcoming party, I can assure you,' he replied.

Bree narrowed her eyes. 'He's so insolent,' she murmured to Áine.

'He's strong and a good fighter,' Áine whispered. 'Which is what we need. He has a true heart.'

'Out of our way,' Lu shouted.

'This is our bridge,' one troll said, and stepped onto the rough stone.

'Since when?' Lu demanded. 'I have always crossed here.'

'Since we said so,' the troll replied. 'You have to pay to cross our bridge.'

'What is your price?' Lu asked.

'One skinny redhead.' The troll laughed.

Corraidhin flared and Lu threw the spear. The giant yelped as the fiery point went into his leg. While the troll was pulling Corraidhin out of his limb, Lu lunged with Cadeyrn. The sword slashed the troll's other leg.

The creature threw Lu's spear aside. Corraidhin landed on the bridge and spat out a small spark, as if in protest at being discarded.

Another troll stepped forward, pushing his mate out of the way. He halted when he reached Corraidhin and stood on the spear to pin it down. 'Come on then,' the troll said. 'You just try and get past me.' He waved a wooden club at Lu.

'Come back here, Lu,' Bree called. She took off the sling with its precious cargo and placed it on the ground. The *argat draiochta* was cold against her hands as she lifted the lid and took some of the fire into her palms. She hoped her idea worked. 'Back here, Lu,' she shouted in a voice that grabbed his attention.

He frowned, his brow drawn tight, but he stepped back.

Bree passed him as she went forward. She looked up and stared the troll in the eye. 'This skinny redhead refuses to pay your price,' she shouted at the creature. 'I'd suggest you get out of my way before I exact my price from you.'

The troll laughed, but his expression didn't hold amusement.

'Very well,' Bree said. She raised her palms and blew the flames. They wavered. She felt her first stab of fear. She blew again and the fire spluttered.

The troll laughed. His mates joined in.

Bree closed her eyes and breathed deeply. For a moment, she imagined the flames growing. She felt their warmth on her palms. She felt their warmth within her. The fire was in her blood. Its heat raged through her. She opened her eyes and blew the flames cocooned in her palms. They roared forth, orange and red fire shooting across the bridge.

The first troll turned and tripped over his cohorts. The ground shuddered as they all fell in a mountainous heap.

Again, Bree blew on the flames. This time, her breath eased out of her mouth and caressed the ancient fire. It felt as if her movements had slowed down as she watched her flames engulf the bridge in a firestorm. The trolls managed to get to their feet. Amidst yelping and cursing at their wounds, they jumped down and disappeared under the bridge.

'We'd best hurry now before they return,' Bree said to her two companions who stared wide-eyed at her. She slipped the fire back into the chest and positioned the sling. 'Are you ready?'

'Allow me to go first, my lady,' Lu said, as he swept a bow, a smirk twisting his lips.

Bree couldn't tell if it was humour or mockery in his expression. She glanced at Áine, who smiled at her.

'Well done, macushla,' Áine said. 'Your gifts come naturally to you.'

Lu lifted Corraidhin from where the spear had been thrown down and returned Cadeyrn to its scabbard. Kuon bounded around Bree, happier than his master that she'd chased away the trolls.

'Come,' Lu said. 'It's not far now.' He took off at a run.

Bree and Áine hurried after him. They entered another forest. Visibility vanished in a heartbeat. The trees rose high above them, cutting out most of the moonlight. The forest floor smelled of damp leaf litter. Buttresses grew at the base of the trees, winding and twisting. Áine tripped over one. Bree grabbed her arm to steady her.

More than anything else, the silence reverberated an endless wave of stillness. Bree's ears hurt. It took a few minutes before she realised she could discern sounds. Strange cries, groans, and shrieks, but all so soft as to be nearly non-existent.

'What are they?' she whispered to Áine.

'Forest sounds,' Áine spoke even more softly. When Bree raised an enquiring eyebrow, Áine added, 'Trees groaning and stretching, small animals…'

'Áine!' Bree interrupted, her voice resounding around

the forest. 'Lu has gone. He was in front of me, but I can't see him anymore.'

'It's all right,' Áine said, and smiled.

Bree took another step and hit something. It was soft and, without meaning to, she walked through it. For a moment, she felt disoriented and lost, as if she floated in a bubble. Then it spat her out and she stumbled into a different wooded area. She gazed about her, amazed at the golden light that shone through the huge, ancient trees.

Kuon barked. Bree saw the hound and his master. Lu chuckled. Before she could say anything to him, Áine appeared.

'What was that?' Bree asked her.

'One of the entrances through the Enchanted Veil,' her aunt said.

'We're safe now,' Lu added. 'This is your dominion, my lady. Tír na nÓg, the Tuatha Dé Danann's Inner Realm.'

He was still mocking her. Bree ignored him and turned to Áine. 'Are we really safe here?'

'We are.' Her aunt took her hands and kissed her cheek.

'Unless Mór discovers some evil power to penetrate the Veil,' Lu said. 'She's laid all the other Tuatha Dé Danann lands to waste and killed the people.'

'Have any sought sanctuary here?' Áine asked.

'We've taken in everyone and every other living being we could,' Lu said. 'Nobles and farmers alike. Centaurs and unicorns too.'

'Thank Danu's spirit,' Áine said.

'Who is Danu?' Bree asked. Her aunt's words were peppered with the name. They hadn't been before.

'She is your grandmother, the mother goddess, and Dagda's wife. Descendants of Danu and Dagda went to the three different realms to forge new colonies, just as I told you.'

'You have never told me about my grandparents!' Bree exclaimed. 'Why have you never told me?'

Before Áine could reply, a large glowing globe caught Bree's attention. It zigzagged at speed through the trees. As it came closer, it seemed to resemble a comet with a tail. Áine had told her about comets but Bree thought they should be in the sky. Had this one fallen to the ground?

Áine gave a happy giggle. Bree had never known her aunt to chortle in such a way.

The comet sped closer and descended on Áine. It encased her head and spun her body around.

Bree's eyes widened. The glowing globe wasn't a comet, nor even one object. It was comprised of small people, each approximately six inches high. Bree watched as some of the little people flew around her head. 'Hello,' she greeted them.

They giggled and then flew to the ground where they formed a rough circle around Áine's feet. Some sat on her shoulders and hung on her hair.

Bree's first fear dissipated as Áine and all the little beings laughed and talked over each other.

'They have wings,' Bree said to Lu, who had his arms crossed over his spear. He had a genuine smile as he watched what was happening. Kuon was sniffing and nudging some of the little people on the ground.

At her words, Lu turned to her, and smirked. 'I assume Áine didn't mention she's Queen of the Fairies.'

The blood drained from Bree's face. 'Queen of the Fairies?'

Lu chuckled at her discomfort. They weren't at the palace yet and she was really starting to hate this man. She guessed as the Triple Goddess, she wasn't supposed to hate anyone, but Lu irritated her. Surely he should be respectful of her rank?

Áine reached out her hand to Bree. Fairies perched on her arm. 'Macushla, please forgive me for not telling you.'

'You had to abandon the fairies because of me. For all those years!' Bree felt her face flame as the blood came back in a rush.

'I didn't abandon them, macushla. I protected you. The fairies understood.'

As if to add emphasis to Áine's words, fairies rushed over to Bree and flew around her once again.

'Welcome! Welcome home! So beautiful!' The fairies' voices were a discordant mix of high pitched little squeaks and other more mellow sounds.

Bree couldn't help but smile when a beautiful, winged being, with large blue eyes, and short golden hair, hovered in front of her. The fairy's wings moved at such a speed they were nothing but a blur to Bree's eyes. A diaphanous gown of pinks and mauves floated in the draught from her wings, and a circlet of wildflowers perched precariously on her head.

'It is lovely to have you with us, my lady,' the fairy said, her voice soft, like whispers on a spring breeze.

'Thank you, er…' Bree said.

'Niamh, my lady.' The fairy bowed her head, holding onto her floral circlet as she did so.

'We should proceed, Niamh,' Bree said. 'I think my Lord Lu tires of our chatter,' she added, nodding her head at Lu.

Niamh laughed, a gentle sound, like crystal breaking. She flew over to Lu and giggled again. 'My Lord Lu's bark is worse than his bite. He doesn't really mind.'

The fairy flew back to Bree. Lu unfolded his arms. 'Don't give my secrets away, Niamh.'

Lu's good-natured words and tone took Bree by surprise. Perhaps only she annoyed him?

'Is everyone ready?' Lu asked. 'We're not home yet.'

'Close enough, my lord,' Niamh said.

'Close enough isn't good enough,' Lu said, his voice gently bantering. 'Come on.' He started off.

'May I sit on your shoulder, my lady?' Niamh asked. 'I know it's impertinent of me, but it would be such an honour.'

'You may indeed, Niamh.'

Bree followed Lu. Niamh talked all the time, but Bree didn't follow half of what she said. Áine proceeded with a golden haze of fairies flying about her. Even Kuon didn't seem to object to twenty or so little people riding on his back. The atmosphere had lightened even as the forest trees had thinned out. Danger wasn't far behind them but, for a few moments, Bree allowed herself to forget why they had fled their home.

A wide spreading oak shut out all light other than the fairies' illumination. Bree recognised the oak with its lobed leaves extending from a centre line. Áine had told her about the magical properties of this wondrous tree.

Bree gasped as she stepped from beneath the oak's canopy. Wide stone stairs ascended to a columned and arched portal that was bathed in golden light. Lu was already halfway up when Bree started her climb. Under the arch an ornate symbol was carved.

'It's a triquetra within another triquetra,' Áine said. 'It's your emblem. The three corners representing the Triple Goddess.'

'I still don't understand what this means,' Bree said.

'All in its right time, macushla.'

As Bree, with Niamh still on her shoulder, reached the archway, she paused, her breath snatched away from her as she stared into the wondrous light. It surrounded her much as the fairies had surrounded Áine. The glow was tangible. Dust motes floated in golden beams and the air moved in silky streams of illumination. Bree could see outlines of trees but nothing else was discernible.

'Come,' Lu said, and waved her on. 'This is an added security before we reach the palace.' He stepped further into the radiance and disappeared. Next Kuon and the fairies that rode on his back vanished in the glow.

Bree followed them. She didn't feel afraid, only joyful with an eagerness she didn't understand.

When she emerged, a whole new world in the hues of a rainbow opened up before her. A river, reflecting an arched bridge crossing it, flowed quietly along with barely a ripple. Quaint buildings, with blue glass sides and cupola roofs, sat on the bridge. They were illuminated by candlelight from within. Above this soared other columned structures. Then higher, as the ground rose, another arched bridge sat beneath a higher level where a magnificent palace with battlements and towers stood in yellow and white shimmering light.

'There it is,' Niamh said. 'Your palace.'

'Home.' Áine sighed the word out.

Bree's eyes widened. She glanced at her aunt. This was Áine's home. Not a dwelling under a tree floating in the ether of the Otherworld. How much Áine had sacrificed for her. Her home, her people, and her fairies. Bree reached out, took her aunt's hand and smiled. No words were needed. What could she say?

Tears swam in Bree's eyes, but not only for what her aunt had done. The beauty of the Tuatha Dé Danann's home filled her with awe and amazement. Yet there was something else. An archetypal memory stirred within her. Perhaps it reached out to her from her mother and other long-dead ancestors. She'd seen her ancestral home in her dreams. It had called out to her, but she hadn't known why. If only her mother would be there to greet her, to take her into loving arms. She wanted to look into her mother's eyes. What had she been like? Like her, Bree was told, but her mother had the wisdom of a lifetime, a long lifetime. Áine said that the Tuatha Dé Danann were immortal, although they could be killed under some circumstances, just as her mother had died by Mór's hand.

Anger rumbled in Bree's chest. Fear, anger, hate— these were new emotions with which Bree had to grapple. She hated Mór without even seeing her. A dark, heavy feeling thundered in her chest. Everything before her gaze was beautiful, and yet it was in danger of being destroyed, just as Mór's hordes had already slaughtered people and devastated their villages.

Bree couldn't allow that to happen here. She could hear her mother's voice in her head. Not the words, but she felt her mother's strength. Waves of encouragement circled within Bree. The warmth of determination and hope replaced the thundering hatred.

She would stop Mór and then rebuild Tír na nÓg. Bree didn't have any ideas about how she'd do it, but she would. She couldn't restore life, but she could revive faith among her people.

Chapter Five

THE MORNING SUN shone by the time they reached the approach to the palace. Golden rays bathed the light cream stone of the towers and crenellated battlements with their saw-tooth merlons. The building rose up to five floors with a square tower in the front above the wooden doors, while two round towers stood, one on each side.

Bree halted. As tired and anxious as she was to reach their destination, she had to pause for a moment. The palace took her breath away as it glimmered in the soft, luminescent light that swathed the building. She could never have imagined that such a huge structure could exist. How did each floor manage to stand on those beneath? After her small cave, she decided the palace was extraordinary.

Guards must have seen them arrive as the heavy wooden gates opened to admit them. They walked beneath the square tower of the gatehouse.

Lu halted in a large entrance with tall columns

framing another wooden door to the left that Bree suspected was the entry to the palace itself. Lu stood at the top of the stairs waiting for them to ascend. Kuon barked, alerting others inside the palace of their arrival. Within moments, people ran down the stairs, cheering and waving their welcome, although Bree thought this had to be but a small percentage of the residents in this immense building.

Bree remained where she stood, overwhelmed by the crowd. Her anxious gaze found Áine, who nodded to her. Women and men alike dipped their heads, smiled, and chattered. Children touched her clothes. Bree couldn't breathe. She'd spent her entire life in a small cave under a tree with only Áine for company. If the open spaces and the tall trees of the forest hadn't alarmed her enough, so many people overwhelmed her entirely, even though everyone was friendly. She wanted nothing more than to find another cave and hide it in.

Niamh flew off her shoulder and returned with Áine, who pushed her way through the throng.

The resounding crash and flare of flames commanded silence, as everyone turned to Lu, who had brought Corraidhin to life.

'Enough!' His voice boomed out over the palace's inhabitants. 'Lady Bree is tired. She needs to rest and refresh herself. There is time enough for welcoming her.'

Without another word, a path opened up. Niamh settled back on Bree's shoulder as she ascended the stairs. Bree nodded and smiled at the people. Chastised and composed, they bowed and allowed her to pass.

At the top of the stairs, Bree turned and waved. Áine joined her.

'The fairies?' Bree questioned.

'They have their homes in the forest. They don't live with me.'

'May I stay?' Niamh asked.

'If the Lady Bree agrees.' Áine smiled.

'Of course,' Bree said.

Kuon followed his master as he led Bree, Áine and Niamh through the great hall, with the walls all made of the same blond stone as the columns outside, while white marble covered the floors. Columns stood everywhere. Ceilings were decorated with paintings of the natural world—trees, forests, animals, waterfalls and streams, all embellished with golden triquetra symbols.

From the great hall, they walked up a narrow staircase and then down a long passageway and in to a large reception room, and on into another long corridor. Lu halted in front of a heavy wooden door, once again decorated by triple triquetra and other ornate symbols Bree had yet to learn. The door handles were made of metal into the shapes of birds.

'Here are your chambers, My Lady.' Lu bowed. One eyebrow arched as he straightened and stared into her eyes.

Bree interpreted his expression as mockery, and it rankled with her. She wished she could've dismissed him and flounced away but, at that moment, three women opened the door and bowed to her.

'Your handmaidens,' Lu explained.

'I'll go on to my room,' Áine said.

Despair cut through Bree. 'No!' she almost shouted. Then with more dignity, she added, 'No, please stay with me, Áine.' Bree hadn't thought ahead to what might happen once they reached their destination. If she had, she wouldn't have imagined not having Áine with her, especially at first, until she'd accustomed herself to her new life. 'Will you, Áine?' Bree implored her.

'Of course, macushla.' Her aunt took her hand and squeezed it.

'Very well,' Lu said. 'There is another bedroom connecting to your chambers. I'll send along your hand-maidens, my Lady Áine.'

'We can manage with three maids,' Bree said. 'We've been living in a cave by ourselves. I'm sure we'll cope.'

'Well now, my lady,' Lu said scornfully, 'you'll have to learn to manage to live with servants. This is how it's done here.'

Bree bristled. 'I will decide how it's done here,' she said.

Lu gave an extravagant bow. 'We shall see,' he muttered as he rose.

Bree felt like wiping the smug look off his face. She turned instead and went into her chambers.

'Sleep well,' Lu called after her. 'You have a lot to do later today.'

Bree kept moving. Of course he'd have to have the last word!

'This isn't all mine, surely?' Bree asked Áine as they walked through the small entrance into another large room. Soft chairs with cushions were placed here and there among low tables set with lamps made of the most extraordinary metal designs. Some chairs also featured intricate metal work. A fireplace was central to the room.

'This is your parlour,' Áine explained. 'Our parlour.'

Bree walked into another room and sucked in her breath. The walls were lined with books and scrolls. Bree had never seen so many books in all of her life. She was beyond amazed. A huge desk and chairs also featured intricate designs around their legs.

'Come and look at your bedchamber.' Áine encouraged her.

The handmaidens opened a door to reveal a room of light cream stone walls, marble floors, with a large, raised, four-poster bed draped with silks in pastel colours. Side tables with lamps were beside the bed and a dressing table with a chair in front of it stood against one wall. All carried elaborate scrollwork. Bree noticed the triquetra about the room, some above her bed and dressing table.

'Am I to sleep in this room by myself?' Bree asked. Dismay plunged through her. She was used to the earthen floors and walls of a small room. Her pallet bed was adequate. Why did she need so much? How could she cope with it? The space alone frightened her. The openness, the light cream that dazzled her eyes… it was too much. She was used to brown earthen walls and floors. How could a place so different even exist?

Áine chuckled but when Bree stared at her aunt, Áine said, 'Oh macushla, you'll adjust. I must too.'

'Yes, of course,' Bree said, and forced a smile. She chided herself for being selfish. Her aunt had lived in their small earthen cave for the last eighteen years too.

'There's a bathroom connected to your bedroom,' Áine said. 'Why don't you refresh yourself and have a sleep. I'll do the same. I'm certain we'll both feel better then.' Áine turned to Bree's handmaidens. 'Will you show Lady Bree the way?' she asked.

Bree nodded and blinked back the tears that threatened to embarrass her.

Áine's handmaidens arrived and her aunt followed them to another bedroom.

Bree walked through to her bathroom. This room was somewhat smaller. It had a huge bathtub in the centre, sitting on the white marble floor. She turned to her handmaidens. 'What are your names?' she asked.

'I am Sorcha, my lady,' a matronly woman said. She stepped forward and bowed her greying head.

Bree smiled. It was a bit of a stretch to think of the mature woman as a handmaiden. The term carried thoughts of young women. She pursed her lips to prevent a grin.

'These are Úna and Doireann,' Sorcha continued.

Úna, a young brunette woman, bowed, followed by Doireann, who was dark-haired and aged somewhere between her two colleagues.

'We have prepared a bath for you, my lady. We heated the water as soon as we heard you were approaching the castle.'

Bree nodded. Bathing had been very different in the cave. They'd had a small copper bathtub that they had to carry into the kitchen, where a natural spring provided drinking and bathing water.

'How did you fill the bathtub?' Bree asked.

'We carried urns of water, my lady,' Sorcha said. 'You need not worry yourself. I will help you disrobe if you are ready.'

'Disrobe?' Bree said. Things were getting worse. 'I can manage, thank you, Sorcha.'

'Oh no, my lady, we can't allow you to manage on your own,' Sorcha said.

Bree stared at the woman. Lu's words about learning to live with servants flashed through her mind. Her jaw set tighter thinking of him. Disrobe? No. She wasn't going to allow anyone to strip her naked. Even Áine hadn't seen her without clothes since she was ten. 'It's very good of you…' Bree started but Sorcha cut in.

'It's my job to do it for you, my lady.'

'Ah,' Bree said, and her heart sunk. 'I wonder if we can compromise for now. I noticed a free-standing screen in my bedroom. Could you bring it in here?'

'Of course, my lady.' Sorcha nodded at the other two handmaidens.

Úna and Doireann hurried into the other room and then carried back the screen, which they placed near the bathtub where Bree directed. She could undress and step into the tub unseen. The screen had four ornately designed panels and was skilfully painted with pink blossoms.

'I am unused to servants,' Bree murmured, feeling foolish.

Sorcha smiled; her matronly instincts stirred. 'I'll

bring a clean shift and throw it over the screen, my lady. Then, when you're ready, we'll help you with the rest of your attire.'

Úna placed towels on a chair and the women departed.

Bree undressed and stepped into the bathtub. The water was warm, and there was so much of it. Áine had only ever partly filled their copper tub. Bree breathed deeply. Her sore and aching muscles relaxed. So much had happened since they'd left the protection of the cave in the Otherworld. She couldn't assimilate all of it.

What now? Tír na nÓg, the land of the Tuatha Dé Danann, this palace, and all of the people. They were her people, and they would now depend on her. How could she help them? She felt lost in this vast building and this new land. She wasn't certain if she could look after herself, let alone a world of other people.

She was startled out of her reverie when she heard a tinkling voice and saw Niamh settle on the end of her bath. Bree checked if the water covered her. Rose petals floating on the surface offered protection to her modesty.

'I thought I'd check on you, my lady,' Niamh said.

'That's kind of you but I'd prefer to bathe alone, if you don't mind,' Bree said.

Niamh giggled, as if she thought that very funny. 'I'll wait in your bedroom,' the fairy said and flew away.

Dressed in her shift, Bree saw that her handmaidens had laid out an assortment of attire from flowing silks in pastels to deep blue and red velvets.

'I think I'll sleep for a while,' Bree said.

Sorcha nodded at Úna who produced a long, flowing

blue nightgown. Bree allowed them to drop it over her head.

She'd washed her hair and towelled it dry. Doireann led her to the dressing table where she sat while the handmaiden brushed her long, thick red locks. Bree could have easily brushed it herself. She had eighteen years of practice.

Úna was waiting by the huge bed with the coverlet drawn back. It was as large as Bree's entire bedroom had been. Bree smiled and slipped beneath the covers. Úna settled the coverlet over her.

'We'll leave you, my lady,' Sorcha said. 'If you require anything, we'll be in quarters through there.' She pointed at a door off Bree's bedroom.

Between the handmaidens, they blew out every lamp, except for one near their own door, and closed long silken drapes until they covered the windows and shut out all other light.

Bree sighed and stared at the darkness around her. The bed felt soft and so comfortable. Maybe too comfortable. Would she get used to silken sheets and downy pillows? Her pallet bed was as hard as a rock by comparison. Tears sprang to her eyes. She gave in to her emotions and sobbed. She was the Triple Goddess, and she was crying like a baby who wanted her mother.

A small glow penetrated Bree's eyelids. She opened her tear-washed eyes to see Niamh, encased by her own magical illumination, sitting on her coverlet.

'I'm here, my lady,' the little fairy whispered. 'You don't need to feel alone.'

Bree blubbered even more at the fairy's words.

After some time of tossing and turning, even Niamh's presence wasn't enough. Bree couldn't cope any longer. She nudged the sleeping fairy awake. 'Follow me,' Bree said, as she pulled the coverlet off her bed.

She went to the door of Áine's bedroom, and slowly opened it. 'Shhh,' she mouthed to Niamh as they entered. Áine was sleeping peacefully, no doubt happy to be back in a comfortable bed in her home land. How had Aine coped all those years living in a small cave and sleeping on a thin, hard bed?

Bree did not want to wake Áine. Bree threw the coverlet from her bed onto the floor, bunched it up into a pillow and lay down. This was better. The fairy flew down and rested next to her.

'We'll sleep better now,' Bree whispered.

Niamh giggled, and then slapped her tiny hand over her minute mouth.

Chapter Six

Lu stood Corraidhin against the wall of his chambers—his spear shooting out a flame as if relieved to be back in the Inner Realm.

'I know how you feel, my friend,' Lu spoke to the spear, not that he expected an answer. That would be magic if Corraidhin vocalised.

Lu reached back and drew Cadeyrn from its scabbard, laying him on a chest worked with symbols of the sun. He threw off the straps that were over his chest, at the same time his manservant entered his bedchamber. Lu lived in one of the front towers, where some of the Immortals, his loyal band of men, also lived. Others lived in Milngavie, the village they'd passed to return to the palace. Lu turned to the man.

'Aongus, I think a bath is in order. Fighting trolls isn't a clean job.'

Kuon groaned and rose from where he'd flopped onto the floor, to hide behind the divan, something he always did when baths were mentioned.

'Yes, my lord.' Aongus bowed his head and left the room. A short man, he had once been powerful and strong, but an injury to his back prevented him from returning to battle. Lu gave him this position, and Aongus had been eternally grateful.

A knock sounded on the front chamber door. Aongus went to open it. Lu followed him into the parlour, a sparsely decorated room of leather divans, no cushions, a bear rug on the floor, a sturdy but old bookcase and a clock. Besides the bedroom and parlour, the chambers consisted of a bathroom, small and meagre, a study, a kitchen and heavy wooden table.

Fionn and Diarmuid strode into the foyer, and spying Lu, crossed over to him. Both men were two of his Immortals, his band of warriors. They were a tight brotherhood. Especially so where Fionn and Diarmuid were concerned. They had been lifelong best of friends and companions.

'You look frazzled,' Fionn said.

'By Dagda's beard, she's nothing but a child!' Lu flopped down on one of the divans. His friends followed suit.

'I told you.' Fionn looked grave. He flicked his long dark fringe off his face. His hair usually hid his eyes that possessed a mesmerising stare.

'We have no chance then against Mór?' Diarmuid asked.

He was a big man, such as they all were, with shoulder length brown hair. Diarmuid was renowned for his beauty, and for his love spot that made him irresistible to women. He told the tale that once when out hunting, he met a beautiful woman. After sleeping with her, she placed a love spot under his eye that made every woman who saw it, fall in love with him.

'Thank Dagda, not every woman,' Fionn had exclaimed at the time. 'Otherwise, my Grainne would leave me.'

Grainne was Fionn's wife and the three were good friends.

'Do you despair,' Diarmuid added.

'I wouldn't say that as yet,' Lu replied to his question. 'If she's her mother's daughter, we may survive.'

'You don't look hopeful,' Diarmuid murmured.

Lu rose and poured some mead, handing a goblet to each of his companions. 'Here's to our survival.'

***

Bree's eyes flew open. Everything was dark. Where was she? What had woken her?

Then the cry came again. Several cries, followed by a clamour of raised voices. Was she dreaming, lying on her pallet in her earthen home fantasising about…

A door burst open, and a horde of people rushed into the room. Bree shook her head. What had happened?

'My lady! My lady!' anxious voices shouted.

Sunlight flooded the room as long curtains were drawn back.

'My Lady Áine, Lady Bree has disappeared.'

'What?' Áine's disembodied voice sounded from somewhere behind Bree. Then Áine appeared at her side. 'Oh no! Have you searched—'

Bree rose. The heat of her embarrassment flamed in her cheeks.

Áine's jaw dropped. The five handmaidens stopped in their tracks.

'Bree,' Áine exclaimed. 'What are you doing here… on the floor?'

'I couldn't sleep in that huge room… on that soft bed.'

Niamh giggled. 'We couldn't sleep,' she added.

Áine wrapped Bree in her arms. 'At least you're all right,' Áine said. Then turning to the servants, she added, 'We have found Lady Bree. Return to your duties. Sorcha, I believe Lady Bree should dress. We must attend to the ancient flame.'

Bree sucked in her breath. She'd left the flame in its small chest in her room. All of her life she'd protected the flame, and now, when it was most at risk in a new dwelling, she'd left it unattended. She ran out of Áine's bedroom, through the parlour and into her bedroom. Relief flooded through her when she saw the *argat draiochta* chest. She sank onto the floor next to it.

After the drama she'd caused, Bree allowed her handmaidens to dress her without a word said between them. At times, she noticed Úna suppressed a giggle. Doireann seemed too taciturn to find the situation amusing. If anything, there was a hint of disdain in her expression.

They dressed Bree in a green velvet gown with long sleeves. A softer fabric fell in two swathes, one from each shoulder. The dress was more beautiful than anything Bree had ever possessed, but it was impractical. How was she supposed to do anything with such a fine dress on?

Áine, dressed in a pale blue gown, entered Bree's

bedroom and kissed her cheek. 'We'll have a drink and some fruit and then we must attend to the flame.'

'Very well,' Bree replied. 'I'm in your hands.'

After they'd refreshed themselves, Áine dismissed all their attendants. 'Are you ready, macushla?' she asked Bree.

A knock pounded on the outside door before Bree could reply.

'I'll go,' Áine said.

Lu and Kuon stepped into the entry and then followed Áine back to the parlour. Bathed, dressed in a fine blue tunic with darker blue trousers, and with his hair washed so that it gleamed yellow like the sunlight, Lu looked different to the man who'd taken them on a perilous journey from their Otherworld home and brought them to this wondrous palace.

For a moment, Bree's heart lurched, and the blood surged through it like a raging tide. Then Lu spied Bree and performed an elaborate bow. When he rose, his eyes laughed at her. The smile she had ready for him vanished.

'My lady,' he said. 'I heard you had trouble sleeping.' Then he laughed.

Bree raised her chin. 'I see gossip, like any ill-wind, travels fast, even in a palace,' she said, lacing her words with condescension.

Lu laughed louder, the sound booming around the chamber.

'Did you want something, my lord?' Bree asked, her tone frosty.

'I merely wanted to ascertain you had everything you needed,' Lu said, his blue eyes still twinkling with amusement.

'I have far more than I require,' Bree said. 'Thank you for your concern.'

'We must go to the flame room,' Áine said.

'Indeed you must,' Lu replied. 'Will you join me later to dine?'

'Of course,' Áine said. 'We—'

'No, we won't,' Bree cut in. The air between them was as sharp as her words. 'We'll eat here. Sorcha can arrange something to be brought to us.'

Áine lowered her gaze. Niamh giggled and flew up to Bree's shoulder from where she'd sat on a divan. Kuon barked.

'Very well,' Lu said. He bowed and headed for the door, chuckling before he closed it after him.

'What an insufferable man!' Bree exclaimed. 'Am I to be made a figure of derision?' She swung around so quickly that Niamh flew off her shoulder. The fairy grabbed her circlet that nearly fell off her head. 'I suppose everyone in the palace knows that I slept on the floor!'

'Please, macushla,' Áine implored, taking Bree's hands. 'Don't let it concern you. Lu has a wicked sense of humour. Come, let's go to the flame room. We must return the fire to its source.'

Bree carried the silver chest and followed Áine to one of the doors in the living room. Áine opened the door and

Bree's eyes widened as she took in all the books that lined the walls.

Bree could have imagined such a wonderous sight. Glass-topped cabinets held scrolls of parchment. Armchairs were placed randomly, and a desk and chair stood in the centre of the room—all designed with intricate scrolls and symbols.

'Oh Áine,' Bree murmured. 'I could stay in this room all day. Is this where the ancient flame is?'

'Not here,' Áine said. 'I thought you might like to see the library first. Follow me, macushla.' Áine led the way back through the grand reception hall, along the corridor and down the stairs to the great hall. 'We must go down to the lowest level, to a room beneath ground, which is where the ancient fire is kept.'

In the great hall, another room decorated in the same manner as all Bree had seen, Áine took some flint and a tinder box and lit a lamp on a table, then lifted it and beckoned Bree to follow as she descended a narrow stone staircase, the steps worn smooth by centuries of use. Bree lost count of the number of steps they trod on, the darkness growing thick as they descended. Once they were both standing in a narrow landing at the bottom—at least they didn't seem to be able to descend any further—Áine whispered words Bree didn't understand and then pulled a lever and a wooden door, covered with triquetra and other symbols Bree didn't know, opened.

'What did you say?' Bree asked.

'I spoke in the High Language. The words I said are like a password to enter,' Áine explained. 'You will have to learn the Tuatha Dé Danann's High Language. For now, come inside.'

'By all that's holy,' Bree murmured, as she cast her eyes around the room. The walls shone silver and were worked with elaborate ornamentations. Bree recognised the triquetra. 'What is this symbol?' She pointed to another that was prominent in the decorations.

'It's a triskele. Another of the triple goddess's signs,' Áine explained, and continued, 'The walls are lined with your mother's magical substance, *argat draiochta*.'

Bree crossed to the centre of the room to the ancient fire, the one true primordial flame. It sparked and danced a merry welcome. Their one lamp dulled into insignificance in its presence. Flames shot from the large cauldron and reflected off every surface, creating a maze of never-ending mirrors.

Warmth coursed through Bree's veins, drawing her to the fire. It cried out to her, and she could do naught but answer it.

She opened the chest that contained the small cauldron. The tiny flame jumped high, as if it too understood it had returned home.

Áine took the chest from Bree and nodded. Bree plunged her hand into the tiny cauldron. The flames slid onto her palm. As before, they didn't burn her. Nor did she expect them to. However, when she confronted the huge cauldron and the leaping flames it contained, she hesitated.

Áine rested her hand on Bree's wrist and chanted words that flowed melodically over Bree and into the fire itself. It roared, shooting flames high. The room blazed as if the sun had descended and blinded them. 'You must say these words. I'll whisper, and you repeat them.'

Bree stared into the ancient, holy fire. 'I am the Triple Goddess. I am maiden, mother, and crone,' Bree recited. 'I am the poetess, the smith and the healer. I am creativity, inspiration and vision. *Bean an ti*, I am she who cares for everything. *Beatha*, I am the livelihood that sustains my people. I am *Comhluadr*, the harmony of being together. *Dochas*, I bring hope to the future. I am *Draiocht*, the magic that is unseen. I am *Fios*, knowledge and understanding. I was at the beginning of creation, in the middle of life and at the end of existence.'

Áine fell silent. Bree knew what to do without being told. She plunged her hands into the fiery inferno. The small flames in her palms immersed themselves with their primeval life force. The conflagration licked Bree's skin with a soft caress that welcomed her and possessed her. Her blood raged with the heat. She saw her mother in the flames, and her mother took on three faces. Just as with the words Bree had recited, she saw the girl, the mother and the old woman. Her mother reached out to her, but Bree stepped back, a movement beyond her volition. Her mother disappeared but Bree carried the fire with her. It burned on both of her palms. When she closed them, the flames disappeared.

'You will be able to summon the fire at your will from now on,' Áine explained.

'I saw my mother,' Bree murmured, in wonder. 'I saw her, Áine!'

'She is with you, macushla.'

'Will I be a true triple goddess one day?' Bree asked. 'I said the words, but I don't have three personae.'

'You will very soon,' Áine assured her.

Bree stared at her palms. 'The flames have disappeared.'

'Of course, they won't be on your hands all the time. Apply your will and they will come,' Áine said.

Bree concentrated and startled herself when the flames appeared. Intrigued, she watched them burn on her palms, but not hurt her. She smiled at Áine and closed her hands together, extinguishing the ancient fire.

Before they left the room, Bree asked, 'Where is she, Áine? My mother?' When her aunt frowned, Bree added, 'Please tell me where her body is.'

'Lu told me she is lying in state. After this fighting is over, she will be cremated.'

Bree's heart soared. 'Then can I see her? I saw her in the ancient flames, but I need to see her in...' She'd been about to say, in real life, but that couldn't happen now. Perhaps seeing her in death would be enough. It would have to be. 'Don't you want to see your sister?'

'Of course, but I didn't want to upset either of us before the battle,' Áine said

'I must see my mother,' Bree said, grabbing her aunt's hands. 'Please. Where is she?'

'I'll ask Lu.'

Chapter Seven

THEY LINGERED in the reception room after they'd eaten. Bree read a book Áine had given her. It told the tale of how her grandmother Danu, the mother goddess, had set out their laws and beliefs. Bree couldn't understand the passages of runes. Niamh, sitting on her shoulder, was of no help either. Bree realised she had so much to learn. In just over twenty-four hours, her life had been turned upside down and around about. Flames burned in her palms now, for goodness sake!

When a heavy thud sounded on the front door, Doireann opened it to Lu. Kuon was beside him. Something inside Bree's chest lurched, a small tug on her heart. Lu leaned forward as he spoke to Doireann, and then she ushered him into the foyer. The light from the lamps glinted off his blond hair. Bree blinked hard and watched as Doireann approached Áine and whispered to her.

Áine rose. 'He wants to speak to me,' she said by way of explanation and headed to the foyer.

Lu leaned into Áine. Bree could hear snatches of the conversation.

'It went well,' Áine said. 'She is at one with the flame.'

'She needs to meet the others,' Lu said.

What others? Bree couldn't believe there could be even more people she had to meet.

'It's a lot for her to take in all at once,' Áine said.

'Tomorrow morning,' Lu added. 'In the grand reception hall.' He stepped away from Áine, turned to the door and then swung back. 'You made grave errors in not educating her enough in our ways.'

Áine drew herself up to her full height. Even then, Lu dwarfed her. 'I did as her mother instructed.'

'By Dagda's beard,' Lu's voice boomed out. 'It doesn't help us now.' Again he leaned into Áine. 'You do know how precarious our situation is?' he asked her.

Bree wanted to rush to her aunt's aid, but something in Lu's voice pinned her to her chair.

'It will soon be Samhain. If Mór is going to make an assault on the Inner Realm, it will be then. She will call upon all her creatures. The dead will rise and do her bidding.'

'Mór will never breach the Inner Realm,' Áine said, her voice sounding less than convincing.

'I wouldn't be too sure,' Lu countered. 'And what do we have to protect us, to save us? An ignorant girl! How can she stand up to the likes of Mór?'

Bree sprang to her feet and hurried into the foyer. Lu saw her coming. He shot an insolent glare her way, and then turned and strode out of the room.

Áine caught Bree to stop her following Lu. 'Let him go, macushla,' she said.

'He has no right to say such things,' Bree countered. Then ignoring her aunt, she swung open the door and called out to Lu in the corridor. 'I want to see my mother before I meet anyone else.'

Lu halted and twirled. It took a moment before he replied, 'Very well.'

'Then arrange it,' Bree said and turned her back on him. Back in her chamber, she felt her breath lifting her chest in a painful rhythm.

Áine led Bree back to the parlour. 'Calm down, macushla.' Áine reached up and pushed back some stray strands of Bree's red hair. 'I've never seen you like this.'

'I've never had to deal with such a rude man before. Anyway, he's going to arrange for us to see my mother's body.'

'That's good. Lu is only concerned for us.'

'He's not worried about me,' Bree scoffed. At least he wore a tunic and wasn't half naked!

Áine led Bree to a divan. 'I understand, to some extent, what he's saying,' Áine said. 'You are ignorant of many of the Tuatha Dé Danann's ways. It was what your mother wanted. She always hoped to bring you here before she died, so she could train you. No one could foresee her early death.'

'I still don't understand why she wouldn't allow you to teach me more about our people. Why couldn't she… and you, Áine, have talked more about our culture, our world? I know I read some things in books, but you never told me about my mother and grandmother.'

'Anything could have disturbed the ether in the Other-world. If Mór had felt the slightest disruption, the slightest tremor, she would have tracked you down and killed you. She's very powerful. One word could have brought her baying at our door.'

Bree had to accept it. It had been her mother's wish. There was no going back. What was done was done. She had remained safe for eighteen years, safe but ignorant of her heritage; oblivious of who she was and of how many people wanted to kill her. She hated to admit that Lu was correct. She'd never tell him so; never give him that satisfaction. There was so much she had to learn, and she didn't know how she was going to do it. How could she save her people against Mór, someone she didn't even know? If Mór was so powerful, how could she be defeated? How could Bree stop her? So many people had been slaughtered. The thought of the village they had passed through on their way here sprang to her mind, the blackened bodies, and the burnt timbers of what once had been the villagers' homes. Tears stung Bree's eyes.

How many more have been killed?

'According to Lu,' she said trying to calm herself, her voice on an even keel at least, 'we have little time before Mór will attack. Tell me more about Samhain.'

Niamh settled again on Bree's shoulder. She'd kept out of the way while Bree was angry.

'Samhain marks the end of the harvest season and the beginning of winter, the darker half of the year,' Áine explained. 'It's a time when the Veil between life and death grows thin. It's the night when ghosts of the dead return to earth.'

'Lu said that the dead will rise and do Mór's bidding,' Bree said. 'Is that what he meant? She will command these ghosts of the dead?'

'She might,' Áine said. 'She has the power to do it.'

'Who else does she command?'

'Scathach,' Niamh said and flew in front of Bree's face. 'She's the Warrior Queen, the Shadowy One.'

'Scathach lives on a remote island at the outer reaches of Tír na nÓg,' Áine commented. 'She may not be a part of Mór's forces.'

'She's been seen,' Niamh explained. 'So has Badb. She's the goddess of fear.' Niamh's wings fluttered faster. 'If she is seen prior to a battle, it foreshadows the carnage to come.'

Áine frowned. 'That isn't good.'

'So we have Mór, Scathach the warrior queen, Badb the goddess of fear, and a horde of ghosts of the dead,' Bree said. Her tone was bantering but her stomach did somersaults.

'Banshees too,' Niamh added. 'Their songs are laced with death curses and hexes. Anyone who hears a banshee song dies.'

Silence sat heavily on them. Then Áine said, 'I think we should forget banshees and Mór for now. The day grows late and you will need a good night's sleep.'

'As if that's likely,' Bree replied. 'I'm tired, but I don't think I'll sleep a wink.'

'You have a big day tomorrow, macushla. Lu has suggested you should meet the others.'

'By all that's holy, who are the others?'

'The other gods and goddess of Tír na nÓg. The immortals, the centaurs and the fairies.'

'I've met the fairies,' Bree pointed out.

'Lu thinks it better for everyone to meet you, macushla.'

Bree sighed. 'So they can see how ignorant and hopeless I am? Great!'

Áine took her niece's hands. Niamh settled on Bree's shoulder. 'They will see you for who you are, a young, intelligent woman, strong and eager to learn about them and the ways of the Tuatha. You already have command of the ancient fire. You need to show them. They will respect you, macushla.'

'Very well,' Bree said. 'I suppose it's for the best.' She had to meet her people sometime. As Lu had said, time was something that was scarce at the moment. Samhain was approaching. There was no time to have a pleasant reception with musical entertainment, if that was the way it was done. She had to meet the others, face them with as much equanimity as she could muster.

Lu returned an hour later, banging on the door as seemed to be his way. When Úna opened it, he strode past her with Kuon following him. 'Come and I'll take you to your mother,' he said, without any greeting, when he spied Bree in the parlour.

Bree, with Niamh on her shoulder, held her aunt's hand as she followed Lu through the corridor outside of Bree's rooms and then into one of the front towers, where on the highest floor her mother waited for them. The room was lined with her mother's magic metal, *argat draiochta*, which caused Bree to squint against its brightness.

'I thought she'd be safe in here,' Lu said.

Bree's heart quaked at what he didn't say. Did he really think they could be defeated and Mór's hordes would defile her mother's body?

Áine entered the room first and crossed to where her sister lay on a high dais. A sob wracked Áine, drawn from somewhere deep within her. It sounded like the cry of a wounded animal. Áine took one of Lady Brigid's hands in hers.

Bree hurried to her aunt's side and took her other hand. At that moment, she felt more distraught for her aunt than for herself. Then, she gazed at her mother and sucked in a breath that rasped its way into her lungs.

Dressed in a green velvet gown, her mother, the Lady Brigid, looked more beautiful than Bree could ever have imagined. An ethereal glow shone on translucent skin. Long red hair fell over her shoulders and draped over the sides of the dais, while red lashes made a fiery arc on her fine cheekbones.

Then, the enormity of their present circumstances, her lost years spent in an earthen cave, her mother's death, washed over Bree like water rushing over a waterfall in pictures she'd seen, and she was at the base of the water-fall being plummeting by its full force. A cry escaped her lips, and she touched her mother's hand. Her beautiful, courageous mother, whom she would never know in life, lay before her in death.

'Why did she send me away with you, Áine? Why? I could have stayed with her, loved her, grown up with her.'

Niamh sniffed and nearly slipped off Bree's shoulder.

'When you were born, macushla, times were troubled. We had come to this realm to grow and prosper but Mór had begun to cause trouble. She was jealous of your mother's popularity, Brigid's power—although your mother never thought of it as power. She simply ruled her people, cared for them and helped them always. When villagers died in random attacks, we all believed it was Mór. She'd started to draw the darker individuals to her. Scathach and others. Then, Mór made a definite threat on Brigid's life. She swore that, as soon as you were born, she would kill you.' Áine sighed. 'Brigid pleaded with me to take you away and protect you. Brigid and I were the only ones who knew that we went to the Otherworld.'

'But Áine, you had to leave your fairies behind… Do you have other family? Children?'

'Only you, macushla.'

Bree glanced at Lu, who had moved closer to Brigid.

'Áine had no choice,' Lu said. 'You had to be protected.'

'Brigid always planned to bring you to her one day,' Áine said, 'when you were old enough and less vulnerable.'

'With you alive,' Lu said as he took over the explanations, 'it meant that if the worst happened and Lady Brigid died, you would be able to claim the crown.'

'Brigid never really thought she'd die,' Áine said. 'The Tuatha Dé Danann are immortal.'

'That's what I don't understand,' Bree said.

'Your mother was stabbed by a dagger forged by black magic by a necromancer,' Lu told her.

'A necromancer? What's that?'

'A necromancer brings forth the dead,' Lu explained. 'Many rituals had to take place to produce a dagger capable of killing one of the Tuatha Dé Danann.'

'I understand now,' Bree murmured. 'Has the necromancer been found?'

'He or she has vanished among Mór's hordes,' Lu said, scornfully.

'And the dagger forged by black magic?' Bree asked Lu. 'Was it found?'

'No. It's still in Mór's grasp.'

'Then… Mór might use it again to try to kill me.'

'It's entirely possible.' Lu stared at her, his gaze intense. 'That's why you're not to leave the palace. You'll be busy enough meeting everyone. Even around the palace, always have a guard with you.' He folded his arms. 'Is that understood?'

'Very well,' Bree said.

She didn't like Lu being so forthright and bossing her around but under the circumstances, she would do as he asked.

Bree stayed a little longer with her mother, until Áine urged her to return to their rooms. She reluctantly agreed but she was determined she would visit her mother every day until the cremation.

CHAPTER EIGHT

Doireann helped Bree disrobe. Bree still didn't feel comfortable removing her shift but allowed her handmaiden to lift her nightgown over her head. Bree was about to move from behind the screen when Doireann pulled a letter from a pocket in her dress.

'My lady,' Doireann started, then lowered her voice. 'This is for you.'

'For me?' Bree took the letter. A wax seal only required her to break it.

'My Lord Lu handed it to me. He said I should give it to you.'

'Lu?' Bree questioned. She recalled that Lu had leaned in close to Doireann in the foyer when she'd opened the door to him earlier. However, Bree couldn't imagine why Lu hadn't given it directly to her or to Áine.

When Bree went to step from behind the screen yet again, Doireann stopped her. 'My lady... perhaps you should read it here... out of sight of Niamh,' she whispered so that Bree could barely hear.

Why shouldn't Niamh see she had a letter? Uncertainty floated around Bree like a cloud. Something wasn't right. She snapped the seal and opened the letter.

Every muscle tensed as Bree read. 'If you want to save your people, meet me at midnight beneath the Yew Walk.' She looked up at Doireann. 'Do you know where the Yew Walk is?'

Doireann paled. 'It is outside the Inner Realm,' she said.

Why would Lu want to meet her there? Perhaps he wanted to see her away from Áine and Niamh. But why outside the Inner Realm? Surely it would be more dangerous? There had to be somewhere around this huge palace where they could meet in private? Hadn't he only said earlier today not to leave the palace? Then why had he sent this note?

'Can you find your way to the Yew Walk?' Bree asked Doireann.

'I can, my lady.'

'Will you take me there?'

'It will not be safe once we're outside the Inner Realm, my lady.'

Bree glanced at the letter. It had to be important if Lu was going to such extremes to speak with her. 'I must go,' Bree said.

'Then I will accompany you, my lady.'

Doireann's taciturn expression darkened. At first, Bree hadn't taken to the young woman but she showed bravery and loyalty in her willingness to lead Bree to the Yew Walk, out in the unprotected part of Tír na nÓg.

Bree smiled. 'We must be there at midnight. I hope

Niamh goes to sleep quickly. She does like to stay close to me. Then I'll change my clothes and we'll leave.'

Bree sank into the soft mattress and pulled the covers up to her chin. Niamh settled on the floral coverlet and eased herself down so Bree could only see her tiny golden head. It seemed that once a fairy slept, their golden effervescent light disappeared. Their wings folded down at will.

Bree thought she could probably get used to this huge bed. It was comfortable in a way, as if she floated on a cloud. Tonight, however, she lay with her senses alert as she waited for Niamh's glow to fade. As soon as it did, Bree eased herself out of the coverlet and dressed in the gown and shoes she'd taken off before bed. She had doubts the shoes would serve her well out in the forests and fields, but it was all she had. From a drawer near her bed, she took the dagger with which she'd fought the trolls and silhouetted figures in the burnt village, and tied its scabbard to her side.

Niamh was still asleep.

Bree tiptoed towards Doireann's door. It opened before she reached it. Doireann nodded her head for Bree to follow. When they reached the outer chambers' door, Doireann turned the handle and peered outside. She nodded again and they slipped out into the passageway. Bree wondered where the two guards, who should be standing outside her door, had gone. It was just as well they weren't there. Bree hadn't thought about them hindering her way. She wasn't used to so many people, so many doors.

Doireann led her down to the courtyard and through a side door that took them outside of the palace, yet again without anyone challenging their movements. Bree followed Doireann through some trees and then across another field and into a small copse of trees.

'Are we close to the Yew Walk?' Bree asked. Her instincts told her something was wrong. She would have turned back if Doireann hadn't replied that it wasn't far.

The moon was high and speared light through the trees to illuminate their way. Nothing seemed familiar. Surely they would have to cross bridges as they did on their journey to the palace? Bree caught a reflection in her peripheral vision and decided it must be the river.

They stepped from the trees. Bree shivered. Was it the darkness that set her nerves on edge? Before she could analyse it, they walked through the other side into the open. Where was the magnificent archway? They should have gone through it.

'We leave the Inner Realm here, my lady,' Doireann whispered. She grabbed Bree's hand, something Bree thought her handmaiden shouldn't do, though she was glad of it.

'Can you go through without saying special words?'

'Yes, we can because we're going from the Inner Realm to the Outer.'

For a second, Doireann disappeared. Then Bree hit something soft. She felt disoriented and lost, as if she floated in a bubble, and then it spat her out. She'd left the

Inner Realm behind. She gazed about her. Another copse of ancient trees faced her.

'We go this way, my lady,' Doireann said, her voice still low.

Bree followed her along an uneven path that traversed the edge of the forest. Even by moonlight, Bree couldn't avoid stumbling. The chill she'd felt a short time ago returned. Why did Lu want to meet out here? Although they hadn't encountered wolves or any other creatures, Bree didn't understand why they couldn't have talked inside the palace somewhere.

Doireann stopped. 'We go through here, my lady.'

Bree stepped between some trees and then came to a halt. This was it. The Yew Walk.

'A little farther, my lady,' Doireann implored.

Bree walked beneath a large, vaulted arch of bare twisting branches, their canopies entwined. Narrow streaks of moonlight found a way through, here and there, offering a teasing glint of the light above. She jumped when a tortured groan filled the cavern.

'It's the trees moaning, my lady,' Doireann whispered.

Bree leaned her head back. The cry came again. Misshapen branches protested as they rubbed against other contorted tree limbs. The name of the Yew Walk had, at first, conjured scenes of a pleasant place to stroll and chat. This couldn't be farther from what Bree had imagined.

Then a different cry came; a scream, thin and shrill, like fingers scratching a slate. Bree shivered. Every hair stood on end. Her skin crawled with fear.

Doireann jumped and scurried away from her

mistress. She pressed her hands over her ears and her mouth opened wide, although she didn't call out.

The scream reverberated through the Yew Walk, one shriek after another, after another. A figure separated itself from the trees. It had the outline of a person, but it possessed the substance of grey smoke. It floated from the canopy and swooped down on them. Long, ragged, grey hair swept behind its skeleton frame. Bony, claw-like fingers reached towards Bree. For a moment, Bree stared at the creature's dark, gnarled face before she bent out of the way of those hands.

The shriek, at close quarters, was deafening. Bree drew her dagger and struck out, catching a shadowy grey arm. The knife went through, as if the being was, indeed, composed of smoke.

The creature circled again, and this time lunged for Doireann. The woman fell to her knees, her hands still over her ears, her face twisted with agony. The gnarled face came close but didn't touch Doireann. Then it flew back to the yew canopy and disappeared.

Doireann toppled to the ground, her features masked in horror.

Bree grabbed Doireann's hands and tried to pull them away from her ears. 'Doireann, Doireann…' It was no use. Doireann was dead, lying contorted in her death throes.

Bree rose to utter silence, as if even the yew branches thought it better not to protest anymore. She turned and stared about her. Cold terror carved a track through her body.

Movement came from deep within the grotto. Bree watched as something walked towards her and slowly

materialised into the shape of a person. Not another creature? At least this one walked. It was difficult to discern
whether it was male or female until it came much closer.
Then long dark hair with a silver streak on each side of a
female face became apparent. She wore a cloak, trousers
and tunic.

She stopped in a section of the Yew Walk that
remained in shadow. 'I see you've met my banshee,' a soft,
silky voice said.

'Banshee?' Bree reiterated. She should have guessed
from what Áine and Niamh had explained earlier in the
evening. The banshee's cry had killed Doireann. Why
wasn't she dead, as well? She stepped forward. 'Your
banshee? You killed my handmaiden!'

The woman made a gesture as if she flicked a piece of
dirt from her sleeve. 'She couldn't live. She'd served her
purpose.'

'Her purpose?'

'She brought you to me.'

Bree looked down at Doireann's body. Confusion
charged through her brain. Doireann had brought her
here at this woman's behest? What about Lu? Where did
he fit in? Bree raised her head. Her stomach tightened. He
didn't have anything to do with this! She'd been tricked.
Despair raged where bewilderment had been.

'Who are you?' Bree demanded.

'My name is Scathach.'

'Scathach,' Bree murmured.

'I see you've heard of me.'

'Don't you live on a remote island? What are you
doing here?'

'I couldn't miss out on witnessing the annihilation of the inner circle. Their obliteration.' Scathach drew her sword. 'I couldn't miss seeing your destruction,' she added.

Bree wanted to step away from Scathach. She wanted to run, but she knew showing weakness would finish her. Instead, she raised her chin. 'Why did you bring me here?' she demanded.

Scathach laughed. 'Why, to kill you, of course.'

'You said in your letter, and I assume you wrote it, that I should meet you if I wanted to help my people.'

'You can't believe everything you read,' Scathach said, and laughed again.

She started to circle Bree, but Bree moved with her, not taking her eyes off the woman.

'What will Mór say if you cheat her of my death?' Bree asked.

Scathach flinched and pointed her sword at Bree. The point of the blade was only inches from her chest.

Bree had sheathed her dagger. Even if she drew it out now, Scathach's steel would hit home first. The flame was her only chance. She focused on her palms. If only she could bring the ancient fire to life. It was a difficult task when Scathach stared her down. Bree couldn't do it. Her palms felt warm, but the flames wouldn't materialise.

Their heads snapped around as the ground beneath their feet vibrated. Something pounded in the near distance. Then it stopped. When it came again seconds later, it was louder.

Scathach's eyes narrowed. Then she lowered her sword, flung her cloak over her shoulder and stepped away from Bree. Scathach clicked her fingers. Something appeared from the shadows where Scathach had at first been hiding. As it came closer, Bree thought it was a horse but wasn't certain. It was black, a dull fathomless black, and it had red eyes.

Bree drew her dagger. This didn't bode well.

Scathach swung herself up onto the horse's bare back. She waved her sword in Bree's direction. 'We'll meet again,' she said. 'I promise you.'

Another horse galloped beneath the twisted canopy and forced itself between Bree and Scathach. 'Not if I can help it,' Lu shouted, his voice resounding beneath the yew trees.

He drew his sword. Blades clashed and sparked. The two horses pranced around one another as their riders fought in a deadly dance. Scathach cried out as Lu's sword, the mighty Cadeyrn, cut her arm. She pulled on her horse's reins and swung away from him.

'I'll meet you at Samhain,' she called to Bree, and galloped away.

Lu turned his horse and, as he drew close to her, he grabbed Bree's hand, dragging her up in front of him.

'That hurt,' she said. She winced in pain and rubbed her shoulder.

'You're lucky you're not dead. By Dagda's beard!' Lu's anger cut through her.

'Doireann...' Bree pointed at the woman's contorted body.

Lu looked behind. Scathach was nowhere to be seen. 'We have to leave her. She betrayed you. She betrayed all of us. Let her people find her; if they will.'

Bree looked into the shadows. 'That was Scathach,' she said.

'I know,' Lu said, and sheathed Cadeyrn.

'What…' Bree hesitated. Perhaps now wasn't the time to ask questions. 'What sort of horse did she have?'

'A púca. It's a shadowy creature, a shape-changer. A bringer of bad fortune.'

Bree didn't reply. Lu tugged her in close to him, and then took his arm away.

'Hold on,' he said. He turned his steed and galloped away from the Yew Walk.

Bree reached down and grabbed the horse's mane.

CHAPTER NINE

BREE DIDN'T SPEAK during the journey back to the palace. Lu's anger radiated from him and enclosed her. She was annoyed too because he made no attempt to help her keep her seat. Her gown forced her to ride side-saddle, which made it harder to stay on the horse's shoulders. Every time she slipped to the side she was forced to tug the poor horse's mane in an effort not to fall off. Even though Lu's arms loosely circled her, he wouldn't help support her.

By the time they reached the palace, and Lu brought his horse to a halt in the entrance way, Bree had borne enough. She pushed against his arm and jumped down, nearly falling in the process.

A pageboy took the horse. She knew Lu had dismounted and was striding up the stairs to catch up with her. He caught her at the top, took her arm and then commenced to drag her behind him.

Bree dug her heels in and stopped. 'Release my arm. I will not be pulled through the corridors of my own palace.'

Lu swung around. 'Your palace? It's a shame you hadn't remembered that earlier and recalled who you are supposed to be.'

The last words rankled, turning in Bree's stomach like a thorn twisting. For a moment, their gazes locked in a battle where sparks flew through the air between them just as Lu's sword had done when fighting Scathach. 'You don't show me any respect,' Bree accused.

'Respect has to be earned,' Lu threw at her.

Bree's jaw clenched and she strode past the tall, powerful warrior with her chin held high. 'I will not discuss things here. I'll be in my chambers if you wish to find me.'

'By all the jumping fleas in Dagda's beard!' Lu's voice boomed out. 'That's where I was taking you. You don't even know the way.'

Lu pushed past her. He bumped her already sore shoulder as he strode by. Bree felt warmth in her palms. Now the flames wanted to materialise! She was tempted to shoot a fiery whip at Lu's back… but she didn't.

Bree followed him to her rooms, but she refused to hurry after him. She walked at her own pace. He was at the door, waiting for her. Two guards now stood sentinel on either side of him. Kuon had found him, and the hound sat at his feet. When Bree approached, Kuon sprang up and licked her hand. Lu opened the door.

Áine was in the foyer and wrapped her arms around Bree as soon as she entered. Niamh flew about them, leaving a trail of golden light behind her.

'Oh macushla,' Áine said. 'I thought we'd lost you.'

Bree stepped back. Áine had been crying, as had

Niamh who settled on Áine's shoulder. Remorse struck Bree. The last thing she'd wanted was to cause distress to someone she loved... and this included the little fairy, of whom she'd already become so fond.

'Come into the other room,' Áine said, and led Bree into the parlour.

Lu was already there, pacing. Kuon knew something was amiss and paced with his master.

'Thank Danu that Niamh woke and saw you leave with Doireann,' Áine said, drawing Bree to a divan.

'I'm sorry, my lady,' Niamh said. 'But I feared all was not right.'

'As it turned out,' Bree said, 'you saved my life, Niamh.'

Lu halted. 'I believe I had something to do with it,' he said and arched a brow.

'I was managing the situation perfectly well,' Bree replied.

'Not from my viewpoint, you weren't.'

'Very well, thank you,' Bree said. She narrowed her gaze and added, 'If you're so conceited you need your actions lauded, then I admit you saved me.'

Lu's eyes widened. 'It was Scathach!' he blurted out. 'You're fortunate she didn't cut you down in a heartbeat.'

'Scathach?' Áine murmured. 'Oh no! Why did you go, macushla?'

'Doireann brought me a note. She said that my Lord Lu had given it to her.' Bree cut him a glare.

'I didn't give her a note.' Lu threw the words at Bree. 'Why would I?'

'My exact thoughts,' Bree said. 'But the note said to meet you if I wanted to save my people.'

Lu paced across the room. The air was charged in his wake. He stopped in front of Áine. 'Do you see? This is what I mean. She knows nothing! Not even enough to keep herself out of trouble.'

'Why can't you sit down and stop storming all over the room?' Bree snapped at Lu. He would never sit down. It drove her to distraction. She directed her next words at her aunt. 'It didn't feel right from the beginning. Even the guards were missing from their posts at the outer door.'

'Doireann had drugged them, and she'd had them removed.'

'Who helped her?' Bree asked. The thought of traitors in their midst sat uneasily.

'She had a confederate,' Áine explained. 'He's been caught and imprisoned.'

'Do we have a prison?' Bree asked. She was ignorant of so much, but less than forty-eight hours had passed since she'd left her Otherworld home. How could she learn everything at once? She'd learned a lesson tonight, though; not to trust so readily.

'Of course we have a prison,' Lu scoffed.

Everything she said dropped her lower in his esteem. She told herself it didn't matter, but of course, it did. If she couldn't gain his respect, how could she achieve the respect of all the other people in Tír na nÓg?

'What did Scathach want?' her aunt asked her.

'She said she wanted to kill me,' Bree said. 'I was in the process of finding out if that was so when a god,' Bree paused for effect, 'on a steed, charged between us.' Lu's jaw tightened and he swung about. Bree ignored him.

'However, she baulked when I mentioned that she'd cheat Mór of the pleasure of killing me.'

'You're here now, safe and sound.' Áine took Bree's hand. 'That's the main thing.'

'The main thing,' Lu said, directing his words at Bree, 'is what the repercussions would have been if Scathach had killed you.'

Bree stared at him. 'You would have had to fight Mór without me,' she said.

Lu shook his head. 'You have no idea.' His tone did more than chastise her. She felt a despair she didn't understand. 'We can fight Mór's hordes without you. You're not here for your battle skills or lack thereof. You're a figurehead. You're the Triple Goddess, daughter of Brigid, granddaughter of Dagda and Danu. You don't have to fight. You have to inspire.'

What could Bree say? Desolation lashed her more than Lu's words could do.

'The repercussions of your death would reach much further than you can imagine,' he continued. 'Your mother is dead. You are her only heir. If you die before you marry, if you die childless, what happens then?'

Bree's head sprang up. 'Am I nothing more than a queen bee to breed a hive?' she asked.

'That's for you to decide,' Lu said. He'd stopped pacing and stared at her.

'Someone else would have to be the triple goddess,' Bree said after a moment.

'That's exactly why Scathach tricked you into coming to her. She would love nothing more than to kill you before we battle, because then we would have internal strife. All the goddesses would vie with each other to take your place. The gods would most likely say, why have a triple goddess at all?' Lu narrowed his gaze. His voice had a cutting edge to it. 'Some might look to me to take your place.'

Was that why Lu disliked her? He was jealous. He wanted to be leader of the Tuatha Dé Danann. He was god of warriors and battle, but he was also the sun god. Lofty ranks!

'Imagine how pleased Mór would be with Scathach if she achieved our downfall from within ourselves,' Lu added.

Bree looked Lu in the eye. Her role was more important than she'd imagined. She must remain strong. It was more vital than ever that she won the respect and support of the Tuatha Dé Danann. Would she win Lu's respect? Did she want to? She saw him in a different light. Was he friend or was he foe?

'I'm tired,' Bree said. 'I'm going to bed.'

Lu bowed. Kuon sprang to his feet. Hound and master left.

Áine kissed Bree's cheek. 'Sleep well, macushla,' she said.

'Doireann is dead, you know,' Bree murmured. 'Killed by a banshee's wail. Why did it not kill me?' Bree wouldn't ask this in Lu's presence.

'It cannot kill gods and goddesses.'

'Then the banshee was for Doireann? After using her, Scathach only wanted to dispose of her?'

'There is no honour among the enemies we're facing.' Áine once again kissed Bree's cheek. 'Try to sleep.'

'I'd like to go to the ancient fire first,' Bree said. 'May I?'

'It is yours, macushla. Can you remember the way?'

Bree nodded. Áine leaned in and whispered the words she must say to open the door. Bree hoped she'd remember them.

She strode back through the great reception room and along the corridor to the great hall. She lit a lamp, as her aunt had previously done—Bree thought of bringing the flames to her hands but decided that might be abusing its special use. She managed to say the correct words to open the door. The room, with the flames reflecting off the *argat draiochta* walls, left Bree in awe. The magical silver metal that her mother had smelted cocooned her from outside influences and thoughts. A sense of freedom lifted her heart and eased away all the negative and conflicting feelings she had surrounding Lu. She traced her fingers over the intricate symbols that had been beaten into the *argat draiochta*. She recognised the triquetra and the triskele. They represented her in her three aspects of maiden, mother, and old woman. Others were spirals and circles laced together. She would learn their meaning in time. The crux of it was she didn't have time. Lu was certain Mór would attack at Samhain, and that was only two days away. But could she trust Lu?

Bree crossed to the cauldron. Its warmth welcomed her into its embrace. She placed her hands on the copper edges. It didn't burn her. Its strength filled her. She plunged her hands into the ancient flames. Warmth spread through her, until the flames raged in her chest. The cares of everyday life slipped away. Thoughts of the approaching battle disintegrated as if they were dandelion seeds thrown into the wind. She was at one with the flames. They cleansed her. Bree stepped back, taking the flames with her. They burned brightly on her hands. Her eyelids closed but the fiery glow still penetrated. Her feet remained on the ground, but she rose and soared above herself and the room. The cauldron was beneath her. The fire still burned. It burned within her.

When she opened her eyes, she was once more standing next to the cauldron. She closed her palms and extinguished the flames.

On previous occasions, with the small cauldron in their Otherworld home and now here, she had felt her mother's strength in the ancient fire. This time, she felt her own strength. She was ready for whatever was about to happen.

Lu opened his chamber door. Kuon ran in ahead of him. Aongus entered the parlour.

'You shouldn't have waited up,' Lu said.

'I couldn't settle until you returned, my lord. Allow me to assist you.'

Lu was pleased to remove his armour. He flopped onto a divan; Kuon jumped onto it next to him.

The outer door opened and Bearach, another of the Immortals, entered. 'I heard you go past my chambers.'

'Did I make a lot of noise?'

'You did, stomping along.' Bearach laughed, a deep hearty sound. A tall man and very broad, he was larger than Lu in that respect. Brown hair looked tousled from sleep and he wore a loose tunic and trousers.

'You wouldn't be laughing if you were me. Confounded woman! She's not even that. She's a child!'

'What happened?'

Aongus carried a tray with two tankards of mead.

'Thank you,' Lu said. 'I need this!' To Bearach, he continued, 'One of her handmaidens tricked her into going into the Outer Realm—supposedly I'd given her a note, claiming I wanted to see her. By Dagda's beard! Would I do such a thing? And who should it be who really wanted to see her? Scathach.'

'No!'

'Yes, along with a banshee and a púca.'

'Of all trolls in Tír na nÓg!' Bearach exclaimed.

Lu rose and strode in front of the divan. 'I can't believe how stupid she is, and she's our Triple Goddess. May the Lady Danu help us. Scathach was about to destroy her when I arrived.'

'Thank Dagda,' Bearach added. 'What do you intend to do?'

'Whatever is necessary, my friend. Whatever is necessary.'

Chapter Ten

Bree didn't sleep well. The huge, soft bed smothered her, but she had no intention of sleeping on the floor again, or indeed, of going to Áine's bedroom out of a need for security. Niamh's presence, as she snuggled into the coverlet, offered some company. Why the little fairy had taken such an instant liking to Bree, she didn't understand, but she didn't suspect Niamh had any ulterior motives.

Doireann's treachery still shook her. From the outset, Bree hadn't liked the handmaiden with her taciturn ways. Why hadn't she had faith in her own feelings? In the Otherworld, in a small cave under a tree, floating in a miasma of ether, and with only Áine for companionship, Bree hadn't had experience with other people. She was too trusting. With Doireann, Bree had dismissed her own instincts. She wasn't used to betrayal. How many other traitors might be in the palace, or in the Inner Realm?

Lu's face flashed into her mind. Her heart somersaulted and her cheeks burned. Why did he cause this reaction? This turmoil? He infuriated her, and yet she liked him. From the first time she saw him, she'd trusted him… well, almost. But now, she wasn't so sure. Did he covet her position as triple goddess? Not that he'd be triple goddess, but he could lead the Tuatha Dé Danann as sun god. He did treat her as if she were a nuisance, and one he didn't want around. Would he betray her? Could she trust him?

Could trust, once lost, be regained?

Sorcha woke her and dressed her with Úna's help.

Áine joined them.

Bree couldn't believe it was morning already.

'You must wear the golden cloak for the reception,' Áine said. Bree glanced at it spread out on her bed. Áine caught Bree's expression and added, 'The cloak is *dath an óir draiochta*, another magical metal. You can put it on later. Let me look at you.' Áine turned Bree around to face a long mirror. 'How beautiful you look.'

Bree stared at her slim figure in the dark green velvet gown. The dress was simple but elegant. She wore a golden belt with a triquetra symbol as its buckle.

Áine took a golden necklace, with the same triquetra design on it, from a small chest and placed it around her neck.

'This necklace and your belt are made from the same *dath an óir draiochta* as the cloak,' Áine explained.

'They're very beautiful,' Niamh said.

'They're so light,' Bree commented. She raised her

hand and traced her fingers along the necklace against her skin. 'I thought the material would be heavy.'

'You'll also find the cloak light to wear.' Áine bent over the chest again. 'This ring belonged to the goddess Danu, your grandmother. Your mother wore it. Now it is yours.'

Wide-eyed, Bree took the ring and slipped it on her third finger. 'It fits.' It also had a triquetra design on it.

'Your people will swear their fealty to you by kissing the ring.'

'Really?' Bree couldn't imagine it. How was this Greeting Ceremony going to work?

'Now,' Áine murmured. 'We should break our fast. I have something to show you before the reception.'

Before they finished eating, pounding shook the outer door.

'Lu,' Bree muttered.

Úna opened it to Lu. Kuon came bounding in ahead of him.

'Good morning, my Lord Lu,' Áine greeted him, a bright tone to her voice.

He entered the parlour and bowed. His gaze found Bree's. She wanted to look away, but his blue eyes darkened and held hers. She couldn't fathom his expression, but it made her uneasy. Was her discomfort only because of his expression? After her disturbing doubts about him, the fact that he came to her room armed troubled her. He held Corraidhin and Cadeyrn was secured at his back, between his shoulder blades. Surely he wouldn't harm her in front of Áine and Niamh?

Áine rose and took Bree's hand. 'We have something to show you, macushla,' she said. 'Will you stay here, Niamh? I leave you in charge of the magical cloak.'

Niamh flew across to it, leaving her glowing, golden luminosity behind her. She giggled and came to rest beside it. 'You can count on me, my ladies,' she said.

Lu led Bree and Áine along a corridor, turning left this time. Kuon followed them. They'd hadn't gone far before Lu took them across a short section of battlement and into what looked to be another tower.

'This is where my chambers are situated,' Lu said. 'Most of my Immortals, my men, also live in rooms in the tower. The armoury is underground at dungeon level.'

Bree didn't reply. It occurred to her that Lu could no doubt see her rooms from his.

Lu lit a lamp that sat on a small table. 'We walk down. Mind the narrow stone steps,' he said, leading the way. Kuon shot past Bree and her aunt and hurried after Lu.

The smooth, worn steps reminded Bree of those leading down to the flame room on the other side of the palace. She was starting to get her bearings.

They stopped at a heavy wooden door and, as she did before, Áine silently muttered words to herself. Lu pulled a lever on the wall and the door opened.

'Come inside,' Áine said.

Bree stepped into a room about the same size as the

chamber that held the ancient flame. This space was also lined with the shiny *argat draiochta* metal.

'Before the reception,' Áine said, her voice more solemn than Bree had ever heard it, 'Lu and I must explain some things to you.'

Bree caught Lu's expression, but it gave nothing away.

'There are four treasures of the Tuatha Dé Danann that the descendants of my Lord Dagda and my Lady Danu brought with them to this world,' Áine said.

'Brought from where?' Bree asked.

'They came from another realm, as I've told you before,' Áine explained. 'For now, that doesn't concern us.'

'If you keep interrupting,' Lu threw at Bree, 'we'll never get it all told to you.'

Bree glared at him but remained silent.

'My Lord Lu is custodian of two of the treasures,' Áine continued.

'Why is that?' Bree demanded, a little more stridently than she intended.

Lu narrowed his gaze and threw a barbed glower at her. 'Corraidhin, my spear, and Cadeyrn, my sword, are two of the treasures,' Lu said, his words as sharp as the blade he drew from behind his back.

That explained why he always had his weapons with him.

'As god of battle and war,' he continued, 'Dagda asked me to be their custodian.'

How old was he to have spoken to Dagda? Áine had said he was twenty-two but, of course, the Tuatha Dé Danann lived long lives. Bree didn't dare ask him for fear of being branded frivolous and empty headed to ask such a question when a solemn matter was being discussed.

'What are the other two?' she asked instead.

'The feasting cauldron,' Áine said, and pointed to a large copper bowl. 'No company ever went away from it unsatisfied.'

'It's like the one we had in our Otherworld home,' Bree said.

'Your mother crafted us a smaller vessel, so that we could live off its bounty.'

'The fourth is this,' Lu said, and went to stand next to a large irregularly shaped stone. It was prostrate and rose to a height of about eighteen inches. 'The stone, Lia, is the most important,' he added.

'I wouldn't have thought that,' Bree said. It had a triquetra chiselled into it but otherwise it looked unre-markable.

'This stone will confirm whether you are worthy to lead the Tuatha Dé Danann,' Lu said.

'How can it do that?' Bree asked.

'If you are the rightful ruler, it will cry out when you stand on it,' Lu explained. His blue eyes darkened into a challenging stare. 'You are required to do so in front of your people this morning. Two of my most trusted men will carry the stone into the reception hall. If it cries out when you stand on it, it will be placed beneath the high throne.'

Bree's stomach lurched. 'May I stand on it now to test it?' she asked.

'No,' Lu snapped. 'You may not.'

Lu's words felt like a slap across the face. 'You mean, in

front of everyone, I have to stand on it for the first time? What if… it doesn't cry out?'

'Then you are not the rightful leader of the Tuatha Dé Danann,' Lu said.

Bree wanted to slap the smug look off Lu's face. He was enjoying her distress.

Áine recognised the tension between them, took Bree's hand and said, 'It will cry out, macushla. You are your mother's daughter.'

'But what if it doesn't? Will someone else try?' Her eyes darted to Lu. 'Will you stand on Lia, my Lord Lu?'

'We are going with the assumption that it will cry out when you step up on it,' Lu commented after a moment. 'You will be required to stand on Lia at the beginning of the reception,' he explained. 'Then my men will move the stone to beneath the throne and, one by one, the other gods and goddess, and the immortals, will step up and offer you their fealty.'

'All will be well, macushla,' Áine assured her.

They left the room and climbed the narrow stairs. At the top, Bree asked, 'How do you get Lia and the cauldron up this spiral staircase?'

Lu frowned at her. 'There is another way out of the room. Nothing for you to worry about.'

'I would have thought I would have everything to worry about,' Bree said, raising her chin.

Lu didn't reply. When they reached the landing once again, he bowed his head and went through a door that obviously led to his chambers.

Áine led the way back to their rooms.

Bree stopped her aunt in the foyer. 'Lu wants me to

fail,' she pronounced. She couldn't throw off her annoyance at him.

'Of course he doesn't.'

'He wants to lead the Tuatha Dé Danann,' Bree continued, ignoring what Áine had said.

'Bree, Lu has always faithfully served Danu and Dagda, and then your mother. None have ever doubted his loyalty.'

'I doubt it!' Bree exclaimed.

'He is only concerned because tomorrow is Samhain. You have so much to learn, macushla,' Áine said. 'Lu is worried that it will all be too much for you in the short time we have.'

'Perhaps you're correct,' Bree said, but she couldn't shake the uncertainty and turmoil she felt when she was in his presence.

'Come and finish dressing,' Áine said.

***

Lu sat down for a few moments. He knew he had been hard on Bree since he brought her here from her secluded life. He expected a lot from her in a short time, but there was so much at stake.

Now he worried that when she stood on the stone, it wouldn't cry out. He'd seen in her eyes that she suspected he might want to rule the Tuatha Dé Danann. He couldn't blame her. She didn't know who to trust. Not that he wanted to rule. Bree had to take her mother's place or there would be chaos between the gods and goddesses. They didn't have time to waste with internal strife.

Yet how could this young woman—this was the first time he'd thought of her as such—succeed to vanquish Mór?

He thought of just moments ago when he had shown Bree the stone and the cauldron. Dressed in her green gown, she had the look of a goddess about her. She was beautiful with her long, red hair falling about her, but too naïve. He worried for her as much as for the realm. When she stood on the stone, it had to cry out.

He had brought the four treasures of the Tuatha Dé Danann with him when they had left their home realm. Yet he couldn't control it. The stone would reveal the true heir, and that was that.

Briefly he remembered his life before. He had been young. With both of his parents dead, Dagda had kept a familial eye on him. He had always thought of the Lord Dagda and Lady Danu as his parents. It was a wrench to leave them behind. Dagda had decreed Lu should be custodion of Cadeyrn and Corraidhin. The sword and spear had served him well over the many years.

He rose, as did Kuon.

'We have a reception to attend, my friend,' Lu told the hound.

CHAPTER ELEVEN

BREE SETTLED the dath an óir draiochta cloak onto her shoulders. It was much lighter than she'd expected it to be. The interwoven links caught the light from the lamps and reflected around the room, painting patterns on the stone walls.

'The cloak is also very important,' Áine said. 'You have or will have the ability to throw it over your people for their protection.'

'I seem to learn something every minute,' Bree said.

'Shall we go?' her aunt asked. 'Don't worry, macushla. You look as regal as Lady Danu and your mother ever looked.'

Bree came to an abrupt halt at the entrance when she saw all the people. Her knees quaked and her feet refused to take another step. The reception room was on the same floor as Bree's rooms. Tall ornately decorated stone columns stood at each end of the room, reaching up to the high ceilings, painted with scenes of Danu and Dagda, and some of Brigid, Bree's mother, hunting. The many festivals were also depicted. Carved symbols of triquetra and triskelion lined the stone walls; not that Bree could see a great many of them. Urns of flowers added more riotous colour, highlighting the hues of the guests' gowns and tunics.

Lu joined her and offered his arm to escort her onto a large dais in the centre of the room. He placed her behind Lia, the recumbent stone, and then stood at her side. His sword was between his shoulder blades. He held the spear with its end on the floor and the point thrust out from his body.

Áine joined them on the dais but she stood on the other side of the throne, the huge cauldron near her.

Bree glanced around the sea of faces. Their hostility cut through her. After the warm welcome when they'd first arrived, she hadn't expected antagonism. Perhaps it was more uncertainty. The outcome for Bree was also the outcome that would affect her people's future. She couldn't find any friendly faces. She guessed Sorcha and Úna, and Cáitín, Áine's handmaiden, weren't included in the ceremony. Bree looked for Niamh but knew the little lady had rejoined the other fairies.

Lu stamped the spear onto the floor, flames shooting out from it. Everyone became silent and looked at those on the dais.

Bree trembled from her feet up. She held her hands at her sides so no one could see them shaking. She'd never imagined so many people existed. An image of her hidden home flashed through her mind. It evoked tranquillity. No such feeling cocooned her now.

Lu reached out for her hand, ready to help her stand

on the recumbent stone—a treasure of the Tuatha Dé Danann, one that would confirm her right to lead her people. Could Lu feel her hand shaking? Bree looked at his face, but he didn't make eye contact. Was he thinking that he should be the one to stand before the Tuatha Dé Danann? Bree didn't know if she could trust him. What if the Lia stone didn't proclaim her right to rule? Would Lu turn against her, cast her down, maybe into the dungeon he had previously mentioned?

Bree moved closer to the recumbent stone. This one moment would define her life from this point onwards.

She put one foot on Lia and a piercing screech emitted from its stony particles. Startled, Bree stepped back down. What was that? Bree didn't expect such a hideous sound. The stone had shrieked like the banshee she'd heard at her meeting with Scathach.

Lu held out his hand to her. 'It's all right. Try again. Everyone cringes at the sound. Just keep your head up and look as if you're meant to be there.'

Bree stared at him. He had never spoken so encouragingly to her. She lifted her other foot. Once again it shrieked but soon ceased when she stood balanced on the stone. A cheer went up. It surprised Bree that Lu started the cheer, but it was picked up and carried around the huge reception room. People clapped and stamped their feet.

At this moment, Bree knew she was meant to be there.

Once again, Lu reached out for Bree's hand and helped her down. The crowd stopped cheering and clapping. The silence unnerved her as much as the screaming. While two brawny men moved the stone to under the high-backed and ornately decorated throne, Bree cast her gaze around the room. Uncertainty had been replaced by more encouraging expressions. It was something. Bree knew she'd have to earn their trust, their respect.

Lu escorted Bree to the throne, and then surprised her when he moved to the front of the dais. He bowed, then stepped forward and grabbed her hand. His lips pressed into the triquetra on her ring. 'Don't forget, everyone will kiss your ring,' he whispered and moved to stand next to her.

He hit the spear on the floor, and announced, 'Ogma, brother of my Lord Dagda of the Tuatha Dé Danann.'

A mature aged man, with black hair and beard and a long brown cloak, approached. He stared with a steady gaze at Bree, and then bowed and kissed her ring. Bree returned the gaze. Dagda's brother. Did he have a claim on the throne?

Corraidhin, the famous spear, hit the floor.

'Airmid,' Lu shouted. 'Goddess of the Healing Arts.'

A lithe young woman with green hair and a short green gown bowed before Bree, and then kissed the triquetra. She wore ornate sandals, with straps that wound about her legs like vine tendrils. She looked as if she had stepped out of the forest, leaving her plants and herbs behind.

Corraidhin stamped the dais.

Lu announced, 'Rhiannon, Goddess of the Night, and of the Underworld.'

A beautiful woman bowed before Bree, and then kissed the triquetra symbol on the ring.

The process repeated, one after another.

Arianrhod, Goddess of the Moon. Oonagh, Goddess of Nature. Ailtiu, Goddess of Midsummer. Vesna, Goddess of Spring. Dodola, Goddess of Rain. Nechtan, God of Water. Manannan, God of the Sea.

On and on it went. God after goddess swore fealty to her. Then the Immortals were presented. Faces swam in front of Bree's eyes. So many people! She wouldn't remember their names.

When Corraidhin flared once more, the fairies headed towards her from the back of the room. Their combined glow looked like a comet swooping down on her. After hundreds of the little beings had kissed her ring, Áine moved across the dais and swore her fealty. Niamh followed her. Then thousands of little people fluttered wings and showered Bree with luminous fairy dust.

The ceremony seemed to be at an end when Lu came closer and said, 'The centaurs and giants are in the court-yard, if you'd follow me out to the balcony.'

Bree blinked. 'Giants?'

'The Daoine ollmhór. Giants from the high country, to the north. Part of their land is outside of the Outer Realm but want to pledge their fealty to you.'

'Very well.'

Lu helped her down from the dais. Áine followed as they stepped out on the ornate balcony overlooking the courtyard. Bree remembered seeing it from the bailey. The metal balustrade featured the triquetra designs.

Bree glanced down at the crowded courtyard, aston-ished by how many individuals inhabited Tír na nÓg, the land of the Tuatha Dé Danann.

The first two centaurs came forward. Both were

female, one with long dark hair, and one whose hair and coat was as ruddy as Bree's own locks. Their torsos and arms were like that of any other woman. The resemblance stopped there. Bree was fascinated how beneath her waist, the centaur's body merged seamlessly to become a horse. Both centaurs carried bows and a quiver filled with arrows on their backs. The centaurs had no trouble bowing but of course they were unable to kiss the triquetra on Bree's ring. More centaurs followed, male and female.

The giants, men and women, came forward in their turn. Standing at least fifteen feet high—Bree had visions of them crawling through the entrance gateway —they bowed and struck their hands over their chests. Bree thought that with at least fifty giants, Mór could surely not defeat them, but perhaps magic could win out.

When the ceremony finished and Bree waved to the assembled crowd as she stepped back into the reception room, she beckoned Áine to her, and asked, 'Where are the people?'

'People?' Áine frowned. 'We've introduced everyone.'

'The ordinary people, the farmers, the villagers. You said some had escaped Mór's hordes and fled to the Inner Realm.'

'They aren't normally presented, macushla.'

'I'd like to meet them,' Bree said. These people were as important to her as the most elegantly clad goddess. They produced the Tír na nÓg's food, tended herds, wove material for gowns and tunics, and worked leather and metal for armour.

'They are simple folk, Bree. It would embarrass them to attend such a fine gathering.'

'Then I'll go to them. Please summon them to the palace. I'll meet them in the courtyard.'

Áine paused for a moment, and then smiled. She squeezed Bree's hand. 'You've always had a good heart, macushla.'

Áine crossed to Lu and whispered to him. His expression belied the fact he was the sun god. His stormy eyes and heavy brows could easily have brought thunder down on them. He stared at Bree, and then beckoned a group of men. They were some of the Immortals. Bree recalled Fionn, with his mesmerising gaze. She'd met Grainne, his wife, a beautiful woman with long dark hair. Lu had also introduced Diarmuid, renowned for his male beauty, Bearach, a big bear of a man, Domhnall, Padraig and Tiomoid, the youngest Immortal. Lu spoke into their ears. They nodded and departed.

Bree stared over the countless faces before her. Everyone had sworn loyalty to her. She wanted to pinch herself to ascertain if she was awake. It seemed more like a dream, and soon she would stir from her slumber to discover she was still in her earthen cave.

While she'd been speaking to Áine and then Áine had spoken to Lu, everyone had started to talk among themselves. Lu asked her to return to the dais. With Bree standing next to him, Lu slammed Corraidhin onto the dais. If not the sudden noise, then the flames that soared above the spear caught everyone's attention.

Bree held her hands together in front of her. It took a moment to find her voice and then persuade it to work.

'My lords and ladies, gods, goddesses, and fairies, I welcome you here today. Thank you for your presence.' Bree swallowed to dispel a knot in her throat. 'My own appearance here has been sudden and unexpected to all of us, including me.' She smiled. 'I vow to serve you, my people, as you have sworn your fealty to me. Tomorrow is Samhain and we may face our greatest challenge ever. I swear on my mother's heart that no one will pierce the Inner Realm. We will defeat Mór and her evil ones and restore our Outer Realm. We will rebuild and prosper.'

Lu groaned. Bree knew she was making rash promises, but she meant them. She wanted to shout at Lu. He'd sworn his fealty to her. Was it sincere? Or had he done so merely for show? How many others might have done the same? Bree's eyes narrowed.

She must push aside her suspicions. Bree had one thing more to show her people. As she stepped to the edge of the dais, she smiled again at all assembled, closed her eyes and focused her thoughts. She felt the warmth in her palms. She opened her hands and spread them wide. Flames flared upwards from her hands. Her eyes flew open.

A hush of breath sucked in by countless people rolled around the room in a wave of awe. Everyone bowed. The fairies flew over the assemblage, their glow brighter than Bree had seen it before.

Bree looked at Lu. He nodded and smiled at her. Bree blinked hard. She didn't understand him. One minute he was snapping at her, the next he smiled... and such a smile... It washed over her like a soft breeze, refreshing and energising. Why, when she didn't know if she could trust him, did she want his approval?

Áine stepped closer to her. Bree knew she'd always have Áine's support and encouragement.

Bree closed her palms. Her people applauded. Expressions of hope stared back at her.

Lu told everyone that feasting was to follow. Servants poured into the room, and gods and goddesses moved aside, while tables were set up. Lu ordered Bearach, Domhnall and Padraig to carry the feasting cauldron to the foot of the dais. Bree stared into its emptiness.

Lu crossed to Bree and said, 'Well done.'

Bree inclined her head in acknowledgment. Lu whispered directions in her ear. She felt a moment's doubt, and then descended the few steps down to the floor. She stood behind the cauldron. A quick glance confirmed that everyone watched her. It didn't make her feel confident.

She focused her thoughts and opened her palms. The flames soared. She concentrated yet again, only this time bringing all her energy to bear on the cauldron. Then she plunged her hands into the huge receptacle and out again. When she stared into it again, she wasn't certain if she had filled it or not. Mists swirled on the surface.

Bree stepped back. Lu nodded to her as if he was pleased.

Servants came, plunged their hands into the mists and withdrew bread, cooked meats, potatoes, and flagons of wine and beer.

Bree shook her head. It was difficult to believe her eyes. Next to her, Lu chuckled.

Diarmuid approached Lu and whispered some words to him.

'Good man,' Lu said, and then turned to Bree. 'The farmers and herders, the blacksmiths and other people are gathered outside beyond the courtyard. Not everyone could fit inside.'

Bree nodded. 'Thank you.' She looked at Áine. 'Will you come with me?'

'Of course, macushla.'

Bree walked through the hall with Áine at her side. Most of those who'd sworn their fealty now indulged themselves in excellent food and wine.

Niamh flew over to them and hovered in front of Bree's face. 'May I still join you, my lady?'

'Of course, Niamh.'

The fairy flew onto her shoulder.

Bree followed Áine down to the ground level and out beyond the castle's entrance. As soon as she stepped outside, a cheer went up. She opened her hands and showed them the flames that burned in her palms. It was instinctively done. Bree knew it would give the people some comfort.

She was about to move among them when Lu surprised her by offering his arm.

'Allow me to accompany you,' he said.

Bree nodded, even though he'd given her a start. She hadn't realised he'd followed her outside. After a moment's reluctance, she placed her fingers on his arm. Muscles moving beneath his skin felt strange to her touch. At least, he had a tunic on, to save her blushes.

At first, everyone was hesitant. They moved aside and

opened paths for her. Bree faltered too. So many people in proximity to her overwhelmed her. She kept her nerve and smiled. Minutes later, she was lost in a sea of people milling around her. They touched her cloak made of magical *dath an óir draiochta* and her emerald velvet gown. They smiled and bowed.

One woman caught Bree's eye. She stood tall and proud, with fiery red hair that fell to beneath her shoulders. She wore a cloak thrown back over a simple green dress, and she held a spear.

'Are you a warrior?' Bree asked her.

The young woman bowed her head. 'I'm a seamstress, my lady, but I fought to try to save our village.'

'That was brave of you,' Bree murmured. She felt in awe of this woman. Bree's life had been so simple, so safe and secure, while this young woman had fought to save the people she loved. 'What's your name?'

'I am called Seraphina, my lady.'

'Has your village been destroyed, Seraphina?'

'It has, my lady. I am the only woman left alive.' Her green eyes swam with tears.

Bree felt Seraphina's grief. Under different circumstances, Bree could have been this woman. She laid her hand on Seraphina's arm. She wasn't going to make any more speeches. Instead, she lifted her cloak and draped it over Seraphina.

Áine made a move to object but other women ran under the cloak's protection. They knew its power. Bree didn't stop them, but she felt Lu stir beside her. As more people stepped beneath the links of *dath an óir draiochta,* the larger the cloak became, until every person outside the palace was sheltered beneath it.

Niamh giggled and flew away to avoid the crush.

Bree closed her eyes and prayed with her people that tomorrow they would win their battle against evil.

When Bree moved aside, her cloak shrank to its usual size. She was stunned by its magical properties.

Bree found Seraphina again. 'Would you like to come into the palace with me?' Bree asked the woman.

Again, Bree felt Áine move restlessly beside her.

Seraphina blinked and gazed behind her as if the words might be directed at someone else. 'My Lady,' she said after her initial shock had settled. 'I don't know how I can be of service to you.'

'You can fight with me tomorrow,' Bree said. She identified with this young woman. By all that was holy, with her red hair and green eyes, Seraphina could have been her sister.

Seraphina raised her chin. 'Fight with you, my lady? I would be honoured to do so… but I am only a humble seamstress.'

'Who fought to save her village,' Bree said. 'Fight beside me and help save our world.'

Tears swam in Seraphina's eyes. 'My spear is yours, my lady.'

'Good,' Bree said, 'and when we've won, you can make me a celebratory gown.'

Seraphina laughed. 'I'd be happy to do so, my lady.'

'Stay with your friends tonight and then come to the palace in the morning. My Lord Lu's men will arm you with a knife and sword.'

Seraphina bowed.

Bree turned, went back to the courtyard and climbed the palace steps with Lu's arm for assistance. His blue eyes smiled at her.

A sense of wonder enveloped Bree. How did she know to throw her cloak over her people? How did she know how to assume a mantle of command? Where did all that come from? Only days ago, she was as humble as Seraphina, and far less capable to deal with Mór's men as the young woman had shown herself to be.

The fire, the warmth of her mother's love and strength, flowed through Bree's veins. She was ready for whatever was to come. She would protect her people, at all costs.

Chapter Twelve

Once back inside the reception room, the noise of talking, laughing, and singing overwhelmed Bree. She was not yet used to so much noise. She didn't get far before Lu tugged on her arm to stop her. Her shoulder still ached from when he'd wrenched it to drag her up into the saddle when she was at the Yew Walk. He stepped in front of her.

'Will you stop doing that!' Bree exclaimed. She rubbed her shoulder.

Lu seemed to take no notice of her protest. Instead, he said, 'You are not fighting tomorrow.'

'Of course I am.' Bree narrowed her gaze.

'You're not.'

'I'm leading my people into battle to fight Mór, and that's all there is to it,' Bree said. Her heart thumped and her blood soared in her head.

'You can't fight,' Lu boomed. Then, he looked around to ascertain who was standing close to them. 'I explained this to you,' he said in a lower tone.

Bree looked for Áine, who was behind her. 'Tell this man, please,' she implored, 'that I must lead my people.'

Áine screwed up her lovely face. 'What would happen if we lost you, macushla?'

'Then what is this all about? Why am I here?' Neither Lu nor Áine spoke for a moment, so Bree continued, 'I thought you brought me out of hiding to save my people, to lead them in this time of crisis. Therefore, I must lead them into battle.'

'You're here to inspire your people, our people,' Lu said, 'but not to fight alongside them. I've told you this.'

'That's absurd,' Bree said, then lowered her voice when she saw those close by turn their heads. 'I must lead my people into battle and fight beside them.'

'Did you not hear me when I said you are to inspire your people, to rally them, to give them faith to go forth?'

Bree saw Lu's jaw tightening and clenching. She felt her teeth grinding in response. 'Am I nothing more than a statue to stand where I'm told, to smile and look benevolent?'

'Macushla,' her aunt started.

'No!' Bree exclaimed. 'I will lead my people.'

Lu huffed out a loud breath. 'By Dagda's beard, you don't know how to fight.'

'Then I'll learn.'

'In one day?' Lu stepped closer and stood over her.

Bree wanted to step backwards but she held her ground. 'If that's all the time there is, then yes.'

Lu flung away from her. 'Stupid, ignorant girl! As stubborn as your mother!'

'I'm pleased to know I inherited her qualities.'

'She died because of her obstinance,' Lu said, swinging back.

'Where were you when she was wounded? I thought your job was to protect her?'

Lu glowered at her. Bree raised her chin despite the fact her legs had weakened to the strength of porridge.

'I fought beside her.'

'Then you failed in your job.'

'I took my eyes off her for a few seconds. I warned her not to force her way through the throng, but would she listen? No. Stubborn. The Tuatha Dé Danann might be immortal, but she believed she could never be harmed.'

'And you let her be killed.' Bree's anger surged, spewing out in her invective. She'd never spoken to anyone in such a manner before, but Lu goaded her and annoyed her beyond belief. 'How could she die?'

His jaw clenched, and one fist making a tight ball, he glared at her. They stood as if held by some unseen force, neither able to move closer or say more, their breaths mingling in the space between them.

Áine spoke. 'Bree, all of us can be killed under exceptional circumstances. It sounds as if Brigid acted rashly. I'm certain her death wasn't Lord Lu's fault.'

Her aunt's words broke the spell and tears filled Bree's eyes. 'She died before I had the chance to know her.'

'I know, macushla,' her aunt said.

Bree sniffed. 'She died doing what she felt was right to protect her people. So will I.'

'We need you to stay safe,' Áine said.

Bree stared at Lu's tall figure and broad back. He

refused to look at her now. Then she swung around and headed out onto the balcony.

Lu and Áine caught up with her. To avoid being tossed off, Niamh had left Bree's shoulder. She settled again once when Bree had halted.

'What are you doing?' Lu demanded.

Bree glared at him. 'Find Seraphina!' she told him. 'Bring her here into the reception room.'

'Macushla, what are you doing?' Áine beseeched. 'I don't think that's wise.'

'Why not? Because she's a seamstress?' Bree raised her chin.

'By Dagda's beard, she is as obstinate as her mother.' Lu strode away and spoke to Bearach.

Ten minutes later, Bearach returned with Seraphina in tow.

'She looks very embarrassed to be in such company,' Áine said.

Bearach delivered Seraphina to Bree. They both bowed. 'My Lady,' Seraphina said.

'You said you are a seamstress.'

'Yes, my lady, I am.'

'Can you make me a shirt and trousers… overnight?'

'Tonight, my lady?'

'Tonight.'

'Of course, my lady.'

Lu bent to deliver a charged whisper into Bree's ear. 'Don't be absurd.'

Bree elbowed Lu away but then turned to him. 'Are you able to provide me with armour, my Lord?' she asked him. Her words were loud and forceful. Lu's eyes reflected his rage, but he held it in check. 'Well, are you?' Bree demanded.

'If we can find something small enough,' he said.

'I'm sure you'll manage, my lord. Perhaps Diarmuid will assist you.'

Lu's jaw worked.

Bree stood her ground and raised her chin.

'These are my wishes,' she said.

Lu didn't move but Diarmuid seemed to appear from nowhere.

'Take Seraphina through to my chambers,' Bree told the man. 'Find Sorcha and explain that Seraphina is to make me some new clothes. Then find some armour that might fit me and give it to Sorcha.'

'Very well, my lady,' Diarmuid said, flicking a gaze at Lu, and then indicated Seraphina should follow him.

'There, that wasn't so difficult, was it?' Bree said to Lu. His anger still raged behind his blue eyes.

'You might dress the part, but it doesn't mean you can swing a sword,' he said.

'That's why I'm relying on you to teach me,' she responded. 'Tonight.'

'You think you can learn everything in one night?' Lu boomed out.

'Not everything. Just enough,' Bree said, her tone smooth, which seemed to stoke Lu's anger.

'By all the jumping fleas in Dagda's beard!' Lu shouted and threw his hands into the air.

'You are creating a scene, my lord,' Bree told him.

'I'm creating a scene?'

'I'm pleased you agree,' Bree said, taking his words as a statement, not a question.

'Dagda help me!' Lu said.

Bree swung away from him, encountering Áine's anxious expression as she turned. She didn't want to cause her aunt to worry but she had no intention of relenting. 'Oh, by the way, Lord Lu, before you attend me for weapon training, will you please send all these gods and goddesses, heroes and centaurs, on their way. Mór will easily defeat drunk deities.'

Bree walked through the feasting tables and the throng of people who were dancing. She smiled and nodded but it was a relief to leave them behind. The quiet palace corridors that led to her chambers provided a certain calm.

Guards opened the outer doors as Bree approached with Áine and Niamh. As soon as they entered the parlour, Áine took Bree's hands.

'Macushla, this is foolhardy. We can't afford to lose you.'

'I know,' Bree replied. 'Lu told me all about the hereditary line, and if I die without having a child first. But Áine,' Bree implored. 'I have had all of my people within the Inner Realm swear loyalty to me, as I swore to protect them. How can I do that sitting here while everyone goes out to battle?'

'No one expects it of you,' Áine said.

'Of course they do. Anyway, I expect it of me.' Bree pulled away from her aunt. 'My mother died in battle. I am my mother's daughter.'

Niamh fluttered her wings and flew in front of Bree's

face. 'You are, Lady Bree. You are indeed your mother's daughter.'

Áine lowered her head. 'Very well,' she murmured. 'I brought you back here, to your home, to assume your mother's position. I don't know what I expected would happen. In peace, it would have been so different.'

'We're not at peace,' Bree said, her tone warmer towards her aunt than it had been with Lu.

'I know, macushla. We are at war with Mór's evil scourge. You are good, with a kind heart and shining soul. If anyone can defeat her, you can, my wonderful girl.' Tears spilled over and ran down Áine's cheeks.

Bree hugged her aunt. 'It will be all right,' Bree whispered, and then kissed Áine. 'I see Sorcha waiting for me,' she added. 'I must allow Seraphina to take my measurements for my new clothes.'

Lu drew a sword from its scabbard and handed it to Bree. 'It was your mother's,' he said.

Bree stared at his expression. His earlier anger had dissipated, and he seemed to have accepted that she would fight Mór. Bree took the sword and held it with reverence.

'It's made of *argat draiochta*,' he added.

Áine stepped forward to look at it. She'd accompanied Bree to a chamber in the tall tower where both Lu's quarters and the armoury were situated. 'I haven't seen it for so many years,' she said.

Bree traced the small triquetra on the pommel; three

points made of one unbroken line, with a circle entwining them. The sword hilt was covered with interwoven knots. It would give her a good grip.

Áine touched the hilt and explained, 'The interwoven knots represent how everything in our world, in nature, in the sky, is all connected.'

Lu pointed at another triquetra that sat on the cross-guard. 'This is also known as the quillon block.'

'The blade is magnificent,' Bree murmured. 'I love these ornate designs.'

'You know the triquetra, of course, and the triskele,' Áine said, 'with its three arms spiralling. It reflects a balance between our inner consciousness and outer self.'

The symbols were joined in an amazing design.

'It is Cara fíor,' Áine said. 'The sword's name is Cara fíor. It means true friend.'

'The sword doesn't know defeat,' Lu added.

Bree's head sprang up. 'Then how did my mother die?'

Áine took Bree's hand. Bree knew her aunt didn't want a repeat of last night's argument. Neither did she, but she wanted to know what had happened. How could her immortal mother be killed if her sword didn't know defeat?

'Exactly what happened?' Bree stared at Lu.

He stared back, and then broke the gaze. 'She pushed through the chaotic battle because she spotted Mór. Then she turned to help someone and Mór cut her down. She didn't have a chance.'

'I see.' Bree felt the sting of tears in her eyes, but she wasn't going to cry in front of Lu. At the end, the reason had been so simple. Her mother tried to help someone, and an evil hand killed her. She glanced down at the sword, weighing it in her hands. She didn't know how she was going to fight tomorrow with such a heavy sword, but she swore Cara fíor would serve her better than it did her mother. She would stare Mór in the eyes when she challenged her.

'For now,' Lu said, 'we will train with another sword.' He handed Bree a blade without any decorations, and at the same time, took Cara fíor from her.

'Are you afraid of my mother's sword?' Bree asked.

'I'm afraid of you wielding it. I'd like to live to fight tomorrow.' Lu chuckled. 'This one is the same weight. Under normal circumstances, I would use sticks with a novice, but we don't have time.'

Bree glared at him but what could she say? At least they weren't arguing.

They started slowly, with Lu showing Bree the various stances, strokes and parries. Held high, the sword felt even heavier. When Bree lunged, she nearly dropped it. Lu groaned. His expression darkened. Bree knew this would be an interesting night.

Much later, after they'd finished, and Bree had washed, she fell into her soft bed. Every muscle ached. Muscles ached that she didn't know she possessed. Not an ideal way to feel the night before a battle, she supposed. Not that she knew what that was meant to feel like, and now she was too tired to care.

Lu had stalked off, shaking his head, after their training. Bree didn't think it a good sign. She'd tried her best. With Cara fíor, her mother's sword, she knew she'd do better.

Bree stared up at the ceiling. Some light came into the room through gaps in curtains. The moon's light was strong. A sharp blade of silver slashed its way across the floor. She'd never been superstitious, but she felt relieved the shaft of light didn't cut across her bed. Bree recalled that Arianrhod, the moon and star goddess, had been at the reception. Perhaps Bree should have sought her advice. She realised that the advice of others would be the key to leading her people. However, tomorrow had to be faced first.

Bree couldn't sleep. She sat up and nearly tossed Niamh off the coverlet as she did so. She'd forgotten the fairy was sleeping there. Bree eased herself out of bed. Her feet on the cold marble sent a shock through her. Her new clothes lay over the back of a chair. Bree padded over to them. They were simply made of a soft fabric that would sit well beneath the armour Lu had presented her with at the end of the training session.

Bree had stared agape at it. 'It's made of *argat draiochta*,' she had managed to say when the lump in her throat cleared.

'It was also your mother's armour,' Lu had said.

'Why didn't you tell me before that my mother had worn armour?'

'Because I didn't want you to fight,' Lu had admitted.

'We wanted to keep you safe,' Áine had added. 'Battle was never your mother's prime objective. She believed in protecting people but not killing others to do so.'

Bree lowered her clothes to the chair. She was pleased Seraphina had finished making them early in the evening so the young woman could get some sleep. Was she sleeping? Or were half the people in the palace awake in anticipation of the battle tomorrow?

Bree crossed to a door with glass panels and pulled aside a drape. The moon rode high. Bree could see little, only some trees, looking like dark giants silhouetted against the sky. The door led to a small balcony, but she didn't feel like stepping out into the night. The darkness, like everything else, was too large and oppressive for her.

She jumped when Niamh landed on her shoulder.

'You should be sleeping, my lady,' the fairy said. Her circlet sat at a crooked angle, almost slipping off her short fair hair.

Bree pushed the headdress into place and smiled with affection at the little lady. 'Do you think Mór might be awake looking at the moon?' Bree asked.

'I don't think she'd care about the moon. Mór seeks darkness.'

Something crashed into the glass door. Bree and Niamh fell backwards together.

'What was that?' Niamh's voice quivered.

'I don't know,' Bree replied. 'It was large and black. At least the glass didn't break.' She stepped closer to inspect it.

A dark shadow swooped again at the window. Niamh screamed in Bree's ear.

This time Bree could discern the shape. It hovered in front of the window, flapping black wings that gleamed in the silvery light. 'It's a raven,' she said.

Niamh screamed again.

Bree hadn't realised they'd woken anyone else until Áine wrenched Bree away.

'It's one of Mór's creatures,' Áine said.

Then, before their eyes, the bird appeared to disintegrate into a black cloud, which reformed seconds later into a face. But not the raven's face. A woman's face, hanging there, disembodied. It hovered, as if taunting or warning.

Bree moved closer to the glass again. Áine tried to pull her back. Bree resisted. She wanted to see, she wanted to look into Mór's eyes... and she knew without being told that this was Mór.

Bright dark eyes, gleaming in the moonlight, stared out of a face that was as white as death. Black brows arched above the glinting eyes. Cheekbones defined with dark paint hung over cadaverous cheeks. Lips that were as black as her long hair stretched in a tight line. Mór opened her mouth and laughed. The next second, she was gone.

Niamh screamed.

'Come away.' Áine tugged at her niece.

This time, Bree allowed her aunt to guide her back into the room. 'So that was Mór,' Bree stated more than asked, her eyes wide, but not with fear, her voice laced with curiosity. 'How can she do that? How can she change a raven into herself... and then only her head?'

'Many creatures can shape-shift,' Áine said.

Bree recalled Lu telling her this after the episode with Scathach and the púca.

'Mór identifies with the raven,' Áine explained.

'But only her head was visible,' Bree added.

'One of Mór's vile tricks,' Áine replied. 'It was most likely a thought projection. Mór can't pierce the Enchanted Veil.'

'Does that mean she has a confederate inside the Veil?' Bree asked, wondering what they would be facing.

'Unfortunately, yes,' Áine said. 'Just as Doireann was one of Mór's creatures. Now stay away from the windows, macushla. It is past midnight.'

Niamh gasped. 'Samhain has begun,' she whispered.

CHAPTER THIRTEEN

LU STARTED AWAKE. He was certain he'd heard a sound, but Kuon hadn't reacted or moved. Lu stared around the room, but he couldn't discern any movement. Then a sound came again. It was outside his door. He swung his feet to the floor at the moment that his bedchamber door opened and a knife flew through the air and into his bed. Fortunately, he had sat up by then.

A moment later a man stepped into the doorway. Lu yanked the door fully open and pounced on the man. They both fell to the marble floor. Kuon barked and jumped around them.

The attacker had another blade. The man was strong and it took Lu some effort to keep the knife away from his throat. With a final heave, Lu threw the man off him, and followed the movement by reversing the situation.

Aongus ran into the room, cried out, and then fled outside. Minutes later, Bearach ran into Lu's bedchamber. By this time, the assailant had pushed Lu off him and the two men were punching each other. Bearach dragged the intruder away from Lu and sent a punch into the man's face. He went down and didn't move.

'Fetch something to tie him up,' Lu said to Aongus.

By the time Aongus returned, the assailant was stirring. Lu dragged him up, pushed him into a chair and tied his hand and feet.

'Now, where did you come from?' Lu said, slapping consciousness back into the intruder.

The man refused to say anything.

By this time, Fionn and Diarmuid had roused and joined them.

'You can do this the easy way by answering my questions here,' Lu said. 'Or do it the hard way. My men will take you to the dungeons to be more persuavely questioned.'

The man kept his head down.

Bearach grabbed his hair and pulled his head backwards.

'I assume you're working for Mór,' Lu said. 'Speak man!' After a few moments, Lu added to Fionn and Diarmuid, 'Take him to the dungeon.'

Both Immortals lifted the man to his feet. They only reached the door before the assailant's knees buckled. He threw his head back, and started to froth at the mouth. In less than a minute, the man drooped, lifeless, in the Immortals arms. They lowered him to the floor.

'He must have taken some before he even came to your room,' Bearach suggested. 'This was obviously a suicide mission.'

'Take his body to the dungeon,' Lu told Fionn and Diarmuid. 'We'll deal with his corpse after the battle.' Lu led Bearach out to his parlour. 'A drink, my friend? Aongus,' Lu called. 'Mead for us both.'

'How by all the gods did the intruder get through the parlour and into your bedchamber?' Bearach asked.

'With stealth. Even Kuon didn't hear him.'

Kuon lifted his head from where he now lay on a divan.

'A lot of good you were, you great beast,' Lu said.

'What do you think the intruder wanted?' Bearach asked.

'To kill me, I'd say. I expect that unable to reach Bree, Mór thought to get me out of the way. An army without its leader can fall into disarray.'

'You're right, of course.'

'The thing I'd like to know is, not just how he found his way to my quarters, but how did he get inside the palace and inside the Inner Realm.' Lu ran his fingers through his hair.

'He must have been planted as a spy when Mór attacked the Outer Realm. Then we invited those left alive into the Inner Realm for their safety,' Bearach said.

'I wonder who he was and where's he has been since then.'

'Hiding in plain sight, I suppose.' Bearach drained the last of his mead. 'Are you unhurt?'

'Yes, I'm all right. Go back to bed, my friend, and thank you.'

Bree knew she should be sleeping. Tomorrow she was going into battle. What did that even mean? She had only the stories in her books to go by. Áine had assured her that her instincts would guide her. Bree placed her hand at the centre of her chest. She wanted to feel her mother's presence. Would she come with Bree into battle?

Oh, she knew that Áine would be with her and Lu with his army... but Bree doubted she'd know what to do. How could she face Mór and her creatures? If the vision at her window was anything to judge by, Bree hated to think how frightening Mór looked in person. After all, so far the woman had killed her mother and laid waste to most of the villages in the Outer Realm. How could Bree defeat her? Yet she must. She had to protect her people. She'd sworn to do so.

What of Lu? Was he friend or foe? He could be jealous of her. If Bree had not been found in her cave, he could have stepped forward and taken her place as ruler of the Tuatha Dé Danann. Yet Lu had found her. Had he hoped that she wouldn't be alive? Bree thought about her mother's death. Lu had been with her. It was only his word that her mother had ridden ahead of him and been attacked and killed. Could Bree trust him? She wanted to do so, but she wasn't totally certain.

Bree sighed and threw back the coverlet. Niamh, sleeping on Bree's pillow, stirred. Bree crossed to the window and stared out. This time neither Mór nor her ravens appeared to frighten the life out of her. The moon rode high, but all Bree could see were the tall trees.

Were there gardens around the palace? Bree would have loved to explore but there hadn't been an opportunity. She knew nothing about her new home, and only slightly more about her people. Yet tomorrow, she would defend them or die trying.

<hr>

As soon as she woke the following morning, Sorcha informed her of what had happened in Lu's tower overnight.

'The palace is abuzz with it, my lady.'

'Is Lord Lu unhurt?'

'Yes, my lady, and the assailant is dead. He took some poison to kill himself.'

Bree dressed and broke her fast with Áine and Niamh.

They'd finished their meal of fruit and bread, when pounding sounded on the door.

'Lu,' Bree said. She wanted to hurry to the door herself, but instead she stayed sitting on the divan.

Kuon ran into the parlour and dropped his head into Bree's lap.

Lu didn't look any worse for wear because of the incident with the attacker.

'I have not long heard about your ordeal last night. You are not injured, my lord?' Bree asked.

'I am not, but the intruder is dead, by his own hand.'

'I assume Mór sent him? Why would she want to harm you?'

'She would want to kill me so that I would not be able to lead the army into battle.'

'I see. Yes, I understand.'

'Are you ready for battle, my lady?' Lu asked.

'I am but why is nothing happening as yet?' Bree asked. 'Perhaps Mór isn't going to attack after all.' She paced the parlour in her chambers.

'That's highly unlikely. It Samhain. She'll attack.'

'Be patient, macushla,' Áine said. 'We don't want to hurry into battle.'

Bree looked at Lu, noticing for the first time that morning that he was dressed in his armour, a combination of metal and leather with intricate designs carved into it—perhaps Lu's symbols as god of war. Although he wore trousers with metal knee pads, he didn't wear a tunic, so his bare chest rippled with muscle as he moved. Bree was still in a gown. She'd change as soon as Lu left them. For some reason, seeing his tall, broad, magnificent frame annoyed her. Or was she frustrated with the wait for battle to begin?

'Don't you ever wear a shirt?' she demanded. 'Surely you need a breastplate for protection?'

Lu smirked. 'I think I have more idea how to intimidate the enemy than you do.'

'So you think strutting around half-naked will frighten Mór's hordes?' Bree heard Áine groan. Niamh tittered.

'Why not? My bare chest seems to have an effect on you.' Lu grinned.

Bree swung her face away from him, mainly to hide the blush that warmed her skin. Kuon nudged her. She looked down into soulful eyes, and patted his head. When she glanced up, feeling she was more in control, Bree asked, 'Do you have any other news?'

His grin dropped from his features in the blink of an

eye, and he became serious. 'It's started,' he said. 'Assaults are being made against the Enchanted Veil.'

'Can it be penetrated?' Bree asked.

'Only if Mór or one of her cronies can break the enchantments that hold it. I think it unlikely. However, they are using magic against it.'

'We should go out to challenge them,' Bree said.

'At the moment, I advise caution,' Lu stated.

'Caution?' Bree had thought Lu was more of an attack and conquer god than one who'd sit down and wait.

'We need Mór to show her hand,' he explained.

'Isn't this showing her hand?'

'No, this is nothing more than a tease. When Mór acts, we'll know it.'

'We should be in the Outer Realm to face her,' Bree said. Her impatience charged through her body and sounded in her voice. She couldn't remain here doing nothing.

'We will be,' Lu agreed. 'But not yet. My spies haven't reported anything to indicate she herself is on the move.'

'You have spies within her forces?' Bree was surprised.

'Of course,' Lu responded. 'I must go back to my men.' He bowed and left them.

'I want to dress,' Bree said. 'Into my armour. I want to be with my people. They should see me. Where's Sorcha?'

The chief handmaiden hurried into the parlour. Bree had known she'd be close by. 'I want my armour and sword.' Bree hurried into her bedroom.

The handmaidens helped her dress. Seraphina slipped the shirt she'd made over Bree's head.

'You did a good job,' Bree told her, as she stepped into her new trousers. 'Do you still want to fight?'

'Yes, my lady,' the seamstress replied.

'You must get dressed,' Bree said.

Seraphina hurried away to don the shirt, trousers, and armour that Diarmuid had found for her.

Áine stood beside Bree. 'I don't think it's wise that Seraphina is to fight. She isn't experienced.'

'I'm less experienced,' Bree said, and then gazed at herself in the long mirror. She didn't know the person looking back at her. The transformation astonished her. With her mother's *argat draiochta* armour in place over her shirt and trousers, her red hair tied back and her sword, Cara fíor, in her hand, it was easy to believe that a quiet girl reading her books in a cave under a tree had never existed.

Her aunt's hand flew to her chest. 'By the Lady Danu, you look like your mother!'

'I am my mother, dear aunt.' Bree smiled. 'Look at you. You have armour too.'

'I wore this so many years ago,' Áine murmured, her words weighted with her memories. She ran her hands over the leather strappings and metal guards. 'I stood next to your mother in this armour long before you were born.'

'Now you will join me in battle.'

'Of course, macushla.'

Seraphina stepped back into the bedroom. Her armour looked to be well-worn. Nevertheless, with spear in hand and sword at her side, Seraphina looked every bit the warrior.

'We are ready,' Bree announced.

On her way outside, Bree came to a halt as she entered the reception room. She still felt overwhelmed by too many people. Gods and goddesses, all dressed in armour ready for what was to come, filled the large chamber. Tables, set with food and tankards of ale and wine, stood against the walls. The huge feasting cauldron sat at the foot of the steps that led to the throne. Was this another feast?

Everyone bowed and opened up a path for Bree as she walked into the hall. Áine followed her, with Niamh sitting on the fairy queen's shoulder. Seraphina had disappeared for the moment. Bree guessed she'd decided to make her way outside using another route.

Bree paused to speak to different deities. She recognised Arianrhod, with her silvery hair falling to the ground.

'Are you fighting?' Bree asked her. She wondered how the moon goddess would tie up all those tresses.

'I will be, my lady, but there is time yet to prepare. Mór will attack tonight.'

'How do you know this?' Bree asked.

'The ghosts of the dead will not be released until my moonlight touches their graves.'

'I see,' Bree replied. She wondered if Lu knew this.

As if he'd been cued, Lu cut a path through the crowd. He was almost a head taller than everyone else.

'My Lady.' He bowed when he reached them. 'May we talk?' He flicked his head to the side. 'In private?' he added.

'Of course,' Bree agreed. She smiled at Arianrhod and Áine. 'You will excuse me.'

Lu led her to an alcove within the room.

'Mór's forces are amassing,' he said. 'Out beyond the forest. Scathach is with her, as is Macha. She's a Goddess of War and has aligned herself with Mór. Badb, the Goddess of Fear, is there. She'll spread her seeds among any farmers and villagers left in the Outer Realm. Mór's banshees have joined her.

'Then we should move into the Outer Realm,' Bree urged.

'Not yet. Mór has trolls and traitorous centaurs yet to join her.'

'I have just been told that Mór won't attack until nightfall. Did you know that the ghosts of the dead need Samhain's moon to touch their graves before they can rise?' Bree demanded.

'I know.'

'Why didn't you tell me?' Bree felt her blood pounding through her veins.

'I was getting to it,' Lu said.

'Getting to it!' Bree snapped.

'There's always the chance Mór might attack before then and have the ghosts as a second advance. I was biding my time.'

'In future,' Bree said, trying to keep her voice calm. 'I would like to be apprised of every detail and then I will understand why you're biding your time.'

Lu's eyes held hers. Bree felt their intensity buffet her. She was determined she wouldn't break the stare.

'I assume I can rely upon you in this regard,' she added.

After a moment, he nodded. The most fleeting of smiles swept across his lips.

'What next?' Bree asked.

'Mingle with your people, as you are now. It's a good idea, I might add.'

Bree inclined her head in acknowledgment.

'I'll go back to my men. They're ready to move at a moment's notice.'

Bree smiled at Lu's back as he strode away. He was infuriating at times, but she should never have doubted his loyalty.

Bree stared up at the centaur's face. She'd gone outside into the courtyard where the centaurs and giants were gathering. The human torso and head towered above her. Her stomach tightened. She was pleased the centaur was on her side. Imagine how intimidating she would be to an enemy on foot!

'What's your name?' Bree asked.

'Hilde, my lady.' The centaur bowed her head.

'I see you have a bow and arrows, Hilde,' Bree commented.

'A good weapon when I'm galloping, my lady. I also have my sword at my back.' Hilde indicated the sword rising behind her head. It was where Lu carried his sword.

Bree's gaze fell to where Hilde's human torso merged into a horse's body. Her muscular front legs raised and tapped the ground, as if Hilde couldn't stand still. 'You have a beautiful coat...' Bree paused. 'Is that the correct term?'

'It is, my lady.'

'What colour is it? Red?' Bree smiled. 'You must forgive my questions. I'm not familiar with horses or centaurs.

'Chestnut,' Hilde said, and returned the smile.

'Your hair is the same colour,' Bree added. 'It's very beautiful.'

Hilde bowed her head. 'Thank you, my lady.'

Bree smiled again. Hilde was indeed beautiful, with a proud set to her jaw.

'My lady.'

Bree turned when she recognised the voice. 'My Lord Lu. You have news?'

'In private.' Lu nodded his head sideways. 'Excuse us, Hilde.'

Bree smiled at Hilde. She was pleased that Lu knew the centaur's name. A tick in his favour. He seemed to care about the people and centaurs that fought with him.

They stepped into the only empty space they could find. The courtyard was teeming with Tuatha Dé Danann.

'I think we must move,' Lu said. 'There are many small attacks on the Enchanted Veil. Once we leave the Inner Realm, I'll deploy forces to deal with them, while we move on.'

'Will we go through the forest?' Now the time had come, Bree's blood chilled and her heartbeat quickened.

'If this was a small skirmish, I would,' Lu explained. 'But the confinement would hinder us. Trees, which may be our allies, would prevent smooth progress. This is only a small portion of our armies.' Lu swept his arm wide. 'Many more wait in the fields close by. In any case,' he added. 'We may need to call upon the tree spirits for aid in the fight. I don't want to put them off-side before we start.'

'Tree spirits?'

Lu huffed out a breath. 'By Danu's spirit, you have a lot to learn!'

Bree's face flamed. 'This is not the time,' she said in a charged whisper. 'If you can't simply tell me the answer, I'll ask someone else.'

Lu glowered at her and then his annoyance fell away. He gave a brief chuckle, and said, 'All trees have spirits. Some are good, some are not.'

'I see.' To some extent, she agreed with Lu. Why hadn't Áine taught her more of the Tuatha Dé Danann's beliefs and customs? Bree had possessed only a limited number of books. 'What do we do?' she asked after a moment.

'We'll skirt the forest. Mór's forces are gathering on the far side of the great plain. We'll meet her on the other side.' He paused and glanced around those gathered here. 'If you get this lot to move, I'll wait with my armies beyond the palace in an assembly ground.' He pointed beyond the courtyard. 'Diarmuid will get your horse.'

Bree hadn't noticed Diarmuid. He stepped away from a group of Immortals and bowed.

'Horse?' Alarm surged through Bree. She couldn't prevent the tremble in her voice. 'I can't ride.'

'If you want to fight, you need to ride,' Lu told her, his voice as sharp as his sword.

Not another hurdle. She was still accustoming herself

to looking at horses, which seemed powerful animals. Bree obviously hadn't thought things through because she hadn't expected she'd have to ride. 'Very well,' Bree agreed. She returned his steely glare. How difficult could it be?

Lu shook his head and marched away. Bree lost sight of Diarmuid but didn't worry. He would no doubt return with a horse.

Bree strode back through the crowd. Áine joined her. Bree raised her hand to forestall her aunt's questions. She must speak to her people, but the noise was deafening. She called out but no one heard. For a moment, Bree felt overwhelmed with hundreds of people milling around. Where was Lu when she needed his booming voice? She halted. No, she didn't need him. She was Bree, the triple goddess, and leader of the Tuatha Dé Danann. She cupped her hands in front of her and focused. Her palms became warm, flames crackled and grew, and then soared into the air in a tower of fire. Silence was almost immediate, and every face turned to her.

Bree closed her palms, took a deep breath from the pit of her stomach, and then drew Cara fíor, her sword. It sparked and cried out as she wrenched it from its scabbard. She held it high. 'It is time,' Bree shouted, her voice strong and steady. 'We march.'

A shout went up. Hundreds moved at once and somehow managed to organise themselves into groups.

Diarmuid stood in the gateway with two horses.

Bree glanced at her aunt. 'I suspect one of these fine beasts is for you.'

'It's been a while.' Áine rolled her eyes.

'That's better than never having ridden.' Bree halted, as if she'd hit a brick wall, as she realised that one horse was a… 'A unicorn?'

Diarmuid bowed his head. 'For you, my lady.'

'Only the triple goddess can ride a unicorn,' Áine explained.

'This is Gealach, my lady,' Diarmuid said.

Bree patted the unicorn's white mane, but her focus was on the spiral horn that rose in golden splendour from the animal's head. Gealach's eye stared in a kindly way at her. Bree moved to stand in front of the unicorn. 'Gealach,' Bree whispered. 'I hope you and I can be friends.' The unicorn snorted out a breath that felt warm on Bree's face. She felt heartened by it.

Diarmuid helped her to mount, and then turned to assist Áine. He bowed his head to Bree. 'Gealach will take care of you, my lady,' he said.

Bree smiled and within seconds Diarmuid had disappeared among the waiting crowd.

'Here we go, Gealach,' Bree declared, and tugged on the reins. She expected to slip off, land on her face and make a fool of herself. She was surprised that she kept her seat as the unicorn carried her through the palace gates. Without a word, everyone followed her.

Áine directed Bree over to her far left, through some trees, and then they made their way onto the assembly ground.

Lu pulled a wry grin when Bree approached him. He nodded at Áine. 'You made it,' he quipped.

'I'm sorry to disappoint you,' Bree said, eyebrows raised.

'Oh, you don't disappoint me at all.'

Bree couldn't tell what he meant. Was he laughing at her? When he wasn't shouting at her, he always mocked her. His next words held gravity.

'Fall in next to me,' Lu commanded her.

Bree suspected this was an honour. She glanced around at Lu's men. Some, like Lu himself, were dressed in armour and rode horses. Others, who gathered farther back, were on foot. Arms and faces were painted in intricate blue designs.

'It's woad,' Áine explained, seeing where her niece was looking. She was on Bree's other side. 'The blue paint is woad. The villagers and Lu's foot soldiers wear it.'

Lu's voice boomed out. He dug his heels into his horse, and it sprang forward.

Gealach moved a moment later. How Bree kept on the unicorn's back, she didn't know. Perhaps it was an enchantment. The unicorn was a magical creature. Bree patted Gealach's neck in thanks and was rewarded with a snort and neigh.

Bree lost track of the time it took to move their forces. At some point, Hilde joined them, as did Seraphina, who carried her spear, her sword at her back. She walked in between Áine and Hilde. Niamh travelled with the fairies.

Moving everyone through the Enchanted Veil took time. 'That's why we came this way,' Lu said.

Bree could understand the reasoning. If they had taken the path on which Lu had brought her and her aunt to the palace, it would take all day to move the troops through.

Finally the entire army was in the Outer Realm, and they moved onto a large, flat plain. Bree caught sight of a glowing streak that darted across the army's front. When it drew close, Niamh settled on Bree's shoulder.

'Ooh, a unicorn,' she said. 'Ah, it's Gealach.' Niamh flittered about the unicorn's head in greeting.

Gealach snorted in a way that was already familiar to Bree. Her breath unsettled Niamh's circlet. The fairy laughed and pushed at it, but it still remained uneven.

Lu chose the place to halt. 'Stay here,' he told Bree. She didn't object to his commands in these circumstances. He rode back along the line of his men, gods and goddesses, centaurs and giants.

Niamh flew high and then settled on Gealach's mane. 'The giants are the Daoine ollmhór. They're from the high country,' she explained. 'I didn't think they would join us. Their land is far away.'

'Is the high country a part of Tír na nÓg?' Bree asked.

'It is,' Áine replied. 'The entire realm is quite large.'

Bree sat back and, for the first time, stared across the great plain. A dark rolling swathe of enemies gathered on the other side not too far away. A smaller force assembled in front of a hillock.

'I can actually discern Scathach,' she told Áine. 'She sits on her devilish púca.' Bree shivered. 'Where's Mór?'

'She'll appear soon enough,' Áine said.

'Who is that next to Scathach?'

'That's Badb,' Áine murmured.

'Ah, so she's the Goddess of Fear.'

'She aims to cause terror and confusion among her enemies.'

'Then we'd best dispatch her early on,' Bree stated.

'A rash claim to make.'

Bree jumped at the sound of Lu's voice. She hadn't seen him return or ride close enough to hear her words. 'We can but try,' he said, but she felt a bit foolish. One minute his words gave her confidence and the next he was shooting her down.

'Badb can shape-shift into a dark cloud and rain down her fear,' Lu said.

Bree shivered. Fear—that was Badb's real power. She'd spread dread and terror. Fear itself was the enemy.

Bree breathed deeply. A strange, unpleasant mix of smells penetrated her nostrils. Damp earth, horse-flesh, sweat and… yes, fear. She could sense it. It weaved itself through their throng. Deep inside, she found the source of her warmth. It radiated from her heart, from her belly. She touched her mother's spirit within her and brought it forth. It was her spirit now and she didn't feel fear.

Bree tapped Gealach's neck, and the unicorn cantered forward.

'Where are you going?' Áine cried.

Bree ignored her aunt. Niamh still sat on her shoulder. 'Hang on,' Bree whispered to the fairy, and pressed her knees into the unicorn's sides. Bree drew her sword and raised it high. 'Sing, Cara fíor,' Bree cried, as Gealach galloped along the front of the army. Bree had never felt such a rush of energy.

Her people shouted out and shook swords, spears and bows in the air.

On the return ride, Bree knew that fear had departed their ranks.

'By Dagda's beard!' Lu shot at her when she returned. 'I can't protect you if you're going to be so rash.'

Bree's elation still floated around her like an aura. 'Protect me?' she questioned. 'I don't need you to protect me.'

'Really?' Lu's gaze darkened. 'You've made a target of yourself. Everyone in Mór's horde now knows who you are!'

'Good!' Bree exclaimed. 'I want them to know who is about to defeat them.'

'You intend to do that single-handedly, do you?'

Bree leaned in close to her. Gealach brushed flanks with Feidlimid, Lu's stallion. 'Don't dress me down in front of everyone. I've spoken to you about that before.'

'Then don't do stupid things.' Lu threw the words back at her.

Bree glared at him. 'Did you hear our people cheer? I think this would be a good time to attack.' Bree flicked the reins on Gealach's neck and, together, unicorn and goddess, leaped forward.

'By Dagda's beard!'

Bree heard Lu's words trail behind her.

Chapter Fourteen

How she didn't fall off Gealach in the riotous crush of horses, men, blades and spears, Bree didn't know. She could only believe the unicorn's magic looked after her, just as Diarmuid had said.

Bree cut a swathe through the throng, heading straight for Badb. Áine followed her, as did Hilde. Bree was surprised to see Seraphina fighting her way through as well. Seraphina was on foot. Bree vowed she'd protect the young woman.

True to its name, Cara fíor proved to be a good friend. No blade stood a chance against it. Arrows came close and, at times, when Bree deflected their trajectory with her sword, she was certain it was Cara fíor directing her hand.

Seraphina fought well. Bree kept an eye on her, impressed by her seamstress's agility. A leap aside, a spin and kick, downed many an enemy.

Hilde stayed with Bree. The centaur's arrows cut the air around her. If anyone came too close, Hilde raised her forelegs and brought her hooves crashing down on her targets.

When they were immersed in the midst of the battle, Bree shouted to Áine, 'We can't all push through Mór's entire army. Better you just fight where we are.'

'What are you going to do?' her aunt asked, shouting.

Gealach reared. 'I have to reach Badb,' Bree called back. 'We can't have her dropping her fear over everyone.'

'You'll never reach her,' Áine cried. 'Bree!'

Niamh flew off Bree's shoulder. 'I'll help. I'll use my sleeping dust,' she said. Without a further word, the fairy flew ahead of Bree and sprinkled a silvery dust over the enemies in front of them. Men and horses staggered into each other.

Not wasting a moment, Bree flicked Gealach's reins and the two of them pushed through, with Áine, Hilde and Seraphina on their heels. Men in dark armour, their hair long and lank, scars twisting their faces into grotesque masks, fell aside.

Niamh flew back to Bree. 'I've used my sleeping dust,' she buzzed in Bree's ear. 'Most will only feel tired, not go to sleep.'

'That's enough,' Bree told her. 'Thank you, my friend.'

The sun was low when Bree looked again. Scathach was nowhere to be seen. Nor was Mór, but Badb clung close to the base of the mound, as if she was cursed by her own fear to fight.

Bree noticed Badb move out of the hillock's shadow.

Gealach reared and then leaped forward. Hilde helped to clear a path with her arrows.

Badb spun on the spot, her grey garb and dark grey

hair becoming one, until she shape-shifted into a small ominous cloud. It grew by the second.

Seraphina threw a spear at Badb. It fell through the cloud onto the ground. Hilde sent three arrows, one after the other in quick succession. They too flew through the dark swirling mist that was Badb.

'Stay back,' Bree commanded.

'Macushla,' Áine cried out as if she was in agony. 'What are you going to do?'

'Keep back.' Bree and Gealach leaped forward, closing the gap between themselves and Badb. Bree sheathed her sword in its scabbard, cupped her hands, hoping the unicorn would keep her on its back, and focused. Flames burned in her palms. She took a deep breath and, just as she'd done with the trolls on their way to the Inner Realm, she blew the flames. A river of fire shot into the middle of Badb's swirling mists.

Badb materialised, screamed and fell heavily to the ground. Her grey clothes burned, and flames encased her. Her cries filled the air but none of her cohorts came to her aid. Badb rolled on the ground and managed to extinguish most of the flames. Then, still screaming, she ran away, around the hillock and out of sight.

The battle closed in around Bree and her friends. They moved steadily back towards their own lines.

Bree spotted Lu fighting a banshee. This creature didn't resemble the one that had attacked Doireann. This banshee looked like the ghost of a beautiful woman. She was dressed in a long flowing blue gown, her long blue hair floating around her. Then she screamed, and any idea that the banshee was beautiful, vanished.

Lu's sword cut through her as she circled him. What could kill a banshee? Bree had shot the ancient fire at the banshee at the Yew Walk. How did Lu hope to kill her?

Lu saw Bree as she rode closer to him, and then, eyes back on the banshee, he split her in two. Or so it seemed. She remained whole. Bree summoned the ancient fire to her palms and blew it at the banshee. The blue apparition screamed as the flames hit her. She fell towards the ground but vanished before she struck dirt.

Bree rode up next to Lu. 'You're lucky I saw you. I don't know how I can protect you if you don't stay near me.' Bree grinned at him.

Lu glared at her for a moment, then laughed, before he turned to deal with a troll. 'I think I can manage this one,' he said.

Bree lost Lu in the crush of men and beasts. Her other comrades stayed with her. Cara fíor rang true with every stroke and Gealach turned aside to protect Bree from swords about to descend on her.

At one point, Bree couldn't find Seraphina. She worried for the young woman. Bree should have insisted that Seraphina have a mount, although Seraphina had probably never ridden. When she fell back in with them, blood poured down Seraphina's left arm.

'A slight wound, my lady,' Seraphina assured her.

Niamh became quite aggressive at times. She spotted another fairy, this one dressed in black. Bree assumed the male fairy was a deserter to the other side. Niamh flew at him and threw red dust she extracted from a pouch at her side into his face. He coughed and rubbed his eyes. Niamh flicked more at him until he gleamed red. Bree couldn't hear what Niamh said to him as she delivered her fairy magic but, going by the male fairy's expression, Niamh's words struck him as harshly as the red dust. He retreated, still coughing and knuckling his eyes.

Arianrhod, her long silvery hair falling over her horse like a cloak, rode close to Bree. Her white owl flew from her arm and dug its claws into one of Mór's men, a black armoured man with a scarred face. The man cried out and tried to hit the bird. The owl pecked at the man's hands and then flew back to its mistress, leaving bloody stripes behind on the enemy.

'It is time for the ghosts of the dead to walk,' Arianrhod said, her voice soft and silky.

Bree heard her despite the din around them. She gazed up at the darkened sky. Arianrhod was the moon goddess and her moon rose above the tree line beyond the great plain.

Oonagh pushed her way through to them. Goddess of nature and love, she wore a long sparkling silver gown that shimmered as if covered with tiny diamonds. Her golden hair was almost as long as Arianrhod's. Oonagh carried a glittering bow and arrows.

Bree couldn't understand how Arianrhod and Oonagh managed to wear dresses while they rode. And their long hair! Bree was pleased she had her shirt and trousers, and her hair fastened back from her face.

'What is it?' Bree asked Oonagh.

'My Lord Lu sent me to find you. He suggests we regroup.'

Bree nodded. She agreed with Lu. If Mór was going to unleash a ghostly army, they should muster their forces.

Before they could move, the enemy army fell back. Perhaps Mór had issued a similar command.

As the dark forces retreated, several Daoine ollmhór followed them, intent on dispensing more grief. The giants' maces sent bodies flying through the night right over the enemy's lines.

'I see you're still alive,' Lu greeted her.

'I see you are too,' Bree threw back at him. His armour and his chest were splattered with blood. 'I told you, you should have worn a shirt.'

Lu chuckled.

'Bree gave Badb a warm welcome and then sent her running,' Áine said.

'I'm impressed.' Lu smiled.

'I think it's best that we should regroup,' Bree said. The great plain had cleared quicker than she could've imagined. A menacing hush remained behind, a void waiting to be refilled.

'Look!' Hilde exclaimed.

A dark figure stood on top of the hillock. Moonlight backlit it. After staring for a couple of minutes, Bree could discern a hooded figure in a black cloak. A white face caught the moonlight and shone with a deathly starkness.

A hum of dread rose from their troops and remained hovering above them.

'Mór,' Bree murmured. She almost savoured the word. 'At last!'

Niamh flew off Bree's shoulder and was soon lost amidst their army. Within minutes, not only Niamh but also all of the fairies flew in a golden, glowing haze in front of the troops.

When Niamh returned to Bree's shoulder, she smiled and said, 'Courage dust.'

'Thank you, little one,' Bree said.

Courage dust aside, everyone was restless.

'What is Mór waiting for?' Bree asked Lu. 'Is she waking the dead or not?'

'You shouldn't be so impatient to see them,' Lu told her.

'I see Corraidhin is also anxious,' Bree added, and nodded at Lu's spear spitting out small flames.

Lu chuckled. 'He loves a good battle.'

Bree sucked in her breath. 'Who is that standing close to Mór?' A tall, darkly robed figure, hooded and with waves of evil emanating from him.

'At a guess,' Lu said, 'I'd say that is the necromancer.'

Before Bree could reply, she saw them—slow moving, ghostly figures, heading across the plain towards them. The moonlight shot through them with its silvery beams.

Arianrhod, the Moon goddess, moved closer to Bree. She seemed perturbed that her wondrous light could raise such evil wraiths. Perhaps not evil spirits but manipulated by the malevolent hands of Mór and her necromancer.

'The ghosts of the dead,' Áine murmured. 'How can we kill them?' Her voice quaked.

'We can't,' Lu said. 'They're already dead.'

'An enchantment?' Bree queried. 'We have enough magical beings with us.'

A goddess Bree recalled meeting at the reception rode up to them.

'Perhaps I can help,' said Rhiannon, Goddess of the Night and the Underworld.

'These are not your dead, Rhiannon,' Áine said. 'These ghosts belong to Mór.'

'I can shape-shift and move among them.'

'To what purpose?' Lu asked. 'They'll turn on you.'

Rhiannon was respected for her knowledge of every plant and tree. She was interwoven with all life on Tír na nÓg, despite her status of Goddess of the Underworld. They couldn't afford to lose Rhiannon.

'There has to be a way,' Bree said. Surely they hadn't fought so hard and come this far to be defeated by ghosts? She cast her gaze over the plain. The ghosts were about halfway across. No one followed them. Mór obviously thought it unnecessary. Bree felt chilled by this thought. She wasn't going to allow the cold to enter her bones. She placed her hands together and felt the warmth churn within her. It grew and charged through her body. It was her mother's spirit. It was her spirit.

Bree swung her leg over Gealach's neck and jumped to the ground. She stroked the unicorn's face.

Everyone around her moved, fidgeting, uneasy.

'What do you think you're doing?' Lu demanded.

'Wait here,' Bree said, and stepped away from them.

'Macushla,' Áine cried.

Bree didn't want to distress her aunt, but she knew what she had to do.

'Niamh, fly over to Áine, your queen,' Bree told the fairy on her shoulder. Niamh's wings were a blur of agitation. 'Go,' Bree added.

Lu jumped down and closed the distance between them. 'I asked you what you thought you're doing?' He grabbed Bree's arm.

Bree wrenched it free, which was not easy with Lu's iron-like grip. 'I know what I'm doing,' she said, and stepped farther onto the great plain.

Seraphina followed her.

'Go back,' Bree commanded. Seraphina and Lu stopped in their tracks. 'I do this alone.'

'Sacrificing yourself won't save your people,' Lu's voice boomed.

Bree kept walking. She didn't feel afraid, even though she was a solitary figure walking towards a sea of ghosts. She felt the unease of those she left behind her, but she couldn't return. Mór and the necromancer still stood on the hillock. Bree felt the woman's evil gaze boring into her. She ignored it. For now, she must focus.

Then Bree halted. Cries and sobs rose in the night behind her. The ghosts were about two hundred yards in front of her. Bree had told Lu she knew what she was doing. But did she? Yes… and no. She must try. That's all she knew.

She held her hands together, closed her eyes and focused. Flames ignited in her palms. Heat raged throughout her body. She took a deep breath. For a moment, she held it in and then slowly, she blew on the flames. They shot out, closed the gap between her and the ghosts. The ghouls burned for a moment, their ash grey faces contorting in silent agony before they disintegrated and vanished.

Bree blew again and another river of fire scorched the next lot of ghostly figures. And again and again, she blew the flames, until a wall of fire rose and then was extinguished, taking the ghostly army with it.

Shocked silence reverberated behind her. A screech emanated from the hillock. Mór's figure seemed to quiver against the moon. A bird, a black raven, flew from her cloak, and then another and another. Within seconds, Mór's trembling cloak turned into a flock of ravens, which swooped in Bree's direction.

Bree looked at the hillock. Mór wasn't there. Had she turned herself into one of the ravens heading Bree's way?

Her stomach lurched, but Bree held her ground, braced herself for the impact. The flock lunged at her and, at the last second before hitting her, vanished, leaving Mór standing in front of Bree, dark eyes gleaming out of a deathly white face. Mór's cloak was gone, leaving only one raven on her shoulder. It leaned forward as if it was about to peck out one of Bree's eyes.

Bree summoned the ancient fire. She raised her burning palms and placed the flames between herself and Mór. 'You cannot win over what is good and right,' Bree told her.

Mór fell back a step as she stared at the flames. Her white face contorted into a mask of fury. 'You are dead! Dead,' she threatened, her words laced with menace, as she drew a dagger from a sheath at her side.

Bree went cold. Her heart pounded. This had to be the dagger forged by black magic by the necromancer, the blade that had killed her mother. Without thinking it through because planning wasn't an option at this moment, Bree blew the flames from her hand into Mór's face. They encompassed the dagger as well.

Mór stepped back, away from the flames. 'You can't destroy this blade with your petty fire.'

Bree stared into the dark, soulless eyes. 'We'll see, but I can certainly destroy you.' Bree blew the flames once more at Mór, pleased to see some long, black strands of the woman's hair had caught alight. 'Your darkness cannot win.'

'We'll see,' Mór replied. Then she swivelled on the spot and vanished into a black cloud, taking her raven with her.

Bree stared at the top of the hillock. The necromancer had vanished also.

The cheer behind Bree became a roar.

Within minutes of the ghosts of the dead turning to dust, the rest of Mór's forces retreated, disappearing from the great plain as if Bree's fire had scorched them too.

Bree turned and stared at her people, who ran towards her, yelping in victory. They surged around her, uttering their thanks, their elation and their love. Bree felt stunned, as surely as if someone had hit her over the head. She had just single-handedly dispatched Mór's horde. It didn't feel real. She'd watched the ghosts disintegrate, she'd watched the horde of evil scurry away, but she could hardly believe it.

Lu's voice boomed out as he cleared a path to her. 'All right, all right, let me through. By Dagda's beard, give Lady Bree room to breathe.'

Bree cried out when Lu grabbed her. What was the man doing now? Then he hoisted her onto his shoulder. She gripped his hands, and then laughed. She could see out over their army. Bloodied gods and goddesses stood beside the Daoine ollmhór and centaurs. All cheered now they could see Bree again. She raised her hands high, nearly slipping until Lu steadied her. He made his way through the army and back across the plain. At its edge, he lifted Bree down. When she turned to face him, he bowed.

'My lady,' he said. When he rose, a smirk twisted his lips. 'You won the war.'

Bree nodded, and she returned his smirk. He always laughed at her. By Danu's spirit, she'd done well, and still he found amusement in it.

Áine wrapped Bree in her arms. 'Oh, macushla, you were astonishing. You have won the love and admiration of all your people.'

'I'm not so sure about *all* my people,' Bree said, and nodded towards where Lu was talking to Diarmuid.

'You couldn't have a truer follower than Lu,' Áine said.

The sincerity in her aunt's eyes should have convinced Bree. If only Lu didn't laugh at her all the time. Bree watched him with some of his men. He slapped them on the back and grabbed their arms in camaraderie. He was respected. At that moment, he swung around and caught her gaze. He held it, his blue eyes darkening. Bree felt her breath catch. So often when she looked at him, her heart leaped, and her pulse beat in her throat. Then Fionn spoke to him. The moment passed.

Seraphina and Hilde had stayed with her during the entire battle. They, along with Áine and Niamh, were talking around her. Arianrhod and Oonagh joined in. Bree gave them her attention. Niamh giggled and flew over them, dropping golden fairy dust.

'For victory, my lady,' she said.

Lu's voice made Bree jump. He stood beside her. 'I

think we'd better make our way back to the palace, and the safety of the Inner Realm,' he said.

'What about our dead?' Bree glanced back over the plain.

Lu followed her gaze. 'My men will take care of everything. The fallen will each receive a hero's burial.'

'What of the Daoine ollmhór? Will the giants return with us into the Inner Realm?'

'I think they will for now. They have a long journey home, so will want to refresh themselves.'

'We must show them our hospitality,' Bree said.

'We will, indeed.'

'And the many skirmishes along the Enchanted Veil?'

'All routed. Our world is safe again... for the time being.'

'Do you suspect another attack?'

'Nothing too soon. But Mór will fight another day.'

'And her necromancer?'

'Her black angel might be harder to kill than Mór. Strong magic will be needed.'

Bree stared up at Lu. Blood streaked through the sweat on his face. 'Why didn't she kill me at the last? She was so close.'

'Mór knew she couldn't defeat the ancient fire. It burned between you.'

'She had the dagger she'd used to kill my mother,' Bree murmured. 'I wish I had killed her.' Something dark stirred in Bree's chest. 'I could have burnt her alive.'

Lu took her hands, turned them palms up, and then looked at Bree's face, his gaze roaming from her eyes to her cheeks to her lips. 'It is not in you to kill in cold blood.

You are here to protect your people. You'd never kill without mercy.'

Bree nodded. She wouldn't allow such dark thoughts to creep into her mind again.

Lu closed her hands together but held them for a moment longer than he needed to. He smiled. 'For now, however, we should get you home. Let me help you mount Gealach.' He patted the unicorn. Bree put her foot in the stirrup and Lu lifted her. 'You did well,' he said, and smiled.

Chapter Fifteen

Samhain was over. Tír na nÓg was safe, for the present.

Bree bathed and fell into her soft bed. It was like floating on a cloud. Niamh returned to her fairy folk but promised she'd see Bree on the morrow. Áine settled in her bedchamber.

Sorcha fussed over her until Bree said, not unkindly, 'Go to bed, Sorcha, for Danu's sake.'

Sorcha bowed. 'I will for your sake, my lady.'

Bree didn't sleep for long. She rose and crossed to the window where Mór's face had appeared to her. Only trees touched by silver light greeted the dawn. As she watched, peach and golden hues painted the leaves, and a gentle breeze caressed them until they blushed a rosy glow. She'd never seen a morning like this. In her earthen cave, only books and Áine's words had hinted at such beauty. Tears spilled onto her cheeks for the many dawns she'd missed. When she'd woken, she'd felt flat and hollow. Now, the sun's rays touched her heart and warmed her. She might have missed the dawn light for eighteen years, but there would be more daybreaks to bring her wonder. Yesterday, she had defeated Mór, who would have destroyed this beauty. How could Mór's heart be so black as to want nothing but darkness? Perhaps Bree was naïve, but she believed this is what Tír na nÓg should look like. Bree swore she would keep it that way.

All that being said, Bree knew little of her homeland. Before she explored the palace and the Inner Realm, she must go to the ancient flame.

Sorcha appeared and tut-tutted that Bree had already risen.

Úna brought a decanter and poured a golden liquid into a glass.

'Peach and apple juice from your orchards, my lady,' Úna said.

Bree drank, and then allowed the handmaidens to dress her in a simple gown, or at least as simple as her wardrobe offered. Seraphina entered last and hovered by Bree's bed, as if she was uncertain what her role would be in peacetime.

'Seraphina,' Bree called, and waved the young seamstress over. 'I need some simple gowns, with not as many pearls and gems as my present dresses have decorating them. Do you think you could sew me something?'

Seraphina smiled. 'Of course, my lady. If you will choose the fabric and the styles.'

Bree frowned, feeling Seraphina's sadness beneath her words. 'You will want to return to your village,' she said. 'How selfish of me.'

'I have nothing there now, my lady,' Seraphina replied.

'Your parents? Family?' Bree silently scolded herself for not asking before.

'My parents died when Mór's men razed our village to the ground.'

Bree took the two steps to reach Seraphina, and then took hold of the young woman's hands. Seraphina was about Bree's age. They'd both lost their mothers. 'I'm so sorry, Seraphina. Your home is here until you choose to leave it, but we will rebuild your village, and you can return to it if you wish—you only have to say. I will decree that the land is yours.'

'My lady.' Seraphina leaned over and kissed Bree's hands. When she raised her russet head, she added, 'I will never leave you. You have my love and my loyalty.'

Áine joined Bree and, after they'd broken their fast, Bree told her aunt she wanted to visit the ancient fire. Before she had a chance to go, Lu banged on the outer door and was ushered into the parlour. Kuon ran ahead of him, and greeted Bree by licking her hands.

Lu smiled and bowed. 'I trust you both slept well,' he said to Bree and Áine. When they nodded, he continued, 'Would you agree to a banquet in the grand reception room to offer thanks to the Tuatha Dé Danann?'

'Indeed,' Bree replied. 'An excellent idea. When did you have in mind?'

'This evening,' Lu said. 'While everyone is still with us in the Inner Realm.'

'Can it be arranged so quickly? Surely food has to be prepared?'

'You forget the feasting cauldron.' Lu smirked.

'Oh... yes, I keep forgetting it, even though it is a

larger version of what we had in our cave.' When would she remember all the things in her new home? 'Very well,' Bree added. 'Why not.'

Lu bowed and turned to depart.

'Before you go, what about my mother's cremation?'

'Does tomorrow, after the feasting, suit?'

'Yes indeed,' Bree said. Her heart quivered as she watched him stride away.

Kuon gave a resounding bark.

Lu spoke to his men, setting the wheels into motion for the banquet. Then, with Kuon at his side, he went to speak to the Daoine ollmhór to ensure they would remain for the feast. There was little else he had to do, so made his way to the stables to see Feidlimid, his stallion. The large black horse nodded his head and neighed when Lu reached his stall. Lu opened it and went inside. He rubbed his hands over the horse's gleaming flank.

'You did well, my friend.'

Feidlimid neighed. Kuon barked.

Lu's thoughts turned to another who had done well, who had surpassed his expectations. How had that naïve young girl he'd met in a cave turned into the fearless woman that had confronted a horde of ghosts and Mór herself? Lu was astonished by her. Then he thought of her amazing emerald eyes and his heart kicked, his breaths came in shallow pants.

'By all the jumping fleas in Dagda's beard,' he said aloud. No other woman had caused him to feel this way.

But she was so young with so much to learn. He was twenty-two-plus years old. He had known Dagda and Danu, while she had only known her aunt.

Once again, he felt amased that she had assumed her destiny in such short a time. Her people loved her, adored her. She didn't need one sun god added to all the rest. He admired her. He'd leave it at that… for now.

Bree went by herself to the flame room. Áine wanted to accompany her but, at the last, Bree wanted to be alone.

The *argat draiochta* that encased the room blinded Bree when she first entered. She crossed to the fire in the cauldron. Its warmth enfolded her and made her feel welcome. Palms together, Bree closed her eyes and focused her thoughts. When she opened her hands, the flames sat on her skin. She plunged her hands and arms into the ancient fire. It didn't burn her. Instead, it replenished her.

Despite feeling energised and complete, when Bree took her hands from the cauldron, she swayed and nearly lost her footing. Her head spun and her eyes wouldn't focus. She grabbed the cauldron so she wouldn't fall. What had happened? Her body trembled. Deep within her, heat raged. Had she kept her hands in the cauldron for too long?

Then the fire within her seemed to separate itself from her and leave her. It swam around her like an aura of flame, red and shimmering, but still not burning. She didn't understand. A moment later, the flames disappeared. The heat inside her was doused as surely as if a bucket of water had been thrown over her.

Bree released her hold on the cauldron. The dizziness had vanished. She took a moment before she returned to her chambers. Should she tell Áine about this strange occurrence? Áine would worry. Perhaps Mór had inflicted injury on her, and Bree was only now feeling it? She calmed herself. Whatever happened had passed. Bree felt well and strong, replenished after becoming one with the ancient fire. She would keep all this to herself. It was probably nothing. Merely a dizzy spell after all that had occurred this past week. She'd gone from recluse to… well, she wasn't certain what she was. Triple goddess, she'd been told, but she wasn't really that yet either.

No, there was no need to mention anything.

Bree wanted to discuss and plan how to rebuild the Outer Realm. So many villages had been razed to the ground. People were homeless. Of course, everyone had been rehoused in the Inner Realm for now, but the villagers would want to return to their own land. Bree spoke to Áine about it but even her aunt was too busy with the forthcoming celebrations that evening. Bree supposed everyone needed to have some merriment after all they'd been through.

Niamh returned in the afternoon. Bree hadn't realised how much she'd missed the fairy until she sat once more on Bree's shoulder.

'Would you like to explore the palace?' Bree asked her.

'Ooh yes,' Niamh said, and giggled. 'I hope we don't get lost.'

'Someone will find us,' Bree said.

Room after corridor after room drew Bree and Niamh through the palace. Huge tapestries decorated with triquetra and triskele interwoven with runes and roses covered so many walls. Bree couldn't even guess what some rooms were used for. Some had to be reception rooms; others had long oak tables and high-backed chairs.

'What do you think, Niamh? A conference room?'

'Perhaps,' Niamh replied.

They headed back to Bree's rooms, and she halted outside a door. Even though this room was next to Bree's, she hadn't been back inside. She opened the door. She didn't have to tell Niamh the purpose of this room. Books on shelves lined every wall. Parchment scrolls were stacked on other shelves. For a moment, Bree couldn't breathe. Had someone hit her in the chest? How could so many books exist? She ran her fingers over aged leather spines. She had her own library in her chambers, of course, but nothing on this scale. One book she took from a shelf had the stories of Danu and Dagda, before their descendants had left the original lands of the Tuatha Dé Danann and founded new colonies.

Bree wondered how much knowledge this library contained. Perhaps she would discover something about her father. She knew only that he was killed before her birth. Áine had told her his name was Bres.

Bree sat in a high-backed chair and read. Some words she couldn't understand. They were, no doubt, written in the old High Language. Runes were beyond her. The urge to understand the symbols burned inside her. She would start learning tomorrow.

As Bree had predicted, Sorcha found her in the library.

'It's time to dress for the celebrations, my lady,' she pronounced. Her tone didn't give Bree any choice but to follow her.

Áine waited for them, with Úna and Seraphina in the background. 'Macushla,' her aunt said. 'I was worried.'

'I was in the library,' Bree said. 'Has the entire day gone already?'

'Ah, that explains it, and yes, it has.' Áine smiled. 'We must hurry now. I laid a gown out for you. I hope you like it.'

A rich emerald-green velvet dress was spread across the bed. Lamplight glinted off small emeralds that looked as if they'd been flung across the velvet and adhered to it. Úna and Seraphina helped ease the gown over Bree's head. Long sleeves fell to her wrists and a small train of velvet spread behind her.

Sorcha led her to a dressing table seat in front of a mirror. Úna brushed her hair until her red tresses shone and then twisted in a style Bree couldn't, at first, see. The end result was a combination of plaits and curls with most of her hair still falling over her shoulders. Sorcha applied a dusting of powder to Bree's face, which seemed to give her an ethereal glow. Red gloss on her lips completed her toilette. Green eyes stared back at her. Bree was happy with her reflection.

Áine had left them for a while but said she'd return. When she did, she held an ornately decorated casket. Sorcha took it from her and Áine extracted a crown.

'I think it's appropriate if you wear your mother's crown this evening.' Áine placed it on Bree head. 'It was originally your grandmother's.'

A golden triquetra pattern, with brilliantly faceted diamonds outlining it, sat centre front. Scrolls and triskeles entwined with runes and smaller triquetras to complete the design.

'It is made of *dath an óir draiochta*, the magical golden metal,' Áine explained.

Bree raised a hand to touch the crown. 'It's so beautiful,' she said with reverence.

'One more thing,' Áine continued. 'Your mother's emerald necklace and ring.' Áine placed the necklace over Bree's head and fastened it, and then slipped the ring on her third finger on her right hand.

'This is too much,' Bree protested, even though the emeralds encased in their golden settings were astonishing.

'Nonsense,' Áine said, and drew Bree to her feet. 'You are the triple goddess, leader of the Tuatha Dé Danann. You must look the part.'

Look the part? Self-doubt plunged through her. This was all an illusion. She was a fraud. She'd assumed her mother's role, but she didn't deserve her crown or her emeralds. How could she face her people this evening? They'd cheered when she'd vanquished Mór and her horde. They would expect more from her now. They would expect to see Brigid, the Triple Goddess of the Tuatha Dé Danann. They would expect to see her mother, not Bree who wasn't a triple goddess at all.

How could she achieve it? If only her mother were still

alive, she could teach her. Bree felt ignorant and undeserving. Lu had laughed at her when he'd first seen her. An ignorant girl, he'd called her. He was correct. She was ignorant of so much.

The reception room gleamed and glittered at her as Bree entered. Áine was a step behind with Niamh on her shoulder.

A cheer soared into the arched ceiling and reverberated around her. Everyone bowed as she approached.

Banqueting tables were laid with golden plates, tall candelabra, and vases brimming over with flowers—roses, peonies, lavender, hollyhocks and so many more. Bree stepped into the centre of the tables and within seconds everyone surged around her to congratulate her, to once again swear their loyalty to her, and to say how pleased they were to have her leading them.

Her personal space breached, Bree felt overwhelmed and unworthy. Why couldn't she be back in her quiet cave with only Áine as her companion? The last few days had been a mass of hectic and confusing events. Now they were over—nearly over. Soon she would be Bree once again and when the Tuatha Dé Danann became aware of her lack of accomplishments, they would most likely banish her back to her cave. They might congratulate her now for saving them, but had she really saved them? She was certain Lu and his men, with a little more time, could have vanquished Mór.

As if he sensed her turmoil, Lu appeared by her side.

Everyone took a step back. He didn't have to say a word. He cut a commanding presence in his rich blue velvet tunic and trousers. His blond hair shone, and his eyes twinkled as he smiled at Bree.

'My lady,' he said, and bowed his head. 'May I say you look very beautiful this evening? Green is your colour. It highlights your incredible eyes.'

Bree inclined her head and smiled. She wasn't used to compliments and didn't know what to say. In any case, Lu's blue eyes held hers and rendered her speechless. Her heart did a somersault. She expected that any minute he'd taunt her and twist his full lips into a smirk.

Instead, he asked, 'May I accompany you around the room? Perhaps I can introduce you to those you don't already know.' He offered his arm.

Bree still couldn't speak. She placed her hand on his arm. Her palm tingled much as it did when she summoned the flame. Lu confused her.

Lu led her through the crowds. No one surged as close to her now that he was with her.

After some time, when Bree felt they must have spoken to everyone, she said, 'What of the centaurs and the Daoine ollmhór?'

'They're outside. Banquet tables have been set up in courtyard. Centaurs and giants need a little more room.'

'I'd like to speak to them.' Bree expected Lu to object and was incredulous when he didn't.

'Of course,' Lu replied, and led her through the palace and outside into the courtyard.

The air was light and pleasant. Bree revived and felt

refreshed, until everyone encircled her once again. Giant men and women leaned over her. She smiled and chatted to them until she felt giddy. Lu sensed this and once again led her away, but not before Bree spoke to Hilde and thanked her. 'Your arrows flew straight and true,' Bree said. 'Not to mention your hooves, which saved me a few times.'

Hilde laughed and reached her hand down. Bree held it firmly.

Bree, still with Lu beside her, went back inside. She found their guests had taken over the great hall for dancing. Several minstrels had followed them to offer accompaniment. They walked silently along the corridors to the reception room. Did they have nothing to say to each other? When they reached the reception room, Bree raised her hand to lean against one of the immense columns at each end of the room.

'Are you not well?' Lu asked.

'I could use a little more fresh air,' Bree explained.

'Perhaps the balcony?' Lu nodded towards the door that opened onto the terrace.

'Yes,' Bree agreed. Once outside, the refreshing air, without a hundred or more people around her, soon revived Bree. She dropped her hand from Lu's arm and instantly missed the touch of it. She stepped back from the ornate balustrade and leaned against the wall. It cast her into shadow.

'It's a beautiful night,' Lu said.

Bree followed his gaze and looked up at the velvet sky with its swathe of stars glinting at her. 'It is lovely. I hope all nights can be as clear and as calm. So different to the nights in my cave. I often wondered what the sky would be like.'

'I understand how difficult it must be for you,' Lu said, after a moment.

'You do?' Bree asked, astonished.

'Of course,' Lu replied. 'You have spent your life in a cavern. Then I come along and drag you from it.'

'You did.' Bree smiled. 'You said I was an ignorant girl.'

'I may have been a bit harsh,' Lu said, and shrugged. His eyes twinkled in the moonlight.

'Can I believe my ears?' Bree laughed.

'You still have a lot to learn.'

'I know. I'm aware of how little I do know.'

'You have time now to absorb everything.' Lu reached out and took Bree's hand. 'Nevertheless, you've come a long way. Like a flower, you've blossomed, petal by petal. I see a beautiful and capable young woman in front of me now, not the girl in the cave, with those angry green eyes staring at me, and her hair in plaits.' He tucked a strand of Bree's hair behind her ear.

Lu's touch awoke every nerve in Bree's body. She stared up into his eyes. His gaze held hers and wouldn't let her go. Lu lowered his head. Certain he was about to kiss her, Bree closed her eyes, but a kiss didn't happen.

Bree's eyes flashed open. Her blood rushed through her veins, like a raging torrent of… what? She'd never felt anything like it. Lu raised his head and moved away from her lips. Bree wanted to stop him, to hold his face to hers.

'We should go back inside,' he whispered. Then, he stepped back from her. He frowned and wouldn't meet her eyes, as if he'd had a sudden change of heart. 'Your people await you,' he said.

Bree felt confused. Why not kiss her and take her into his arms? Why step so quickly away from her? Did he think he'd acted inappropriately? She didn't know how to behave in a situation like this. Áine hadn't prepared her for it. Bree hadn't mixed with other young women, to share secrets and to giggle behind their hands. All she could do was to nod. 'Very well.' She took his proffered arm but avoided looking at him.

Lu led her to the top banqueting table and held out a high-backed chair for her to sit. He sat on her right side, while Áine was on her left. As soon as she sat down, servants carried huge golden platters to the tables—boar and venison, and vegetable dishes—more than Bree had ever seen or tasted before. Lu helped serve her and indicated that she should eat. As soon as she began, everyone else followed suit.

Conversation during the meal was lively. Lu paid her extravagant attention and joked and teased her. Perhaps, he regretted not kissing her, and was trying to make up for it.

'You gave me a hard time too,' he said, when they were discussing his arrival at the cave.

'I thought the wall was about to crumble and then you opened the door.' Bree laughed.

Áine joined in. 'You were unkind to her, Lu.'

'I have already been chastised for it.' He chuckled.

His laughter rumbled like distant thunder. Bree could listen to it all day.

When the long meal finished, servants rushed to clear the tables and then moved them out of the way.

Minstrels, in a mezzanine gallery at the end of the reception room, had played during the banquet. They now changed to more lively music.

'May I escort you onto the floor?' Lu asked.

'What for?'

Lu laughed. 'For dancing.'

Bree felt the blood drain from her face. She'd rather tackle Mór again than try to dance. 'I can't,' she murmured.

'Why not?' Lu countered.

'I can't dance,' Bree admitted. 'I wouldn't know what to do.'

'Didn't Áine teach you to dance? I remember a certain hop, step and kick during our flight here when you floored one of Mór's men.'

'I can dance on my own,' Bree said, feeling the blood surging back to her face.

'Very well, dance on your own.' Lu took her hand and led her onto the floor. She had no choice but to do it. It wouldn't be seemly to pull away from him or to argue in front of everyone.

Lu dropped her hand. 'Dance,' he commanded, his lips smirking.

Bree glared at him. She wished she could shout at him.

'No one will be able to dance if you don't go first,' Lu said.

Bree took a deep breath. She could do this. If she could defeat Mór, she could do a simple dance. She smiled at everyone in the hall. Their expressions of anticipation didn't help the butterflies that already pirouetted in her stomach. She recalled the little jig Áine had taught her. It was simple enough. Step, kick, step, kick, spin and repeat. Jump to the side and kick. Jump back and kick and repeat. Finish with two higher kicks and bow.

It was over before Bree realised she'd done it. The room broke into rapturous applause.

Lu strode to her side, took her hands and led her into a dance. Everyone else swarmed onto the floor.

'You see,' he said. 'Now no one can see what you're doing. You can stumble about like an ungainly foal if you want to.'

Bree pulled a wry face at him and did exactly as he'd predicted. Her legs felt like a newborn foal's, dipping here, staggering there. The only good part about it was that Lu held her hands and, at times, he placed his hand on her back or waist.

When the dance finished, he left her and danced with Áine. Ogma, Dagda's brother, claimed Bree. She could tell that he didn't often dance, so she relaxed and chatted to him.

Lu returned to her after an hour or so of dancing. 'We should do the formal part of the evening,' he said. 'You must address everyone.'

The butterflies swooped again in Bree's stomach as Lu led her onto the dais. Áine accompanied them and stood on her left side. Lu remained on her right.

'Quiet!' Lu bellowed in an undignified manner.

The assemblage fell silent and turned to look at them.

Bree didn't know what to say. She could swear she'd always protect them. She could vow that peace would remain with them. But how could she promise those things? Mór was out there, no doubt already plotting her next step. The necromancer could even now be forging a new dagger with black magic. Instead, Bree stepped forward and cupped her hands, concentrating on the ancient flame. Seconds later, she opened her palms. The flames rose in front of her.

Everyone bowed.

Bree felt her head spin. She swayed and nearly lost her footing. Lu stepped forward and placed his hand under her elbow to steady her.

Not again! This was what happened when she'd gone to the flame room and thrust her hands into the ancient fire in the cauldron. Just when she'd defeated Mór, just when Lu had brought her back to her people, something had to go wrong. She couldn't understand what was happening to her.

She focused on the flames in her hands. Her body trembled but deep within her, she felt the flames' warmth. It grew, until heat raged through her body. Then, as had happened before, the blaze within seemed to separate and leave her. It swam around her like an aura of fire, red and shimmering, and yet, not burning.

Bree didn't understand. She lost awareness of Lu near her, of Áine too, of her people waiting in front of her. She could feel only the flames. Without knowing why, Bree reached out her arms. Two columns of fire shot towards the ceiling. At the same moment, the fiery aura separated from her, and yet she still felt a part of it.

A hush fell over the Tuatha Dé Danann. Bree became aware that they were on their knees.

Six hands reached out with flames in their palms. Six hands… and they were all hers. It took a further minute for Bree to realise that two clones of herself stood next to her; joined but separate. Three bodies were entwined with the one heart, one soul.

Bree felt her mother's spirit within each incarnation. Bree closed her palms. The ancient fire extinguished. Three bodies became one again. Bree floated in a sea of calm. She felt at one with herself, with her mother's spirit, and with the universe.

Áine crushed her in an embrace. 'How wonderful, macushla,' she murmured in Bree's ear. 'You are indeed the Triple Goddess.'

Bree didn't understand what had happened. Nor why it happened then. Perhaps she had always been taking small steps towards it. At least she wasn't ill as she'd thought she might be.

Lu reached out his hand and bowed his head. 'My Lady, allow me to take you down to your people. You have proved yourself beyond measure.'

His hand felt large and warm and familiar. Bree took it, but this time, she didn't want to let it go. The wonderful feeling she felt from contact with him didn't last for long. As everyone came up to her, he dropped her hand. If she could have, she would have tied their hands together. As each person bowed before her, Lu took a step away. At least people weren't crowding her this time. Bree smiled and thanked them for their sworn fealty. Then she looked for Lu. He was farther away from her.

For a long moment, she met his eyes. It seemed as if time had paused, and they were held frozen. Lu's eyes held sadness, which she'd never seen before. She wanted to shout out, to stop everyone else from getting between them. She wanted to bring Lu closer to her. Why was he moving away from her? Then the moment was gone. Bree lost sight of his tall figure; his golden hair. Why did she feel she'd lost Lu altogether?

Áine took her arm and hugged her once again. 'Oh macushla, I am so happy. Your mother would be delighted if she could have seen you become the Triple Goddess.'

'But she's not here,' Bree lamented. She knew she was incorrect. Her mother would always be in her heart. Her mother had been with her every step of the way.

'You are the Triple Goddess,' Áine said. 'You have achieved so much.' Áine took hold of Bree's shoulders. 'You have become everything your mother desired for you. Be happy, Bree.'

Bree kissed her aunt's cheek. 'I'll try,' she murmured and attempted to smile. 'Dear Áine. You have protected me all of my life and for that, I thank you. You know I love you.'

'Of course, macushla. As I love you.'

Did Bree want to hear those words from Lu? She didn't know. Bree couldn't see him in the reception room. Why had he left her? She'd ask him tomorrow.

For now she must smile and nod and be happy for her people. After all, now she was truly the Triple Goddess.

Chapter Sixteen

When Lu sat in his parlour later than night, more like early hours of the morning, he looked around at his men… some of the Immortals, who'd brought the party back to his chambers. Fionn, Grainne and Diarmuid sat huddled together, as they were usually found. Bearach bellowed and guffawed at something Domhnall had said. Domhnall was a rugged man, battle-worn, and with a good heart. Tiomoid, the youngest Immortal, nodded his head and nearly spilled his mead every time he did so. He was a quiet man. Physically, he had the muscle, the vigour to be an Immortal, but he had a timid heart and a softer nature. Padraig's snores almost drowned out the conversations. He was a shorter man but thick-set and muscular.

They were his band of warriors, and his friends, but Lu felt separated from them at this moment. His thoughts should have been about the battle and their victory, but instead, they took him back to the reception hall and a young woman who had danced in his arms. He could hardly believe that she had defeated Mór and her evil hordes. Only days ago he had dragged her from a cave and now she shone as Triple Goddess.

He'd nearly kissed her. Dagda only knew why! It was the moment they were both caught up in. It wouldn't happen again. She infuriated him. Well… she had done so since he first saw her… but he couldn't get Bree's sparkling green eyes out of his mind. He couldn't forget how luscious her lips had looked.

Lu sprang to his feet. Dagda help him!

Kuon jumped up and barked.

Everyone stopped talking and stared at him.

Lu poured himself another tankard of mead and drank half of it in one breath. 'Drink up, my friends.'

Everyone laughed and went back to their conversations… or snoring, in the case of Padraig.

Lu banged on her door early the following morning. Bree, her aunt, Niamh and Seraphina sat chatting in the parlour. All were tired from the reception.

Úna brought Lu to them. Kuon raced ahead and nudged Bree for a pat.

'I have arranged for Brigid's cremation this afternoon,' Lu said.

'Good morning to you too, my Lord Lu,' Áine said.

'Good morning, my ladies,' Lu said and grimaced. 'You can see I'm more suited to the battlefield than a palace.'

Bree gazed at him from under lowered eyelashes. He didn't seem out of place last evening when they danced, or when he almost kissed her. Or did she imagine he was going to kiss her? After they had danced, he'd moved away and left her to cope alone speaking with everyone.

No, no, it wasn't after they'd danced. He left her after she'd become the triple goddess, after she showed the full aspects of womanhood—the girl, the mature woman and the old woman. Why? Had she been correct about him all along? Did he covet her throne? Perhaps before she'd assumed her full triple goddess aspects, there had been some hope for him, but now, when she was ensconced in her position, he might not be able to take her place as easily.

Lu avoided her gaze. Even her aunt raised her eyebrows at Bree, as if to ask why she was staring at Lu. He never sat down and joined them. This morning was no exception. He nodded and left them. Kuon turned and followed his master.

Bree, with her aunt and Niamh, followed Lu to a field at the side of the palace but some distance away. Seraphina followed discreetly with Sorcha and Úna. Bree was amazed at how quickly Lu had organised the ceremony. It was the best time to hold the cremation while the Daoine ollmhór—the giants from the high country, the centaurs and all the other gods and goddesses were still within the Inner Realm.

The sun shone in all its golden glory—Bree had never imagined sunshine could feel so wonderful, a warm caress on her skin. Birds sang in the hedges. Bree caught a glimpse of a tiny blue wren. It was difficult to believe that two days ago they had lived in fear of their lives. Now Mór had escaped, and her mother lay dead.

A dais had been set up for Bree, Áine, Lu and Ogma. Áine stepped forward and spoke about her sister, as anyone would of their sibling. Then Áine chanted words in what had to be the High Language. Bree couldn't understand any of it, but a sense of calm eased into her.

Then Lu rose and held his hand out for Bree's. She didn't know why but, at this moment, she trusted him as she had most of the time during the last few days. When he led her down to stand in front of her mother's pyre, Bree asked in a side-whisper what they were doing.

'You must light the kindling.'

Bree sucked in her breath. 'No, I don't want to.' Her heart pounded in her chest. 'I can't.'

'It's expected of you. You have the ancient fire.'

Bree thought of her mother as she'd seen her lying in state. Brigid had looked beautiful, serene and ethereal. Bree couldn't light the fire that would burn that beloved person. She threw a glance over her shoulder to her aunt. Áine nodded her encouragement. Seconds ticked by. Bree realised that at this stage she couldn't refuse to do what was expected of her. She would lose the respect of her people. She shot a glance at Lu, who nodded.

Cupping her hands and focusing her mind, Bree opened her palms to see the ancient fire. She looked around at her people and then stepped up to the platform on which her mother's body rested. Bree blew on the flames in her palms, and they ignited the pyre. She felt dizzy but understood now what it meant. Her persona had split into her three aspects.

When her three aspects had become one again, Lu took her hand and led her back to the dais. Bree stood next to her aunt for a few minutes, but she didn't want to watch her mother's entire cremation.

'I must go back to the palace,' she whispered to her aunt.

'It is all right, macushla, I'll accompany you.'

Lu wouldn't allow anyone back into the Outer Realm for another week, not until his men had searched every part of it to ascertain none of Mór's horde lingered, hiding in burned out farm houses or in the forests.

Bree agreed to his directives. It gave everyone time to recover from the ordeal of battle. Bree and her aunt had to grieve their mother and sister.

Seraphina stayed and made Bree quite a few gowns, as well as some trousers that had a half-skirt covering them at the back, while at the same time leaving the front free for riding and practising the sword. Lu didn't attend her lessons but sent Diarmuid to instruct her. The man was a great hunter, by all accounts, so was suited to teaching Bree swordplay and how to shoot an arrow. Bree knew Diarmuid had a lot of work ahead of him, but he was a kindly and patient man. Nevertheless, Bree still hoped that Lu would attend her lessons and teach her again.

Bree, with Niamh on her shoulder, and Áine beside her, often walked in the formal gardens which stood directly behind the palace, with parterres made of clipped hedges encasing roses of every colour. What a revelation and surprise it was to find the gardens so close to the palace.

'I could never have imagined a flower could be so beautiful,' Bree said. 'And look at these trees.' She gazed up at an avenue of trees massed in pink blossoms that grew behind the rose parterres. 'They are delicate and magical.'

Niamh flew to one of the trees and carried a few blossoms back for Bree. Niamh sneezed and had to push her circlet back in place.

'Are you happy, macushla?' her aunt asked.

'I am. Who wouldn't be in such an idyllic garden and a beautiful palace?' Bree smiled. She glanced back at her new home. Wonderful intricate metalwork with triquetra entwined among leaves and rose designs adorned the rear of the palace where there was a seating area from which one could gaze out over the gardens. 'Although, I do miss our quiet cave at times.'

Áine nodded. 'It takes a while to accustom oneself to the noise of everyday life.'

'As long as Mór stays away, I'll be happy.'

'That's not a given, unfortunately.'

Bree went with Áine, Niamh and Seraphina to the latter's devastated village in the Outer Realm. Lu insisted he accompany them, along with his most trusted men—Diarmuid, Fionn, and Bearach, Domhnall, Tiomoid and Padraig.

They all rode. Bree was pleased to see her unicorn

Gealach once again. Her white coat shimmered, and the golden horn picked up hints of silver from Gealach's white mane. Bree must ride her more often. She took Seraphina up behind her, even though the young seamstress was reluctant.

Niamh flew to Áine shoulder.

Kuon, nearly as large as a horse, bounded along beside them.

Once they'd ridden through the Enchanted Veil, Bree's heart contracted at the devastation that lay before her. Fields of crop had been burned to a cinder, and whole villages erased, leaving only a few tortured timbers reaching to the sky as if pleading for mercy.

They halted on the outskirts of what was left of Seraphina's village. Bree felt Seraphina's gasp of horror behind her back. Everything had been razed to the ground, with only the bitterness of burned timbers to sting their noses and eyes.

Bearach rushed over to Bree and smiled but lifted his hand to Seraphina. 'May I help you down?'

Bree smiled. She caught her aunt watching them, a strange expression in her eyes. It seemed that Áine was assessing them, even though Bree couldn't think why.

Seraphina slid to the ground, which allowed Bree to dismount. No one rushed forward to assist her, but then, she didn't require assistance.

Lu strode across to her. 'We'll go into the village on foot. Everything has been checked over and is completely safe.'

Bree nodded ruefully. 'At least it's safe now. We must add more enchantments to the Outer Realm. This can't be allowed to happen again. The Outer Realm should have no less protection than the Inner Realm.'

'I have added more,' Lu replied, 'but you could bestow some extra enchantments. I'm certain Áine will help you.'

'Yes, indeed,' Áine replied.

Niamh flew onto Bree's shoulder. 'I have some rose dust to help the unpleasant odour.'

'Thank you, Niamh,' Bree told the little fairy, her circlet lopsided as usual, 'but I think we should smell the burnt timbers and crops to make us realise how dreadful it is to have an entire village destroyed.'

Niamh gave a sad smile and flew over to Seraphina's shoulder.

'Niamh has a sweet and kind heart,' Bree said.

'Shall we move on?' Lu suggested.

Seraphina walked ahead of them, Bearach at her side, as she picked her way through the embers. When she halted in front of the remains of a hut, Bree knew it had to have been Seraphina's home. Bree joined her, placing a hand around the other woman's shoulders. They were nearly the same height and, even though their red hair was similar, Seraphina's face, with the ravages of her grief showing, looked ten years older.

'Are you certain your parents couldn't have escaped?' Bree knew it was a shallow question, but she felt she had to say something. No one could have escaped this conflagration. Then Bree glanced at Seraphina, thinking that one person had escaped... Seraphina.

Seraphina shook her head and tears rolled down her cheeks. 'I only lived to stand here today because my mother had sent me into the forest for mushrooms. We knew Mór had attacked other villages on the rim of the Outer Realm, but her hordes hadn't penetrated this far.' Seraphina paused. Bree could see how difficult it was for Seraphina to control her emotions. 'When I went into the forest, I never suspected it would be the last time I would ever see my mother.'

Bree turned Seraphina around and hugged her. 'I know.' At least Seraphina had explained what had happened. When Bree glanced over Seraphina's shoulder, she once again noticed her aunt's narrowed gaze. Then Seraphina stood back, sniffing.

'Thank you, my lady. I know you understand. We have both lost our mothers.'

Áine coughed, her eyes watering. 'I think the acrid embers are affecting me.'

'We'll move on,' Bree said. She turned to Seraphina. 'Do you want your village rebuilt upon the old ground or would you like a new location?'

'There's fertile land over yonder,' Lu said and pointed to an area that was to the side of the devastated village.

'That land is fertile,' Seraphina agreed. 'Baile Meánach is… was a village of farmers. I would prefer the village to start afresh… although we don't have any people left alive.'

'There are villagers from other settlements,' Lu said. 'Some who were close to the perimeter of the Enchanted Veil. I think it best if they resettle elsewhere.'

'Ah yes,' Bree agreed. 'This would be an ideal place for them.'

Seraphina smiled—the first time Bree had seen some genuine pleasure in her green eyes.

'Then it's settled.' Bree squeezed Seraphina's hand. 'Once we're back at the palace, we'll draw up some plans for the village layout and designs for the houses.'

'You are too good, my lady.'

'We must look to the future,' Bree said. 'What other villages are there?' Bree turned to Lu.

'Cruithnecht is another village for raising crops and general farming. Figid is a village of weavers of cloth. They are both close to the Inner Realm. You know, of course, Daoine ollmhór is the home of the giants. Other villages are close to the mountains— Goibniu inhabitants are miners of iron ore; Gobán Saor villagers smelts the ore; Clachcerd's people are stone workers; while Cran-ncoill is close to a dense forest. The villagers fell the trees that are required for buildings, but they also plant a new tree for every one they chop down.'

'I must visit all of them one day,' Bree said. 'And the Fae Realm.'

Áine spoke now. 'The Sidhe or Fae Realm, is entered through an oak tree, just as the Otherworld is accessed.'

'I would love to see your realm,' Bree said, remembering that Áine was Queen of the Fairies.'

'One day soon,' her aunt agreed.

Bree was pleased Lu came back to her rooms with them. He sat down in the parlour for the first time, after leaving Corraidhin, his fiery spear, and Cadeyrn, his sword, in the foyer. He looked out of place sitting among the small embroidered cushions. His legs were too long and he fidgeted. At least, he wore a tunic, and spared... or deprived... the women the sight of his muscular chest.

They soon had a rough layout for a village and several houses. Bree left the village draft to Lu, but she enjoyed contributing to the house design.

Seraphina explained that the houses were made of daub. 'It's a mixture of straw and mud, with a conical roof made of straw. They're round houses, so we can light a fire in the middle for cooking and heating. The thatched roof reaches almost to the ground, meeting a stone wall with a door in it.' Seraphina took a quill, dipped it in the ink and sketched a rough outline. 'Sleeping quarters are at the top of the house, reached by a ladder.'

'It sounds wonderful,' Bree said. 'Much finer than our earthen cave.'

Lu pointed to the wall that surrounded the house. 'It's a drystone wall. I hope we have enough skilled people left to build them.'

'Then we must search all over the Outer Realm,' Bree said.

Lu stood suddenly, disturbing Kuon who'd been snoring at his master's feet. 'I must away, but first, would you care for a walk in the gardens, my lady?' He bowed to Bree.

She raised an eyebrow and then rose. 'That sounds pleasant.' Bree smiled at Áine and Seraphina and then followed Lu and Kuon.

Lu grabbed his sword and replaced it in the scabbard behind his back and then took a firm hold of Corraidhin, who coughed out a sizeable flame, as if complaining that he'd been left in the foyer. Lu even opened the door for Bree but he avoided her gaze.

They walked behind the palace, where it was quieter, strolling along the paths meandering around the various parterres.

'What sort of tree is this?' Bree asked, pointing to the avenue edged with pink blossoms.

'I have no idea,' Lu replied. 'I'm the wrong person to ask about trees and flowers. I would ask Oonagh. She is the goddess of nature, love and relationships.'

'I see. Where can I find her now she has returned to her home?'

'She is often at the palace or out in nature somewhere.'

Bree wondered if she should also consult Oonagh about love. Bree had thought Lu might have harboured feelings for her, but it was obvious he didn't. After that almost-kiss, he had put a distance between them. He'd either changed his mind or he'd never had feelings for her. Ignorant of men and women, Bree had mistaken his movement towards her as something more than merely congratulating her on becoming triple goddess.

'Come and I'll show you a secluded place.' Lu led the way past the avenue of pink trees to a viewing platform where a small waterfall fell into a pool at its base.

Bree gasped at the beauty of the scene.

'If we cross the stream that flows into it, we'll see a higher waterfall that ultimately flows into the lower one. Perhaps we can leave that for another time.'

Bree smiled up into his blue eyes, pleased to hear there would be another day when they might stroll together.

'I wanted to give this to you.' Lu handed her a metal

symbol made up of three conjoined spirals and rotational symmetry. 'It's a Triskelion. You've seen the symbol previously. Nature and the movement of life are believed to be one of the meanings of this symbol; it's thought by some to describe the past, present, and future. Your mother gave it to me as a symbol of the strength of the family. You could wear it as a brooch.'

'Is it made of *argat draiochta*?' Bree asked.

'It is.'

'It's beautiful, but you must keep it if my mother gave it to you.'

'I would like to pass it on to you. We are family now. You have joined the Tuatha Dé Danann and become the triple goddess.'

Family? Bree wondered what that really meant. Did Lu see her as a sister? She didn't know what he thought of her or what she thought of him.

'Thank you,' she said, not knowing what else to say.

'I'll be away for a few weeks.' Lu said. 'I'll take most of my Immortals and travel throughout the Outer Realm to make certain all of Mór's fiends have gone. I'll lay even more enchantments on the Enchanted Veil.'

'When are you leaving?'

'Tomorrow at dawn.'

'I see,' Bree murmured. She felt unaccountably disappointed.

'I'm sure you will ably manage.' Lu slapped his thigh. 'Kuon, heel.' He smiled and walked away.

With the rushing water of the falls in her ear, Bree stared at the triskelion in her hand. When she raised her head, Lu had vanished from her sight.

To walk away from Bree wasn't easy, but Lu couldn't stay. He'd given her the Triskelion, and that was that.

He would spend a few weeks away with his men riding through the Outer Realm. It was a sizeable area, taking in all the villages, or what remained of them. Each village had worked in a specialty field or craft. Goibniu was where the miners who extracted iron ore lived; Gobán Saor, the village that smelted the ore; Clachcerd, the village for those working and shaping stone; Cranncoill inhabitants felled forest trees for building; and Cruith-necht, a farming village. The fairies surveyed the Fae Realm, which was in the Inner Realm but was not for other beings.

Lu would miss her. When she smiled at him, and thanked him for the Trikelion, it had almost undone his resolve to keep his distance. But no! Now that Brigid had been cremated, he would take his men and help the villagers rebuild. It was wrong of him to suggest a relationship between them, other than the one they had. She was young—only eighteen. He might be twenty-two but the years had treated them differently. He felt it only right to allow her to find her feet, find her way of doing things without any complications. That way, people would turn more to her. Whereas now, many still came to him with requests, or mediation issues. Better he go to Feidlimid in the stables, find his men and prepare to depart.

Áine and Niamh found her in the garden. 'Lu said he'd left you here. You still should have someone with you at all times.'

'Surely that's not necessary now.'

'Perhaps not. I'm being overly protective of you.'

'Lu gave me this,' Bree showed her aunt.

Niamh twittered and Bree pulled a face.

'Ah, a Triskelion. That's…'

'*Argat draiochta.* I know. My mother had given it to Lu. He thought I might like to have it.'

'That was kind of him.'

Bree stopped and looked her aunt in the eyes. 'Is he kind?'

'Yes, of course. Why would you ask?'

Bree huffed out a breath. 'I don't know. He did nothing but taunt me when he first found us.'

Áine smiled. 'It's just his way, and you must remember things were in dire straits at that time.'

'Not so long ago,' Bree pointed out.

Áine took Bree's hands in hers. 'Life has changed so drastically for you. I'm so sorry I couldn't tell you the full truth.'

'It doesn't matter now. I'm not sure as yet how to cope, but I suppose I will.'

'You're your mother's daughter.' Áine took something from a pocket in her gown. 'It's a day for gifts. I wanted you to have this. Your mother gave it to me.'

'Oh no, not you too, Áine.' Bree grinned. Her aunt slipped a ring on the third finger of her right hand. 'It's made with your mother's *dath an óir draiochta*—her golden metal.'

Bree turned her hand from side to side. At the front of the band, two hands cradled a heart on which sat a crown.

'It's a Claddagh ring,' Áine explained. 'Its design represents love, loyalty, and friendship—the hands represent friendship, the heart embodies love, and the crown symbolises loyalty. It encompasses all that Brigid stood for.'

Bree wrapped her arms around her aunt, nearly unseating the fairy from her shoulder. 'I hope you will stay by my side.'

'Of course, macushla. Always.'

'Me too,' Niamh said.

Bree smiled. 'Thank you, my dearest friends—my family.'

That night as Bree tried to sleep, Áine's Claddagh ring on her finger, Lu's Triskelion next to her bed, she thought of Lu and wondered why he gave her the brooch. She couldn't understand the man he was—he'd shown her so many faces. The booming, impatient god, the taunting and teasing man, the good man as he was with his men, his kindness showing at times with Bree.

His almost-kiss. She couldn't forget how he leaned down to her. If not to kiss her, then what?

What a fool she was to think he was attracted to her. All he'd done was congratulate her and then he couldn't get away from her quickly enough. No, Lu wasn't interested in her.

From tomorrow onwards, she had to give all her time to her people. Seraphina needed a village to be built, as did so many others. Bree must place more enchantments on the Outer Veil. She had the High Language of the

Tuatha Dé Danann to learn and her mother's skill with the forge to master. Mór and her necromancer had to be rooted out and put in the dungeons. There would be no time for romance and love. No time for imagined kisses.

Bree reached across and picked up the Triskelion. As she fell asleep with it in her hand, her dreams centred on a pair of very blue eyes and golden hair.

Chapter Seventeen

Beltane was approaching and there'd been no sign or sound of Mór.

Bree stood out on the balcony that was off her chambers. She told herself not to think of Mór, not to expend any energy on the woman, not to disturb the ether lest Mór should feel it… but she couldn't help herself. It had been roughly six months since Samhain, and Mór and her necromancer had not been seen. Bree knew she should be happy and relieved, but Mór's presence hung over her as if she saw the woman daily.

'Are you ready, my lady?' Niamh flew out to the balcony.

Bree turned and smiled. She often seemed to have to switch on her smile… when she was thinking of Mór, or when she thought of Lu—he'd been away for months, and since his return, she'd hardly ever seen him. In fact, if she didn't have to smile, Bree wondered if she would. 'I'm ready.'

'So are we,' the fairy said, and flew over to Bree's

shoulder, pushing back her circlet of flowers before it slipped off her head.

Áine and Seraphina were waiting in the parlour, as were Sorcha and Úna, the handmaidens laden with towels and fresh clothes.

They headed to the ground floor and to the rear of the palace where the terrace, framed by intricate metal work detailing triquetra and designs from nature, always gave Bree a euphoric boost. Although the palace had a conservatory—she had added roses in large pots to this area—Bree was delighted that no matter the season, flowers and plants within the Inner Realm always bloomed.

Bree led the way through the gardens with their parterres and the beautifully flowering cherry trees and their pink blossoms. Bree had asked the Goddess Rhiannon the names of the trees. She'd been happy to oblige. She'd also told Bree that the reason the flowers always blossomed was because she'd placed an enchantment on them. Bree had laughed.

When they reached the end of the path, Bree stared over the balustrade at the small waterfall and pond. Today, they were taking another path that led to the higher waterfall and larger pool.

Bearach joined them. Bree was expecting him. Not that it had been arranged but the big man seemed never to be too far away from Seraphina. Niamh giggled. Bree grinned at her aunt.

When they had walked through to the pool and Bearach had cast his keen gaze around the area, he stood watching Seraphina.

'Are you swimming with us, Bearach?' Bree asked,

trying to keep her amusement out of her voice. 'You're welcome, but we are swimming... naked,' Bree whispered the last word.

Bearach went red from the tips of his fingers to his hairline. 'Oh no, my lady. No, no. I'll stand guard close by so that no one will disturb you.' He dipped his head several times and retraced the path.

As soon as he was far enough away, the women all broke into laughter.

Bree, who'd been so shy at disrobing in front of her handmaidens when she first arrived at the palace, now stripped off her gown and jumped into the pool. The others quickly followed, except for Sorcha and Úna, who sat and watched. Niamh flew around the pool and settled close enough to the waterfall to feel its spray but not too close to be battered by it.

The water was cool. Bree dived and resurfaced near Niamh. Wisteria grew behind where the fairy sat, and other plants—ferns and small mosses— edged the pool.

'Tell us, Seraphina,' Bree called across the water, 'has Bearach proposed yet?'

'No, my lady,' Seraphina was quick to say.

'Shall I sprinkle some love dust over the big man?' Niamh asked. She giggled. 'Or over you?'

'I'm very fond of him,' Seraphina admitted, 'but...'

'But?' Bree asked. 'He cares for you.'

'I know, but it's embarrassing. He follows me around like a little lamb.'

'Perhaps you should ask Bearach to marry you, if he's shy?' Bree said.

'I wouldn't act rashly,' Áine said.

Bree frowned at her aunt. There were times when Áine didn't seem to like Seraphina or approve of things she did. Bree couldn't understand why and Áine would never say. It didn't make any sense. Seraphina had been a good friend since she had come to the palace. Bree knew Seraphina wasn't a goddess or an Immortal. Áine had made an occasional comment about Seraphina's village, emphasising that she worked the land. Bree always followed such comments with her own, that Seraphina was a wonderful seamstress. Bree had never before known her aunt to be biased but she was definitely prejudiced against Seraphina. The conversation moved on and Bree tried not to worry about it.

Later in the day when Seraphina and Bearach had gone to Seraphina's village in the Outer Realm, Bree, Niamh and Áine sat in the conservatory reading. It could be accessed via a staircase from the first floor or through the grand double gates on ground level. The conservatory and the stables on its far side were outside of the palace. The conservatory was made of glass panels set into metal frames, each section of smaller panels arched and held by intricate metalwork, with the delicate designs of triquetra and runes of flames, because this building had been built by Brigid, Bree's mother. What made a wondrous difference was that the roof was decorated by colourful stained glass, so that multicoloured shafts of light fell on ferns, potted primroses in yellow and blue, and tall delphiniums.

Bree paused to gaze at a seat she had made after

having a lot of instructions from Goibniu, the metalsmith of the Tuatha Dé Danann. He was named after a village in the Outer Realm. It had been hard work learning to use the forge—hot work too. Bree wished it had been her mother who had taught her but Goibniu, a huge man with bulging muscles, was undoubtedly the next best choice. The seat was partially of timber, but Bree had smelted metal for the sides and legs, decorating them with triquetra symbols.

'You have come a long way,' her aunt said, after obviously noticing where Bree was looking.

'Yes, indeed, my lady,' Niamh said.

'Thank you, Áine. I do feel as if I've achieved some success.'

'Your knowledge of the High Language is progressing well.'

'I enjoy learning it, as I do the runes.'

Áine smiled. 'Your mother would be so proud of you.'

Bree looked up when she heard a sound on the path. Then a shadow fell over the entrance.

'Lady Áine,' Lu said in greeting. Then, he looked at Bree. 'I've come to rescue you from your boredom.'

Bree raised her chin. 'Reading is not boring, as you would discover if you sat down for long enough. What do you do all day when we're not at war?'

'Frequently I look after triple goddesses.'

Bree's eyes narrowed. 'This triple goddess doesn't need looking after.'

'You will if you come with me to the Outer Realm.'

Bree flushed cold. At first she felt like uttering a cutting remark, telling him she managed when he wasn't at the palace. Instead, she asked, 'There isn't any trouble?'

'Not at all. I thought you might like to see Seraphina's village. It's all but completed.'

'Oh yes, indeed.' Bree sprang to her feet, nearly unseating Niamh on her shoulder. 'Will you come too, Áine?'

'No, I... I don't think I will just now. You two enjoy your ride.'

Again, Bree felt her aunt's resistance to something connected with Seraphina. 'Very well.' Then, to Lu, she added, 'I'll change my clothes and meet you at the stables.'

Úna helped Bree change into a riding outfit that Seraphina had made for her, this time dispensing with the half-skirt, leaving only the trousers and a tunic, with a leather corset outside and a cloak attached at her shoulders. She always wore the triskelion and the Claddagh ring and carried Cara fíor in a scabbard between her shoulder blades whenever she left the Inner Realm.

'Are you certain you won't join us, Áine?' Bree asked.

'I think Niamh and I might find our fairy sisters.'

'Oh yes,' Niamh said, excitement lighting her eyes.

'Very well. I'll see you later.' Bree left her aunt and the little fairy and made her way to the stables.

Next to the conservatory, the stables housed the horses of all the Immortals and any of the gods and goddesses who rode. Bree's unicorn, Gealach, was also housed in a special room. Bree rode Gealach as often as she could. The unicorn was always happy to see her.

When they'd ridden through the Enchanted Veil, Lu commented, 'You pass through more easily now.'

'I do indeed. I'm becoming accustomed to most things, I hope.' Including your aloofness, Bree thought. In the six months since Samhain, Lu had never made a move to become closer to her. The imagined kiss was nothing more than a memory on Bree's part. How stupid she'd been to think he found her attractive. When she glanced at him, she found Lu's blue gaze on her. Perhaps he wondered what she was musing upon.

'You've achieved a great deal.' Lu broke their locked gazes. 'Not only in what you've learned but in what you've constructed. You must be pleased to see the Outer Realm villages being rebuilt.'

'I am pleased. It is good to see people settled and happy once again.'

They'd reached Seraphina's village. It spread out before them in a jumble of roundhouses, which once she stepped among them, Bree saw were actually well set out and organised.

Seraphina, delighted to see them, took them on a tour. Bree wasn't surprised to see Bearach at the village. Even Lu must have witnessed the growing attraction between his immortal and Seraphina because Lu raised an eyebrow at Bree and grinned.

Amidst a ring of fortifications, the roundhouses were at one end of the village, with bakers, a tiny inn, a metal-smith and a small marketplace at the other.

'We couldn't have done any of this without you, my lady,' Seraphina said, her green eyes sparkling.

'I haven't laid one stone since that first one,' Bree said. She'd been honoured when the villages had asked her to lay the first stone.

'You have given us your support, my lady.'

'That's what I once told you. You are here to inspire your people,' Lu whispered to Bree.

Bree pursed her lips at Lu and said aloud to Seraphina, 'I'm so pleased to see you happy and to know that the Outer Realm will be better than ever before.'

'Would you be willing to light our Beltane fire, my lady?' Seraphina asked.

'Of course. I would be delighted to be a part of your village's celebrations.' Beltane was an important time—the beginning of summer when all hearth fires were extinguished and all relit by the Beltane fire that was central to all. People danced around the sacred bonfire to be cleansed and to have their animals purified. It was a time for casting the dark days aside and welcoming the light. It was also a time for courtship.

'What do you say, my Lord Lu?' Bree asked on their ride back to the palace.

'About what?'

'Me lighting the village's Beltane fire?'

'A good idea. You can light the main fire on the field near the palace first and then move on to Baile Meánach, Seraphina's village.'

'Do you think Bearach and Seraphina might start officially courting?'

'It looks likely.'

'It's obvious they're in love,' Bree murmured.

'Do you think so?' Lu wouldn't look at her.

'You must be aware that they are always together,' Bree added. 'What of yourself, Lu? Do you wish to marry one day?' Bree almost didn't dare look at him... but she couldn't resist. His features grew taut.

'One day perhaps. I am too busy to think of marriage.'

'I'm surprised you're not trying to marry me off to someone. Isn't that one of my duties... to produce an heir?' Bree asked, archly.

Lu turned his head to look at her, his blue eyes darkening. 'Do you wish to marry?'

'One day perhaps. I'm too busy to want to marry now,' Bree said, mirroring his words.

They passed the remainder of the journey in silence. Bree was aware of the fraught air between them.

Chapter Eighteen

THE PREPARATIONS for Beltane filled everyone's days. The main bonfire was made ready in the field near the palace where six months earlier Lu's army had assembled. Bree thought that at least they shouldn't have any threats from Mór during Beltane.

The palace was decorated with banners depicting the ubiquitous triquetra and the Beltane fires. A general air of merriment pervaded the palace and beyond into the town and villages.

With Bearach and Seraphina in tow, along with Niamh on her shoulder, Bree walked into the town she'd first noticed on the night of her flight to the palace. Again, Áine didn't want to join them. Bree knew she was reaching the point where she'd have to ask her aunt why she didn't like Seraphina.

The path descended until they stepped into the Inner Realm township of Milngavie where some of the Immortals lived, along with minor goddesses and gods who didn't have their own domain. The houses here were more elaborate than those in the Outer Realm. Many had small turrets and arched windows and were decorated with similar Beltane banners to the palace. Bree crossed an arched bridge spanning the river. From here she could see the lower bridge that was covered by small houses with arched windows made of blue glass and domed roofs. Bree remembered seeing this on her way to the palace. Many of the people came outside to welcome Bree. Overall, an aura of jollity lay over the township.

Seraphina had made Bree a new dress for the celebrations—a green velvet with long flowing sleeves with triquetra sown in gilt stitches over the gown that sat slightly off the shoulders.

'Do you think it is too… too revealing?' Bree asked her aunt after Sorcha and Úna helped her dress. Seraphina had already returned to her village.

'Not at all, macushla.' Áine kissed her cheek and slipped a sprig of white cherry blossom into Bree's hair. 'You look beautiful.'

'Very beautiful,' Niamh agreed.

'You look lovely too in your diaphanous pink gown,' Bree said. She noticed that Niamh's circlet was entwined with pink petals. One sprig of cherry blossoms caused the circlet to dip to one side. Not that this was something new because Niamh's circlet never sat straight.

'Thank you, my lady.' Niamh giggled.

Pounding rocked the chamber door.

'Lu has arrived,' Bree muttered.

Niamh giggled again.

Lu strode into the parlour and stopped abruptly as if he'd hit a wall. He stared at Bree but then dragged his gaze away to include Áine and Niamh before he said, 'You look beautiful, my ladies.'

Niamh flew to hover in front of Lu's face. 'You look handsome too, my lord.' Niamh giggled.

Bree agreed. Lu took her breath away. Dressed in deep blue tunic and trousers, that were simple but elegant and outlined his muscular frame, Lu looked to be everything a god should be, as far as appearance went.

Kuon nudged Bree.

She patted his wiry hair. 'You look handsome too,' Bree said, and smiled.

'Are you ready?' Lu asked.

'We are indeed,' Bree said.

Lu held out his arm to Bree, and they headed outside, with Áine following with Niamh on her shoulder.

A golden haze soared through the air as they approached the field. It surrounded them; the small fairies flying in front of Bree as a cacophony of small voices swelled in greeting. The fairies drew Áine and Niamh away to the side of the field.

Bree was so pleased to see Hilde and her other centaur friends, along with Arianrhod, the Moon Goddess, Goddess Rhiannon, Airmid the Goddess of Healing, who looked resplendent with her long green hair and gown, that was split at the sides to reveal her bare feet entwined with leafy scrolls, and Ninlil, the Wind Goddess, who promised that she wouldn't allow the wind to blow too strongly this night. Oonagh also joined them. Goddess of nature and love, she wore a long silver gown that shimmered as if covered with tiny diamonds.

Lu's Immortals hurried over, except for Bearach who was with Seraphina at Baile Meánach. Fionn's wife Grainne was with him, along with Diarmuid, Domhnall and Padraig. They spoke as a group for a while, until Lu whispered to Bree that they should start proceedings. He escorted her to the huge bonfire. Once there, Lu slammed Corraidhin into the ground. It coughed out enough flames to gain the attention of those closest to them and, after a few minutes, everyone fell silent.

Bree placed her palms together, focused, and immediately felt the warm sensation. When she opened her hands, the ancient fire burned in her palms. She said aloud, 'I am the Triple Goddess. I am maiden, mother, and crone. I am the poetess, the smith and the healer. I am creativity, inspiration and vision. *Bean an ti*, I am she who cares for everything. *Beatha*, I am the livelihood that sustains my people. I am *Comhluadr*, the harmony of being together. *Dochas*, I bring hope to the future. I am *Draiocht*, the magic that is unseen. I am *Fios*, knowledge and understanding. I was at the beginning of creation, in the middle of life and at the end of existence.' Bree blew on the flames, nothing more than a caress. The bonfire flared and within minutes, it roared.

The Beltane fire was alight.

The field erupted into cheers and laughter. The goddesses and gods started to dance around the flames, bathing in the smoke to cleanse and purify themselves.

Bree stepped back, away from the conflagration, Lu still beside her. Niamh and Áine found them. Niamh flew around, doing somersaults and twirls in the air. Bree noticed that Lu drifted away to talk to Diarmuid, Fionn and Grainne. The latter three were often together.

Niamh and Áine drew Bree closer to the fire, so they could all bathe in the smoke from the sacred flame. After a while, Bree told her companions she was going to Baile Meánach—Seraphina's village.

'You can't go alone,' her aunt told her, frowning.

'There are enough people abroad tonight for it to be safe.'

'I'll come with you, my lady,' Niamh said.

Bree smiled. 'Very well, if that will appease you both.'

'At least, you'll have someone with you,' Áine said.

Bree, with Niamh in her usual spot on her shoulder, crossed to where Gealach was tethered. She was about to place her foot in the stirrup when a tug on her arm stopped her.

'Where in Danu's name do you think you're going?'

Even if she hadn't recognised Lu's voice, there was no doubt who spoke. Kuon nudged her for pats.

Bree turned to look at Lu. 'You may recall I'm lighting Baile Meánach's Beltane fire.'

'You're not going on your own,' Lu said, his hands on his hips.

'I'm not. Niamh is with me.'

Niamh rose, did a twirl and sat back on Bree's shoulder.

'I'm sorry, Niamh, but you're not adequate protection for Lady Bree.'

'Honestly, I'll be quite safe. I know the way.'

'Yes, you will be safe because I'm coming with you,' Lu insisted.

Bree let out a huge sigh. 'It looks as if we'll have company, Niamh, whether we like it or not.'

'My Lord Lu is only concerned about you,' the fairy said.

Lu went to fetch Feidlimid. Once he'd returned, he helped Bree to mount and they set out, with Kuon trotting beside his master.

The villagers of Baile Meánach were already dancing, singing and drinking mead by the time Bree arrived. Villagers took Feidlimid and Gealach's reins from Bree and Lu. Seraphina and Bearach ran to them. Bree hugged Seraphina and then held her at arm's length, noticing an extra glint in her eyes.

Seraphina laughed and whispered in Bree's ear. 'Bearach and I wish to marry.'

Bree hugged her again.

Niamh gave a twirl, her diaphanous gown floating out around her.

'That's wonderful,' Bree said. She heard Bearach telling Lu. 'When?' Bree asked. She hadn't ever seen Seraphina so happy.

'Tonight, my lady, if you will see us bound.'

'Tonight?' Bree laughed.

'It is a good time to marry at Beltane,' Lu said. 'The time for new beginnings.'

'Very well, but I should light the fire first,' Bree said.

Seraphina and Bearach led the way. Everyone separated for them, bowing and nodding to Bree and Lu.

Bree looked at the smaller bonfire and closed her

hands together. Silence fell over the village, an air of anticipation taking the place of the revelry. When she opened her hands, the ancient fire burned in her palms. Bree turned around so that all could see. An awed hush rippled through the evening air as if it were water and someone had thrown a stone into it. Then Bree turned back and blew on the flames. They shot across and ignited the bonfire. Bree uttered the words she had already said this night.

'I am the Triple Goddess. I am maiden, mother, and crone,' Bree recited. 'I am the poetess, the smith and the healer. I am creativity, inspiration and vision. *Bean an ti*, I am she who cares for everything. *Beatha*, I am the livelihood that sustains my people. I am *Comhluadr*, the harmony of being together. *Dochas*, I bring hope to the future. I am *Draiocht*, the magic that is unseen. I am *Fios*, knowledge and understanding. I was at the beginning of creation, in the middle of life and at the end of existence.'

Everyone cheered and clapped.

Before dancing started again, Bree turned back and held up her hands. 'At this wondrous time of year, in front of all the people of Baile Meánach, I ask Seraphina and Bearach to step forward, so that I may bind them together as husband and wife.'

A raucous cheer soared out over the village as Seraphina and Bearach moved forward, some of the men slapping Bearach on the back as he passed them by.

When they stood in front of Bree, she realised she didn't know what to do. Her first instinct was to take the sprig of white cherry blossom from her hair and slip it into Seraphina's hair. Bree kissed her cheek. Then she bade the couple to take each other's hands—four hands held together. Bree took a ribbon from Seraphina's hair and wrapped it around their hands.

'May you love and cherish each other for ever more. Do you swear to do this?'

The couple replied as one.

'May you have a happy home with many children. May you grow old together.' Bree smiled at them. 'I bind you together, to love and cherish, to never be torn asunder. Do you pledge your fealty to each other?'

Again the couple spoke as one. 'We do, my lady.'

Bree stepped closer and tied the ribbon that was already wrapped around their hands. 'You are bound together in this life as tightly as this ribbon binds your hands. You have my blessing.' Bree kissed Seraphina on the cheek. Bearach bent down so she could repeat the action, and then he kissed his new wife, lifting her off her feet in a bearhug.

Cheering erupted and the villagers surged around the couple, leading them to the Beltane fire.

Bree was left standing next to Lu.

'You did well,' he said, gazing at her intensely. 'I think you deserve a tankard of mead.'

Bree laughed. 'Perhaps a small tankard.'

Lu offered her his arm. He led her to a roughly hewn seat and went in search of the drinks at the small inn. When he returned, he sat down close to her. Kuon on his other side.

As Bree had spoken the binding words, her thoughts had strayed to Lu, wondering what he was thinking. Did the ceremony stir any feelings in him for her? Perhaps his closeness now signified that. Bree wasn't certain. She was aware of his thigh close to hers, not that she could feel its warmth through her gown. Imagining it caused heat to flush over her face.

'I hope they'll be happy,' Lu murmured.

'They love each other.' Bree looked at Lu and wondered yet again what he was thinking. She thought of his almost-kiss. She always tried not to because she'd been mistaken, but she couldn't help it. She'd imagined he was going to kiss her. She had to be honest with herself. Her attraction to Lu had grown. Gazing at his strong profile made her tremble inside. She often imagined his arms around her, holding her tightly. After all these months, he'd made it obvious that he felt nothing for her.

Lu lifted his tankard. 'Well, here's to their happiness.'

'To their happiness.'

Lu's eyes held hers and she wondered if he did care for her. He was angry that she attempted to come here alone but that could have been for other reasons. He didn't tease her in the same way as he used to. He didn't call her ignorant anymore. Bree supposed that was a step in the right direction.

When they'd finished, Lu rose and reached out for her hand—something he didn't usually do. Bree took it, her hand feeling so small in his. His palms were calloused, but she gained comfort from his hold on her fingers. Even though he was a god of... everything, Bree smiled to herself at her thought... he was a warrior. He didn't laze around like many of the lesser gods. Lu and his Immortals were the backbone of Tír na nÓg. She might be their triple goddess, but it was Lu who held it all together. Bree was aware of his strength and height as they strolled along together. She hoped he couldn't feel her hand shaking, or he would start teasing her again.

'If you want to join in the festivities,' Bree said. 'I'll be safe here with Niamh and the villagers.'

'I'm happy to remain with you. I'm not worried about the festival and drinking too much. Someone has to keep a clear head just in case trouble erupts.'

'Oh, of course,' Bree said, hoping she didn't sound as disappointed as she felt. For a few seconds she'd thought Lu wanted to be with her. How foolish of her. He was only concerned for the safety of everyone.

He smiled and squeezed her hand. 'Your company has its attractions.' He was teasing her again.

'Oh really,' Bree replied, playing along.

'You don't argue with me as much now.'

'You are the one who argued with me,' Bree told him.

'That's not how I remember it.' Lu laughed.

'It wouldn't be, would it?'

'You're very beautiful when you're annoyed.'

Bree stopped in her tracks. She hadn't expected that. He looked as if he hadn't expected to make the comment.

Lu turned to her, and then hooked a stray strand of hair behind her ear. 'Don't you think you're beautiful?'

'It seems an immodest assumption if I did.'

'Well, I'm telling you that you are.'

'Are you certain it's not the romance in the air that's affecting your senses?' Bree asked, even though she wished she hadn't. She still always doubted him.

'I don't think so. I've wanted to tell you before, but we are always so caught up with other matters.' Lu placed his finger under her chin. 'We're not now. We're here together.'

Bree stared up at him as his head lowered. She could almost feel his lips on hers in anticipation. Her eyes closed. Then she felt him wrenched away from her. Her eyes flew open.

Diarmuid, looking alarmed and anxious, stared at both of them. 'I'm sorry to interrupt, my lady, my lord but… Seraphina has gone missing.'

Lu frowned, his sharp tone showing his annoyance at being disturbed. 'She must be somewhere among the villagers. Perhaps she and Bearach have sneaked away to find some privacy.'

'No, my lord. Bearach is looking for her.'

Bree felt a chill through her body. 'Has he looked in her roundhouse?'

'Yes, my lady.'

At that moment, Bearach ran up to them. 'Seraphina has gone… gone! I turned away to speak to Padraig and when I turned back, she wasn't there.'

Bree didn't think she'd ever seen anyone look so distraught. She gazed around them. Villagers were everywhere, dancing, singing. 'Surely Seraphina must be somewhere in the village?'

'I'm going to search further afield for her,' Bearach told them.

'Wait,' Lu said. 'Let us all search the village first.'

'Mór might have taken her,' Bearach said, his desperation making his voice ragged.

'Mór can't get inside the Outer Realm now,' Lu said. 'You know that.'

'Well, Seraphina is gone,' Bearach replied. He turned and ran away.

'Surely, it couldn't be Mór,' Bree said.

'I can't see how but I'd better go after him.'

'Of course.'

Lu took her hand again and brought it up to his chest. 'You are not to go back to the palace without me.'

'I won't. I'll help search here for her.'

Lu brought her hand to his lips and kissed it. Then he was gone.

Niamh flew back to Bree and hovered before her. 'Are you all right, my lady?'

Bree didn't know how she felt. Lu had nearly kissed her and then this… Seraphina gone. How could it be? 'I just can't believe how Seraphina could have disappeared.'

'Perhaps she's been kidnapped. It could be Mór. She has her ways,' Niamh said.

'That's not very reassuring, Niamh.' But Bree knew it was true. If Mór wanted to achieve something, she'd find a way to do it. The question that wouldn't be denied was, why. Why would Mór want to kidnap Seraphina?

Chapter Nineteen

Bree helped search the village. No sign of Seraphina could be found. She saw Lu ride back on Feidlimid. He dismounted and strode towards her, his gaze thunderous.

'The fool has ridden off and with so many people trampling the ground, I can't see his tracks.'

Bree knew Lu meant Bearach. 'Should we get a group together to go after him?'

'Yes, I'll head back to the palace with my men and get us organised. It's not just a matter of following Bearach. We don't know what else we'll come up against. I'll organise some provisions.'

'I'll come with you.'

'Good. It's best you stay with Áine at the palace.'

'I'm not staying at the palace. I'm coming with you when you search for Bearach.'

'Don't you be a fool too!' Lu exclaimed, as he helped her mount Gealach.

'Ooh no, my lady,' Niamh said, from where the fairy sat on Bree's shoulder. 'It could be dangerous.'

'Of course it'll be dangerous,' Lu added.

'I'm joining you,' Bree said, 'and that's the end of it.'

Lu scowled. 'We won't have time to mollycoddle you.'

'I don't need to be protected and pampered,' Bree said, and indicated to the unicorn to move. Gealach shot ahead. Niamh had to hold on.

Lu soon caught up with her but said nothing.

'Seraphina has disappeared?' Áine reiterated, her face whitening. 'How?'

'That's what we don't know,' Bree said. 'Apparently, one second she was standing next to Bearach and the next she'd gone. Bearach has ridden off after her. Lu is getting his men ready now to go after them.'

'You're not going too?' Áine grabbed Bree's hand as she was stripping off her gown.

'Of course I am.' Bree turned to Sorcha. 'Please help me with my trousers and armour, and then get together the bare essentials I'll need. Send for some food for every-one. We don't know how long we'll be.'

'No!' Áine exclaimed. She swung away from Bree, her hands going to her face. 'This can't be happening.' Then, to her niece, 'You can't go. You can't endanger yourself. Oh, this is all my fault!'

Bree stopped what she was doing. 'What do you mean it's your fault?'

'I did the wrong thing, macushla. I never thought it would come to this.'

Bree felt chilled, a cold hand of fear gripping her heart.

'You didn't arrange for Seraphina to be taken? I know you don't like her but…'

'No!' Áine cried out. 'By Danu's love, I wouldn't do such a thing.'

'Then what?'

Áine stood still and stared at Bree. 'I must talk to you and Lu… alone. Now.'

Bree stared, her breath catching. 'Úna, find Lord Lu and ask him to attend us here.' When the servants had gone, Bree turned back to her aunt. 'Please tell me what this is about. You're frightening me.'

'I will, macushla. I should have told you before.' Áine flopped into a chair.

Bree had never seen her aunt like this. Even Niamh must have been concerned because the fairy flew over to her queen and sat on her shoulder.

The door flew open. No pounding on this occasion. Lu stormed into the living room. He was already dressed in his armour. With a shirt on, Bree noted at the back of her mind.

'What is this about? We must leave. Time is of the essence.'

Áine rose and straightened her shoulders. 'I have something to tell you.'

'Can't it wait?' Lu cried, his brow furrowing.

'No, it can't. It must be said… and it must be said now.'

Lu stamped Corraidhin on the floor. 'Well, get on with it.' Kuon gave a bark, as if to agree with his master.

'Seraphina… Seraphina is your sister, Bree.'

Bree felt as if someone had thrown a bucket of water over her. 'What…?'

'Your twin sister.'

'We don't have time for ridiculous jokes,' Lu said, and once again stamped Corraidhin on the floor.

'It's not a joke. Please just bear with me for a few minutes.' Áine took a steadying breath. 'When you were born, Bree, Brigid implored me to hide you, to guard you with my life so that Mór could never find you until you were old enough to fight back, if necessary.'

'We know this,' Lu said, folding his arms.

'What you don't know is that five minutes later a second baby was born... Seraphina.'

Bree's chest felt so tight she couldn't breathe. She strode to the balcony door, swung it open and stood out in the fresh air. This couldn't be true... and yet, Bree thought of the times someone had commented that they could be sisters. They both had red hair and green eyes. Seraphina was a little shorter than Bree, and her face reflected the hardships she'd known throughout her life. Could it be true? Bree had always felt a connection to Seraphina, since the first time she'd seen her. Perhaps their sibling relationship had drawn her to Seraphina? They got on well together.

Bree turned and walked back into the room. 'Seraphina doesn't know, I assume.'

Áine looked pained. 'No one knows. Or, at least, I thought no one knew.'

'Finish your story, Áine,' Lu said.

'Well... we didn't expect a second baby.' Áine wrung her hands together. 'Brigid said to take both and hide them but not together. Then if one was found—Mór wouldn't suspect there could be two children—the other one would remain safe. I prepared to depart.' Áine sighed. 'The trouble was, I didn't know where to hide the second baby. We—Brigid and I—had worked for months to make the cave in the Otherworld comfortable. At the last minute, such as it was, I didn't know what to do. Then I thought of a woman, a seamstress whom Brigid and I occasionally asked to sew for us. She lived in Baile Meánach.'

'Seraphina's village,' Bree said.

Áine nodded. 'I asked her to take the baby and to care for it as her own. I hoped that, hidden in plain sight, Seraphina would be safe. As the first born, Bree, you were the rightful heir, but I still wanted Seraphina to have a good life.'

Bree flopped into a chair. Even Lu sat down.

'I can't assimilate all you've said,' Bree told her aunt. 'Seraphina… my sister, my twin sister.'

'When we returned to the palace, I should have told you… told you both,' Áine continued. 'Especially when you brought Seraphina into the palace.'

Bree sat forward. 'You've never liked Seraphina. Your dislike became stronger all the time. Why?'

'I didn't dislike Seraphina,' Áine said, shaking her head. 'I was concerned. I kept worrying about your partiality to her, Bree. Both sisters together. I was afraid something might happen.'

'As it has now!' Lu sprang to his feet. Kuon jumped up as well. 'By Dagda's beard, I can't believe how foolish you've been, Áine!'

'I know, I know. I'm sorry.' Áine went to her niece and took her hands. 'I'm so sorry, macushla.'

'Now,' Lu went on. 'Seraphina going missing is much more fraught with danger than it was half an hour ago. She's been kidnapped because she's the sister of the Triple Goddess.'

'This is why I feel so devastated,' Áine said, once again wringing her hands. 'That's why I had to tell you now.'

'You know what this means?' Lu asked. He didn't wait for a reply. 'It means that, not only does someone else know Seraphina's true identity, but she might not be the real target. Seraphina is the bait to catch you.' Lu stopped his pacing and faced Bree.

Bree felt her stomach lurch. 'You might be correct.'

'I know I'm right,' Lu said. 'Mór… and let's face it, it can be no one else but Mór… knows that you will go charging off in search of your twin sister. So, you won't be going anywhere, my lady. You'll walk straight into a trap.'

Bree faced him. 'It can't be a trap if we know about it. We are forewarned.'

Lu groaned and ground his teeth. 'What about Mór's necromancer? We don't know what he'll do.'

'That's exactly why I should go with you. We'll have more chance of success if I'm with you.' Bree turned and lifted a roll of clothes and a bag of food that had been prepared for her. She placed *Cara fíor* in its scabbard behind her back. 'We don't have more time to waste. Are you coming, my lord?'

'I'm coming along too,' Áine said.

'By all the jumping fleas in Dagda's beard!' Lu roared, lifted Corraidhin, and strode for the door. Kuon followed him.

Áine caught up with them in the great hall. 'We should take some of the fairies,' she said to Bree.

'Some centaurs too. I saw Hilde at the Beltane fire.'

'We can't travel with an army,' Lu said.

They moved outside. Hilde must have heard about Seraphina's abduction because she was in the courtyard ready to go, along with her partner Heremon, a large centaur with a black coat and a scarred face. Bree greeted them both. Then she looked over the men who waited with them—Diarmuid, Fionn, Domhnall, Padraig, and Tiomoid. Cythala, one of the Daoine ollmhór giants from the high country whom Bree had met, stood with them, along with Rhiannon, Goddess of the Night and the Underworld and the Dead, joined them. Bree thought Rhiannon might be useful on the journey. She could shape-shift, and had a strong connection to all life.

Bree moved her unicorn closer to Lu. 'I think we're ready to proceed, but where are we heading?'

Lu groaned when he looked out over the group and then his gaze came back to Niamh sitting on Bree's shoulder. 'South. It's the most likely direction. We'll have to go through the swamplands first. I hope this lot will be up to it.'

'You lack faith, my lord. Not a good start. This lot will surprise you. Shall we go? I have a sister to save.'

Chapter Twenty

THEY RODE OR WALKED, as the case may be, through the night. Only Cythala was on foot. Bree had no idea where they were. They'd gone over fairly flat land for two hours before Lu called a halt in a lightly wooded area.

'We'll stay here and get some rest until daylight. If Lady Bree will make a fire, I'll have first watch.'

Everyone dismounted and moved to do a task. Domhnall and Padraig sought out kindling for a fire. Áine, Bree, Niamh and Rhiannon unloaded food and drink. Cythala ripped small branches off trees and fashioned some rough and temporary dwellings. Hilde and Heremon shot fresh game. Lu, Diarmuid and Fionn scouted around the area.

They sat around the fire to have something to eat and drink. Bree couldn't swallow too much. A knot sat in her chest and her throat.

'Eat up,' Lu said. 'We don't know what daylight will bring. This could be our last meal for a while.'

Bree made a little more effort.

No one felt like talking. They cleared up and settled

down in either a makeshift dwelling of branches or slept in the open, as all Lu's men did.

Bree couldn't sleep. She slipped out of the make-shift tent she shared with her aunt, Niamh and Rhiannon, and walked over to where Lu leaned back against a tree, lowering herself to sit next to him. His blond hair glinted in the firelight, but his face was partially in shadow.

'You should be sleeping,' he said.

'I can't. I just keep thinking about Seraphina and the enormity of Áine's confession.'

'It rocked me too,' Lu agreed. 'I can't believe Áine kept it a secret from you and me.' He looked at her and held her gaze. 'You must be shocked.'

'To say the least.'

'Now we have not only Seraphina to rescue but Bearach as well, the stupid idiot.'

Bree could hear the annoyance in his voice. 'Are you still angry with me for insisting on coming along?'

Lu groaned. 'I know when I can't win.'

'Are you used to winning?'

'For the most part... until you came out of hiding.' Then he chuckled. 'I'm not angry with you. You're the Triple Goddess in any case; you outrank me.'

'So I am,' Bree said, and smiled.

Lu took her hand and held it in his. 'I can't guarantee I won't be cross with you again.'

'Nor can I guarantee I won't be annoyed with you. You're a very infuriating man.'

'Am I, indeed?'

Bree laughed softly. 'You are.'

They fell into silence. Bree was supremely conscious

of her hand in his. Every nerve tingled. Lu didn't do anything else, didn't take it to his lips… just held her hand. Bree felt woefully inexperienced and wasn't certain if she should do something.

What could she do? What could…

Bree startled awake, disoriented for a moment. It seemed that she'd gone to sleep. Blood suffused her face— she'd been leaning against Lu. He'd put his arm around her and held her. She sat up and stared now at Fionn, who'd come to take over watch from Lu. Lu jumped up and held out his hand to her.

'Try to get back to sleep,' Lu told her. 'It's only a couple of hours until dawn.'

Bree went inside her makeshift tent but couldn't sleep. She could only keep thinking she wished she'd been awake when Lu had put his arm around her.

So much went through Lu's mind. Áine's confession and extraordinary tale more profound than any other. How could she keep such a thing from them? From Bree, more than anyone else! Now, look at the dangerous situation they were in. It could have been avoided, if only they'd known. Lu would have persuaded Bree to place guards on her sister. He would have insisted. And yet, Seraphina and Bearach had just married. She'd stood close to him. The entire village was feasting around them, and she had disappeared. Nothing had protected her. Mór had to have spies in the Outer Realm. Too many enchantments had been placed on the Enchanted Veil for anyone to break through. Leaving was another matter… a simple matter.

Lu would have to right that when they returned. A process would have to be set up. Bree would no doubt have some ideas.

Bree! By Dagda's beard! What did he think he was doing? After all his resolves, they'd vanished as soon as he was alone with her. Perhaps it was fortunate he hadn't kissed her at Baile Meánach. However, it was becoming more difficult to deny his feelings for her. Now she was in danger again, and he felt overcome by an urge to protect her… even though, she claimed she didn't need protecting. It didn't remove his desire to do so.

They set out soon after dawn, quickly leaving the forested areas behind. Flat plains stretched out around them with not even the sounds of birds. The ground became swampy, with huge areas swimming with water. They soon realised they couldn't ride for much longer. Some of the swamps turned into foul smelling bogs where noxious gases rose to mingle with fog that had descended upon them.

'I know a way through,' Rhiannon said. 'We'll have to walk. It's too treacherous on our mounts. We'll need to feel the firmness of the ground beneath our feet.'

'You realise it could be difficult for us,' Hilde said.

'We'll go slowly,' Lu promised.

'I hope Bearach got through the swampland,' Fionn murmured.

'The great fool!' Lu exclaimed at his absent friend. 'I hope so.'

Lady Rhiannon went first, with Lu and then Bree following her. Nevertheless, each step was a concern. Bree had overheard Áine tell Niamh that the swamps changed shapes and sizes. What was safe one day could be treacherous the next.

Bree found the noxious odours nearly worse than the worry that they'd take one small step in the wrong place and fall into the swamp. She was especially afraid for Cythala, who not only had huge feet but weighed more than anyone else. Lu had said some bogs had quicksands that could drag you down to your death.

When they heard a plaintive cry, Bree halted. Lu looked back at her. 'What is it?' she asked.

'It difficult to tell.'

A black shape flew through the fog. Bree tried to see through the thick grey clouds. 'It could be a raven. I think I just saw one.'

'Mór,' Niamh uttered, from her position on Bree's shoulder.

'It could be, or it could be one of her evil flock,' Áine said.

'Either way,' Lu pointed out, 'a raven didn't make that sound.'

Then it came again. They moved along.

A cry and scuffle came from behind Bree. She halted again. Heremon had slipped and was struggling to keep his balance. One of his back legs had slid off the track. Cythala, who was walking behind everyone else lifted Heremon physically back onto the narrow track. Relief washed over Bree. It was just as well they had a giant with them!

'Help…'

A new cry. Or was it the first one? Bree looked around but couldn't see anything through the fog. She could only just discern Cythala at the end of the group.

Then it came again. 'Help.' A faint voice carried through the mists.

'Where are you?' Lu shouted. He stood up in his stirrups. 'I can't see anyone,' he said as he sat down.

'Let me try,' Rhiannon said.

Bree knew that Rhiannon could shape-shift, but she'd never witnessed it. It happened quicker than Bree could have imagined. She'd seen Mór manifest herself as a raven. The Goddess Rhiannon's shift was to a white dove. She flapped her wings and the fog swallowed her.

'I could have gone,' Niamh whispered. 'My glow could have lit the way.'

'Don't worry little one,' Áine said. 'Rhiannon will find her way better than any of us.'

Then, a dove remerged out of the mist and, before their eyes, became a woman.

'It's Bearach,' Rhiannon said. 'He's caught in a bog and halfway submerged.'

'The fool!' Lu exclaimed. 'Very well, we'll have to free him.'

'Let me.' Cythala's voice reached them from behind. 'I can pull him free.'

'I'll show you the way,' Rhiannon said.

'We don't have a great deal of choice,' Lu said.

Bree wondered if she could help. Surely as Triple

Goddess she should be able to do something. 'I could light the way for Cythala,' she said.

'You're going nowhere,' Lu said, frowning at her.

'I can light the way,' Niamh said.

Rhiannon's dove fluttered above them waiting while Cythala waded through the swamp, skirting them. Niamh flew with the dove and the three of them disappeared.

'By Danu's love, I hope they will remain safe,' Áine murmured.

The horses and the centaurs fidgeted, but only slightly more so than Bree. She wanted to jump down and move around but the path didn't offer any room to do this.

Then, they heard sounds… grunts and splashing and swearing.

'Bearach's on form,' Lu said, and uttered a relieved laugh.

Minutes later Bearach stepped through the fog, walking ahead of Cythala. Niamh and Rhiannon flew close to them. The dove materialised as the woman.

'I'd jump down and hug you, you great bear, if there was room,' Lu exclaimed. 'It will have to wait until we're out of the swamplands. Then I'll kick your backside as well.'

Bearach laughed. He stood dripping mud and slime.

'We need to move through quickly,' Bree said. 'Bearach must be cold.' She sucked in her breath as another dark shape cut through the fog. 'Mór's raven.'

'Who'll go back to her and tell her where we are.'

'We must hurry then,' Bree said.

It took another hour before they'd picked their way through the swamps, only to enter a dark forest. At least they could halt. The trees reminded Bree of the Yew Walk. Branches denuded of leaves reached out in tortuous embraces to others of their kind. Some branches bent and twisted down to the damp and dank ground, giving the appearance that their trunks were old. Bree felt certain the entire forest was ancient. It was in its death throes if the smell was anything to go on.

Padraig gathered kindling. Lu warned him not to go out of sight of them. When the Immortal returned, Bree ignited the sticks and leaves until a decent fire burned.

Bearach, after apologising for his actions, stripped off his tunic and boots, and sat huddled in front of the fire. Cythala sat on the other side, taking his boots off to dry too.

'I'm sorry for running off like that,' Bearach said.

Bree thought it amusing to hear such a big man as contrite as a child who had disobeyed its mother. She suppressed the urge to smile. 'It's good to have you with us.'

'Thank you, my lady.'

'You great bear,' Lu said, and cuffed his friend's head.

Bear was a name Bree had often heard Bearach's companions use. He was a great bear of a man.

'You haven't found Seraphina, I assume?' Bearach asked.

'Not yet, my friend,' Lu replied. 'However, from here on, we stay together.'

Bearach nodded. He went on to thank his saviours.

'Who would have thought a giant would have the brawn to pull me out of the bog,' Bearach said.

Bree could tell he was teasing, as Cythala threw a stick at Bearach and the two fell to laughing.

Laughter didn't seem to belong in this forest. It was as if the ancient trees wouldn't abide it and they quashed it, until it lay damp beneath their feet, leaving only melancholy behind. Bree felt it creep into her bones. Niamh felt it too. The little fairy huddled close to her. Bree half expected a banshee to scream or a púca with its wild red eyes to ride by, but nothing moved, except for things slithering almost silently close to their feet.

Bree shivered. She wished they could move on... but there was no guarantee that anywhere in this southern realm would be any better. She went to sit with Lu. 'Where do we go next?'

He sighed. 'Get out of this forest, to start with. It has an air of despondency about it.'

'You feel it too.'

Lu nodded. 'We need to give Bearach a chance to recover and then we'll be on our way but to where, I don't know. This part of the realm has never been explored. We hear stories about it at times, but nothing definite.'

'Has it been left to Mór and her followers?'

'Basically. No one really knows where she lives. Sometimes she's with Scathach or Brandubh, who can shapeshift into a raven like his mistress.'

'I don't remember him from our battle with Mór.' Bree frowned.

'He would have been there... somewhere.'

'Along with Mór's necromancer.'

Lu groaned. 'I'm not sure how to get rid of him.'

'I could use the ancient fire,' Bree suggested.

'That might work.' Lu gazed at her searchingly. 'Just remember that this is a trap to catch you.'

'This is about saving Seraphina.'

'That too.' Lu grabbed her hand. 'But it's more about destroying you.'

Chapter Twenty-One

BEARACH DECLARED himself ready to go on. He put his wet clothes back on, eager to continue the search… Bree didn't think, for all his strength, that Bearach had regained enough energy, but the truth was they had to hurry.

Tiomoid's cry further persuaded her of this. He was a quiet man with a gentle heart. He sprang to his feet as his moan wrenched from the depths of his soul. He held his head in his hands and his dark gaze shot around as if he was looking for someone. Then he ran, wildly through the twisted trees.

'By Dagda's beard!' Lu exclaimed, jumping to his feet.

'What's the matter with him?' Padraig asked.

'He's gone mad,' Domhnall said.

'It's the melancholy of this forest,' Rhiannon explained. 'We've been here for too long.'

Bree didn't doubt her words. She'd felt the gloom of this place, and Rhiannon was connected to all the trees and plants.

'We'll catch him,' Hilde said, and she and Heremon galloped after Tiomoid.

Lu didn't let them go alone. He mounted Feidlimid and hurried after the centaurs. Bree followed seconds later on Gealach.

They caught Tiomoid more by accident than anything else. He'd staggered and tripped into the aged and tangled branches of a yew tree. By this time he was screaming.

Hilde and Heremon reached him first.

Lu sprang down and pulled Tiomoid to his feet but the man who was his friend started flailing his arms about, hitting Lu several times in the face.

The others had caught up with them and Diarmuid dragged Tiomoid off Lu. Bearach took aim and sent a resounding punch into Tiomoid's jaw. The man fell to the forest floor.

'Let's get out of here before someone else runs amok.' Lu lifted the unconscious man and, with Bearach's help, placed him, face down, over his horse's saddle.

It took another hour to leave the woeful forest behind. By that time, Bree noticed that Padraig was becoming irritable, and she guessed he would have been the next victim to succumb to melancholy. Within ten minutes of leaving the forest behind, Padraig recovered and Tiomoid stirred. Lu called a halt and they all dismounted while Cythala lifted Tiomoid to the ground.

They paused long enough for a drink and for Tiomoid to punch Bearach in the shoulder.

'I have a headache now, you great bear!'

'Be thankful it's not worse,' Bearach told him.

The landscape had changed, the ground so flat that not

a tree could be seen, just hard land that cracked and gaped open in places. They all had to be careful lest their horses stepped into the hollows. Hilda and Heremon had their own problems with it. Only Cythala could easily step on the holes and not be bothered by them.

The afternoon grew late, but the sky was a slate grey as if the sun didn't exist here. The air was colder, and a chill wind blew.

At least they didn't have to ride in single file here. Bree rode in the front with Lu.

'I'm hoping we find some shelter before nightfall,' he said.

'Do you think we're even going in the right direction?' Bree asked.

'I'm certain of it. If we weren't, I think Mór would find a way of diverting our course.'

'Do you think she's watching us?' The words were barely out of Bree's mouth when a raven appeared in the sky above them. 'Mór's raven?'

'I'd say so.'

Cythala walked up alongside them. 'I can see something up ahead. It's too far to identify as yet.'

'What sort of thing?' Bree asked.

'It could be two large pillars side by side.'

'Out here in the middle of nowhere?' Lu asked.

'I can't see more yet,' the giant said.

Another raven flew over them and then was gone. Bree didn't like it.

As they drew closer to the pillars, Cythala squinted. 'They look like hands… enormous stone hands.'

Bree couldn't understand why anyone would erect

statues of hands but as they drew closer, they all saw the grey stone hands from wrists upwards buried into the ground. What was even more alarming was that the ground on either side of the statues, as far as the eyes could see, had become huge gaping chasms, with no way across. The crevasses were too wide for their horses to jump and even for Cythala to try to hurdle the fissures.

Bree turned to Lu. 'We're being forced to go between the hands.' She hoped this wasn't Mór's idea of a joke that they'd now be within her grasp.

'I'm not surprised,' he said.

'Do you want me to fly through and check the other side?' Niamh asked.

'We all stay together,' Áine said.

Bree's stomach tightened. Strangely enough, she couldn't see far past the hands. The light was failing but only a short distance ahead the landscape seemed to be in total blackness. 'Should we stay on this side and settle for the night?' she asked.

'We must go on, my lady,' Bearach implored.

'We must rest,' Lu said, 'but I think we should go through the hands. We don't have any shelter here.'

'We don't know what we'll find.' Áine's expression showed her anxiety.

'I think Lu is correct,' Bree said.

Lu smirked at her. 'Do my ears deceive me?'

Bree sneered back at him and shook the reins for Gealach to walk on. Lu caught up with her.

'We go through together,' he said.

Bree felt daunted and overwhelmed upon walking through the hands, the huge palms facing in, the fingers reaching skyward. It wasn't just their size. The ground around the hands was thrust upwards, as if the hands themselves were attempting to escape the land that held them imprisoned. Bree felt a ripple of fear pass through her. It was as she'd thought, the hands represented being held but not in a good way. They made Bree feel as if she were their captive, just as the hands themselves were held captive in the ground. She shook her head. That was the last thing she wanted to feel now.

Once they'd all walked through without anything untoward happening, they were soon aware that night had fallen early. Niamh's glow was the only illumination they had, even though Bree knew she could use the ancient fire.

Then before they could proceed, a deep rumble filled their ears. It came from the ground. As the rumble turned to a roar, the land began to shake. The horses moved restlessly. The shuddering became worse, and chasms opened up.

As Gaelach pranced skittishly, Bree saw that a long crack was opening up between Hilde and Heremon. Heremon leaped across it to join Hilde. Kuon barked and jumped about.

Rhiannon shape-shifted into a dove, while Niamh could no longer remain on Bree's shoulder.

Even Lu and the Immortals were struggling to keep their mounts from stepping into fissures and breaking their legs. Bree fared the best on Gaelach, as if the unicorn didn't possess the fear of the other horses. Cythala too had little trouble stepping across the fractures in the ground.

Then the land settled, and the grumbling stopped.

'Is everyone unhurt?' Lu called out. When all replied that no harm had been done, Lu said. 'We should go on for a while to put enough distance between ourselves and the Hands.

They walked on for a few hundred yards before Lu drew a halt.

'We can't go on without enough light.'

'Wait,' said Bree. 'What's that up ahead? I can see small flashing lights.'

'I'll check,' Niamh said, before anyone could stop her. Fortunately, she returned after only a few minutes. 'Fire-flies,' she informed them. 'There's a cave.'

'Good. Let's bed down there for the night,' Lu said.

Once Bree had lit a fire, she looked around the cave, while everyone brought in food and water for their horses. The cave was large enough for all of them and they would feel safer this way. The roof was far above them and cut deep into what had to be a hill or mountain. Niamh had flown around outside before they entered but couldn't discern a great deal. Bree thought it strange that out of all the flat land on the other side of the hand stat-ues, this side should immediately have a hill. Yet perhaps nothing should seem strange in this unknown part of the realm.

They sat and ate but soon settled. Lu took first watch. He built another small fire near the cave's entrance and sat close enough for some warmth but far enough away from the fire's illumination so he could see if anything moved in the darkness.

Bree joined him as she had on the previous night,

sitting on the ground next to him. After her entire life spent living in a cave, admittedly more comfortable than this one, she wondered how Lu fared, although he was used to fighting and bunking down in all sorts of conditions.

'Do you think it strange that we went through the statues and immediately found a cave in a hill?'

'No, I don't think anything's strange. I'm sure when we entered the portals, and I'm certain that's what those hands were, that we're now in Mór's territory.'

'I thought so too.'

'We need to be on our guard, even more so now,' Lu added. He gazed at her. 'How are you coping?'

'I used to live in a cave, remember. As for the rest, I'm tired, dirty and anxious.' Bree gave a faint smile.

'You're doing well.'

'Can I believe my ears?'

Lu smirked. 'It's not the first time I've said you've done well.' A smile replaced the sneer. 'You've come a long way from the girl you were.'

'The ignorant girl…?' Bree suggested, mockingly.

'All right, I know. I was tough on you to start with.' Lu took her hand. Then said, 'You should get some rest.'

Bree looked at him and smiled. She knew this memory of him sitting with Corraidhin angled against a raised knee, Cadeyrn still between his shoulder blades, and Kuon snoring beside him, would always stay with her. If someone painted Lu, they couldn't imagine a better pose to suit him. He was a man of action, strong and dependable. Bree knew she should never have doubted his sincerity. He would never want to depose her. For her part, she didn't know what she'd do without him. She recalled the time after she'd fully become the Triple Goddess, when she thought he intended kissing her—her mistake?—that he'd seemed aloof. He'd kept away from her, and she never understood why.

'Did you mean to kiss me?' Bree asked. She grimaced as she hadn't meant to say it. The words escaped her with the thoughts. When Lu didn't respond, didn't even look at her, she felt a wave of embarrassment wash over her. Idiot! Why had she asked? Then they both spoke at the same time. Bree indicated Lu should speak first.

'When?' he said.

'After I'd become the Triple Goddess, after my three aspects showed.' Although after Seraphina and Bearach's wedding he almost kissed her too.

'You looked very beautiful that evening and you'd surprised me. Witnessing your growth, your courage and determination. I wanted to kiss you but...'

'But you changed your mind, almost straight away, I think.'

Lu ran a finger down her cheek. 'I did change my mind.'

Bree frowned. 'You became aloof and indifferent to me.'

'I stepped away because you'd only just become the triple goddess. You'd defeated Mór... for the time being. You'd been through so much. Yet you still had so much to learn. I didn't want to complicate things for you. I thought there would be enough time later for... whatever might happen.'

For us? Was that what he was saying? Time for us?

Perhaps Bree should have felt pleased but instead, she felt anger stir in her chest. 'Why couldn't you let me decide how much I could cope with? What gives you the right to decide anything for me?' Bree looked around to ascertain if her raised voice had woken anyone. If it had, everyone must have been pretending they hadn't heard because no one moved.

Lu's eyebrow rose. 'I was only thinking of you. Not deciding for you.' He took her hand. 'Also, at that early stage, I didn't think you'd welcome my attentions.'

'Like now?' Bree pulled her hand out of his. All this time they could have been developing a relationship instead of her nursing her hurt and wondering if he was actually betraying her, or at the least, wanting to usurp her. Bree rose, glared at him and went back to where she planned to sleep next to her aunt and Niamh. She cast him a last glance as she lay down. He was still staring at her.

Lu groaned. Kuon grumbled in his sleep.

'I've done it again, my friend.' Lu ruffled Kuon's head. He watched as Bree settled. Trouble was, she asked the questions, and then didn't like the answers. In all his many years, Lu had never understood women. 'What do you say, my hulking hound? Nothing? Better I say nothing too.'

Chapter Twenty-Two

Having had little sleep, Bree was nevertheless pleased to see a thin grey light outside the cave. They quickly ate and made their horses ready. Hilde and Heremon went outside to stamp their feet. Bree avoided looking at Lu, partly because she felt embarrassed over her behaviour. She may have acted a little childishly, storming off as she'd done, but even now, her anger stirred.

'Are you well?' her aunt asked.

The question made Bree realise that her annoyance could be seen. She smiled slightly for Áine's benefit.

Niamh settled on Bree's shoulder, and they went outside.

A grey sky hung above a looming mountain that had seemed to have sprung up from nowhere. At least it had provided them with a place to sleep. Bree had feared that once they were inside the cave, Mór might have attacked them. She obviously wanted them to keep going. But to where?

The mountain looked to be a range, going on out of

sight. This forced the band to stay on this side of it, unless…

'Do you think we're meant to cross this mountain?' Bree asked her aunt—she wouldn't ride with Lu at the moment.

'There doesn't look to be a way across so far,' Áine said.

'No, there doesn't. It appears we have no choice but to go into a forest again.' Bree stared at what appeared to be an entrance to a large, wooded area. 'Talk about being led to where Mór wants us!'

'I know,' Niamh agreed.

'Mór isn't known as the phantom queen for nothing,' Áine said.

'Another gloomy forest,' Bree commented as they stepped inside.

This forest was darker than the previous one. Everything this side of the hand statues seemed bleaker. Trees twisted as if in agony. Sounds of things scurrying through the leaf litter startled Bree as Gealach's feet squelched into it. She had the feeling eyes were watching them. Then Bree saw two red eyes and something black moved through the trees at her side.

'It's a púca,' Bree whispered to Áine. 'I saw one with Scathach in the Yew Walk.'

'I see it,' Áine said.

'Do you think Scathach might be close by?'

'Perhaps.'

Niamh pressed herself closer into Bree's neck. 'What should we do?'

Bree moved Gealach forward and joined Lu. 'Did you see the púca?'

Lu raised his eyebrow at her. 'I did.'

'Aren't they supposed to bring bad fortune?'

'You mean more than we have already?' Lu asked dryly.

Bree turned away. 'I can see there's no use talking to you.' She rejoined her aunt.

The forest stretched on and by the time they halted to eat, there still seemed no end in sight. They ate in silence, all no doubt brooding over their journey, just as Bree fretted. Were they even going in the right direction to find Seraphina? Bree glanced over to where Bearach stood. He'd finished eating and was staring into the trees. He must feel despairing. He'd no sooner married the woman he loved, than she was snatched away from him. Bree wished she could do something to help. She felt guilty. It was partially her fault, even though she hadn't known Seraphina was her twin when she bound Seraphina and Bearach together. If she'd known... would it have changed things? Perhaps.

They kept threading their way through the interminable forest. Cythala took the lead for a change. Bree noticed that Lu's shoulders dropped, as if it took a degree of responsibility off him. Again, Bree felt guilty. This wasn't the time to be bickering with Lu. She was the Triple Goddess, and she should be supporting him, helping to keep everyone's spirits high.

She led Gealach to ride beside Lu. 'We shouldn't be arguing now. We need to stand together against Mór's evil.'

Lu nodded and gave a faint smile. 'I agree.'

Bree sighed. 'Has nothing of this southern part of the realm been explored and mapped out?'

'The Lady Rhiannon has shape-shifted and flown over the area a couple of times. From her observations, the lands alter every time she's surveyed it. It's impossible to know.'

'Mór's evil magic?' Bree asked.

'Most likely.'

'It looks lighter up ahead. Or do my eyes deceive me?'

'I believe it is. I'll be pleased to get out of this forest before nightfall.'

'It's all taking so long,' Bree muttered. 'I hope Seraphina is all right.'

'We can't go any faster.'

The forest didn't end, only thinned out. Lu halted and called to Padraig and Domhnall to scout the area. They all dismounted to stretch their legs. Cythala flopped down on the forest floor, as pleased to sit down as they were to stand and move around. Hilde and Heremon stood quietly together.

The two Immortals returned and reported to Lu and Bree.

'The forest continues, while a mountain rises on its other side and becomes a valley,' Domhnall said.

'I don't like the sound of that,' Lu said. 'With mountains either side of us, we could walk into a trap. We'd be bottlenecked.'

'But only half a mile along from here, there's a huge door cut into the new mountain,' Padraig said.

'How huge?' Bree asked.

'Gigantic!' Domhnall exclaimed. 'The height of fifty men or more.'

Lu frowned. 'By Dagda's beard.' He then beckoned everyone closer and informed them of this new discovery.

'The area in front of the door is fairly open,' Padraig said. 'We could stop there for the night.'

'It sounds like a good idea,' Lu said.

Everyone agreed and they rode on. When they reached the clearing, they stopped and stared at the door.

Bree felt her breath sucked away at the sheer size of it. No matter what the Immortals had said, it couldn't prepare her for the size of this door cut into the mountainside. Twenty or more steps led up to it from the forest floor. An unusual pattern covered it. At first, Bree thought it was of tree roots entwined but soon realised it was of forearms and hands criss-crossing over each other. Here again hands were significant.

'Could Mór have built this?' Bree whispered to Áine. Although why she whispered, she didn't know. Somehow, this discovery made her feel small and humble.

'Perhaps,' Áine replied. 'I wonder, though, if an earlier civilisation could have built it.'

'They must have been giants,' Niamh said. 'Even more gigantic than Cythala's race of the Daoine ollmhór.'

The sound of a raven above them startled everyone.

'We should do our usual routine,' Lu said. 'Search for kindling, tend the horses, eat, sleep.'

'I'd love to have a bath,' Bree murmured and sighed. 'I'll never complain that my bathroom at the palace is too large ever again.'

Niamh giggled.

Bree brushed Gealach down and wiped her golden horn clean of dust, then gave her food and water.

It didn't take long before they all sat around a fire that Bree had lit. Conversation revolved around the huge door —who could have built it and why, and what was behind it.

'Will we see if we can open the door and go inside tomorrow?' Hilde asked.

'How can we open it?' Fionn asked. 'I can't even see a keyhole.'

'We don't have a key in any case,' Diarmuid added.

'If it's a choice between riding in between two mountains or going through a door, I'd choose the door,' Tiomoid said.

'What would you know?' Bearach cuffed him. 'You're only a baby.'

'I have more sense than you, running off and getting stuck in a bog,' Tiomoid replied.

Bearach grunted and pushed the younger Immortal off the log he was sitting on. Everyone laughed, including Tiomoid.

It helped lighten the mood.

Lu took first watch as he'd been doing.

Bree sat down beside him once everyone else had bunked down. 'Are we really going to try to open the door?' she asked. Lu looked tired and dishevelled, his golden hair a little dull. She hated to think how she must look.

'We might not have any choice. Mór has led us where she willed thus far. I suspect she might convince us to try the door.'

'That's nothing to look forward to.' Bree sighed. 'I just want to find Seraphina.'

'I want to keep you safe.'

Bree gazed at Lu's blue eyes that he'd turned on her. She found it more and more difficult to resist those eyes. Her heart did a flip. 'I'm sorry about last night.'

'It's my fault too. I should never have become aloof when all I wanted to do was to get to know you better.'

'It's in the past now. Shall we forget it?' Bree asked.

'I think we should.'

'I have a confession though.'

'Oh?' Lu gazed askance at her.

'I thought you might have wanted to usurp me, so that you could take control.'

Lu's expression darkened. 'You thought that?'

'I'm sorry. I shouldn't have doubted you.'

'I should think not.' Then his eyes twinkled with amusement. 'I wouldn't make a very good triple goddess.'

Bree laughed but softly, so as not to wake anyone. After a few moments, she asked, 'Do you think the palace and the realms will be safe with us not there?'

'Ogma will look after things, and he has some of my men and the army if anything did happen. I don't think it will. I think we're the ones walking into a trap.'

'The trouble is we know it but can't do anything to prevent it, not if we want to find Seraphina,' Bree said.

'You should get some sleep,' Lu said.

Bree knew she should but underneath it all she was enjoying her quiet time with Lu.

'Go on. Even Kuon is asleep before you.'

Bree smiled. 'Good night.' However, before she could stand up, Lu grabbed her hand and kissed the back of it.

'Good night, my lady.'

Bree shuddered awake to the loudest noise she thought she'd ever heard. Louder even than when Lu was breaking the enchantments that protected Bree's cave home in the Otherworld.

Everyone jumped to their feet. Bearach, on watch, was the first to go running into the forest ahead of them. Lu was seconds behind him. Cythala followed. The others talked among themselves, wondering what had happened.

Bree thought she knew. Mór had done something to prevent their progress through the wood. When the men came back, she knew she was correct.

'The mountainside has collapsed,' Lu said. He caught Bree's gaze.

So Mór had decreed they should open the door. They only needed to discover how to do so.

Chapter Twenty-Three

Everyone climbed the steps to the gigantic door, and then puzzled over what to do.

'It must have been closed by magic,' Bree suggested. 'Perhaps magic can open it.'

'You could burn it down, my lady,' said Tiomoid.

'Be quiet,' Bearach chided. 'Speak to my lady when she speaks to you.'

'It's quite all right,' Bree said. 'Although I don't think burning it down is a good idea. We don't know what's on the other side.'

Cythala stepped forward and leaned against the door but even he looked small against its height. The door wouldn't budge. All the men put their weight behind it but couldn't open it.

Bree and the women scrutinised the hand design over the entry. 'There must be some way to open it.' Bree leaned her head back and doubted her words. The entrance stretched far above her.

Rhiannon placed her hands on the carved timber. 'I believe it is closed with dark magic.'

'If we are to enter, then perhaps good magic will open it.' Bree stepped forward. She placed her hands, as Rhiannon had done. The hand design felt strangely real, as if Bree was touching flesh. A coldness rushed through her body. She started to shake. She saw images in her head of tall statues standing in light amidst darkness, with an overall feeling of evil flowing into her body. Bree stepped back and doubled over, breathing hard, but the coldness had left her.

Áine and Lu hurried to her.

'I'm all right,' Bree said, straightening. 'That door was definitely sealed with dark magic.' Bree took a few more moments to steady herself. 'I'll try to open it with good magic.'

Everyone stepped back, except for her aunt and Lu, who remained beside her. Bree took a breath and focused on her hands. She felt the warmth and when she opened her hands, the ancient fire burned on her palms. She closed her eyes and then recited, 'I am the Triple Goddess. I am maiden, mother, and crone. I am the poetess, the smith and the healer. I am creativity, inspiration and vision. *Bean an ti*, I am she who cares for everything. *Beatha*, I am the livelihood that sustains my people. I am *Comhluadr*, the harmony of being together. *Dochas*, I bring hope to the future. I am *Draiocht*, the magic that is unseen. I am *Fios*, knowledge and understanding. I was at the beginning of creation, in the middle of life and at the end of existence.' Bree paused for a moment and then, continued, '*Ciar draiochta* will bow to the power of *Feidhlim*.' The fire in Bree's hands soared.

Bree stepped back. Nothing happened.

'What did you say,' Niamh asked.

'Dark magic will bow to the power of great goodness,' Áine explained.

Still nothing happened. Lu moved restlessly beside Bree. She heard Hilde and Heremon stamp their feet.

Then, the door shook, much as Bree had done, visibly shaking, with dust raining down on those close enough. Everyone moved backwards to avoid the debris landing on them. The huge entrance split in two and swung open, as if by a spring or by magic.

Bree stepped forward into the doorway. She'd seen this in her vision. Tall statues placed in a circle stood in the centre of the room, with beams of light highlighting them from a huge oculus in the ceiling. The statues, five in all, and all women, were dressed in long gowns, the stone chiselled to give the appearance that the garments flowed and moved around the stone figurines.

The rest of the room was cast into shadow, but Bree could discern its lofty dimensions.

'By Dagda's beard,' Lu murmured. 'Where did this come from?'

Everyone entered the room but some with more hesitation than others.

Bree turned to Hilde and Heremon, and asked if they'd wait outside and keep an eye on the horses.

'Very well, my lady,' Hilde said.

When the rest were all inside, the enormous doors

shuddered and then closed with a resounding crash that made everyone jump.

'Well, we're inside now whether we like it or not,' Lu muttered. He stamped Corraidhin on the ground. Kuon barked.

Judging by the size of the door, Bree knew the room had to be vast. Yet there didn't appear to be anything else in the chamber. Bree stepped forward and walked cautiously to the statues. Áine and Lu remained on either side of her, Kuon stood next to his master.

Bree said, 'I saw these statues in my mind's eye when I placed my hands on the door. What could they be? Their position beneath the oculus has to be significant.'

'Perhaps they are from an earlier civilisation. We, the Tuatha Dé Danann of Tír na nÓg, have been here for only a few generations,' Lu said.

Bree realised they were all whispering, as if this room was a holy place… and maybe it was.

'I bid you welcome.'

A voice filled the room, reverberating through each of the group. Then it laughed but no mirth sounded in the chortle.

Bree's gaze shot around the room. At first, she couldn't see anything or anyone. The massive chamber was too dark. Then she caught a movement high up in the black shadows. Bree couldn't comprehend if a ledge or another small room was up near the ceiling. Before she could alert anyone, the shape flew and dived towards them, manifesting itself as a raven. Seconds later, the one bird became a flock of ravens, diving straight for Bree. Her knees trembled but she didn't flinch. This had happened before. Inches short of her face, the ravens merged and metamorphosed into a woman in a black gown and cape.

Mór.

Bright dark eyes, gleaming even in the dim lighting of the chamber, stared out of a face that was as white as death. Her cheekbones defined with dark paint sat above cadaverous cheeks. Lips that were as black as her long hair stretched in a tight line.

'You have arrived.' Mór stated the obvious.

Lu pointed Corraidhin at her. 'What's stopping me from killing you at this moment?' Bree could see his jaw tensing.

'I'm pleased you asked that question. At this moment?' Mór mused. 'Allow me to introduce my necromancer to you. If you kill me, I'm certain he would cast you all into a different kind of Underworld than the one the Goddess Rhiannon presides over.'

A man stepped out of the shadows. His tall skeletal figure hunched as he walked, as if he couldn't stand straight. A skull-like head seemed a match for his body, with stringy grey hair that hung below his shoulders and eyes as dark as jet, as dead and soulless as the man himself appeared to be. Bree inwardly shuddered as she stared into his eyes.

'I wouldn't look at him,' Lu said, and took Bree's hand. 'He is an undead, born of dark magic. He'll rip your soul from your body in the blink of an eye.'

'Even faster,' Mór said and laughed. 'Now where are my manners. This is Brandubh, my black raven man. Isn't he beautiful?'

Beautiful wasn't a word Bree would use to describe

Brandubh, although with his black skin stretched over a large muscular frame, he was impressive.

Arms folded over his massive chest, Brandubh stood behind Mór.

'I think you know Scathach,' Mór continued her introductions. Scathach had also stepped out the of darkness.

Bree remembered the woman with her long dark hair, with a silver streak on each side of her face. She wore a cloak, trousers and tunic, as Bree had seen her dressed before. Bree recognised the same designs scrolled over her face.

'We've come for Seraphina,' Bree said.

Mór tutted and turned to Lu. 'You haven't taught the girl any manners, I see. One must be cordial before attending to business.'

'We're not here to socialise with you,' Lu replied.

Mór stepped closer to him, briefly stroking his face with one finger. 'You and I could have ruled all of Tír na nÓg. We would have been good together.'

Lu tossed her hand away from him. 'Only in your nightmares, Mór.'

'Ah, now you have said something relevant. If only you knew what lived and died in my dreams. The nightmares would be yours.' Mór swirled, so that her black cape swung around her, transforming into a multitude of ravens that flew to the lofty shadows.

Bree frowned, wondering what was happening. A moment later a terrifying screech filled the room. Over and over it sounded, as if more than one banshee cried out. Bree recognised the horrendous creatures descending on them one second before she collapsed.

CHAPTER TWENTY-FOUR

BREE COULDN'T THINK where she was or what had happened. She heard a woman's voice, but it seemed to be a long way off. Bree couldn't understand why she was sleeping. What had she been doing? Then she startled awake. The banshees had descended on them. She remembered being in the Yew Walk with Mór and her banshee. The banshee's cry had killed Doireann. Only goddesses, gods and immortals could survive a banshee's screech. In the Yew Walk, Bree hadn't collapsed. Here in this strange place five or six banshees had swooped over them.

Was anyone dead?

Bree stared around, realising that she could hardly move. One hand and arm was tied behind her back. The other arm was tied to her waist with her palm against her body. Bree could tell, Mór didn't want her to use the ancient fire. Bree's ankles were also secured, and she sat on the ground, just out of the light from the oculus.

Bree noticed that a huge circle, with stones marking it,

surrounded the tall figurines. The stones were also in the light. Bree gasped, her stomach lurching, her heart tightening. The necromancer stood inside the circle of stones, leaning over a table that had been placed there. All this had been done since Bree had collapsed. She couldn't see clearly from her position on the floor. The necromancer also blocked her view. Then the man moved, and a cry was wrenched from Bree. Tiomoid had been stretched out on top of the table and tied down. The young Immortal seemed unconscious. Had they all been made comatose by the banshees' wails?

'Ah, so you are awake?' Mór strolled over to Bree. 'You are stronger than before and have woken quickly. Other than you, only Lu is awake.'

'Where is he?' Bree asked. 'Lu!' she shouted.

'Bree. Are you all right?' he called back.

From the direction of his voice, Lu had to be on the other side of this vast room.

'Yes, are you?'

'How touching,' Mór murmured, sneering. 'I'll make certain that you are buried together.'

'Where are the others?' Bree demanded.

'They're around.' Mór waved a dismissive hand.

During the next few minutes, everyone else gradually woke up. They were scattered around the circle.

'Where's Seraphina?' Bree asked.

'Ah… your sister. A family reunion.' Mór walked around to where Áine was tied up. 'Really Áine, you shouldn't have hidden the sister's existence from me for all those years. It's only made me angrier with you. At least Brigid is dead. That's one victory.'

Bree cried out and struggled against her bonds.

'You can't escape, my Lady Bree. The ropes securing you have a glamour on them. My necromancer made it. It's the opposite of your enchantments. None of you can break a glamour. Not even you.'

'Then why am I bound in this way, so that my palms can't touch each other?' Bree demanded.

'I always say it's better to be safe than sorry.'

'I want to know where Seraphina is,' Bree said. She kept her voice firm and strong even though she was inwardly trembling.

'She's hanging around, being looked after by my faithful banshees.'

Hanging around? Bree's gaze shot upwards. In the shadows she saw movement; one of the banshees. Then, as she stared, Bree discerned a cage with a figure inside. 'Seraphina!' Bree shouted.

'She can't reply. Her mouth is covered.'

Bree's terror mounted and she took some deep breaths to control it. 'What do you want of us?'

'I want your lives, nothing less. Perhaps more. I want your realms. Everyone who doesn't bow down to me will die. As you can see my banshees are on top form. Your giant needed a crack on his head to take him down.'

Bree frowned. Why was Mór playing this game, trying to be glib?

'Untie Tiomoid,' Lu called to Mór. 'Whatever you plan to do, I'll take his place.'

The young Immortal had just woken and struggled against his bonds.

The necromancer moved to stand close to Tiomoid,

the man's skeletal figure hunched over the young man, chanting words as he did so. Bree couldn't understand what the necromancer was saying. Then the evil man drew a scian, a long dagger from his robes. He held a bowl and in one fast, unexpected motion, the necromancer used the scian to cut off Tiomoid's left hand. It fell into the bowl.

Bree screamed out, as did Áine and Niamh. The fairy was tied to her queen. Perhaps the others couldn't see what had happened.

'By Dagda's beard, when I get out of here—' Lu started.

Her glib act vanishing with her steps, Mór seized the bowl and thrust Tiomoid's hand under Lu's nose. 'You will not get out of here,' Mór said through decades of anger.

Bree heard Lu's frustration and fury, heard him struggling to get out of his bonds.

'My lady,' the necromancer said, following Mór. Bree could barely hear his thin voice. 'The blood must be fresh.'

'Here.' Mór thrust the bloody receptacle at him.

The necromancer might have looked pleased if such an emotion could exist across his cadaverous face.

Tiomoid screamed in pain. Bree wished she could do something to help him. She focused on the hand behind her back. She felt flames on her palm but as soon as she tried to make the fire flare, they burned her back. Her other palm rested on her stomach, making it useless.

'Will you shut up!' Mór cried out at Tiomoid.

'He's in agony,' Bree shouted at Mór.

Mór grabbed a dagger from her side and stabbed it into Tiomoid's chest. Her vicious gaze seared Bree's heart.

'Now he's not in agony.' Mór waved the blood coated blade in front of Bree. She recognised it as the dagger that had been forged by black magic.

Everyone cried out in abhorrence at what had happened. Bree could tell now that everyone was scattered over the room, including Cythala. They were hidden in the shadows. The ancient fire flared in Bree's palm but once again she burned herself and could achieve nothing of any use.

'You evil, black hearted devil!' Bree cried out.

'You flatter me,' Mór said.

Bree's tears ran down her cheeks. She couldn't go to pieces. She wouldn't allow herself to quake under Mór's evil. Tiomoid was dead. Bree had to think what to do before anyone else was killed.

Mór went to stand close to the necromancer. Whatever the vile man was chanting over the bowl with its gruesome contents, it looked as though Tiomoid had been a sacrifice needed for whatever else the necromancer was conjuring. The necromancer doubled over, his thin stringy hair falling over his face. His voice grew higher in pitch. The floor shook, a little at first and then as if an earthquake was upon them. Mór took a step backwards into the darkness. Bree wondered if this was more than even Mór expected. The Shadow Queen was alarmed.

The earth roared and shuddered. The five large statues facing each other in the centre of the room, beneath the bright light shining through the oculus, trembled and then the stone platform on which they stood cracked. A second fracture saw them toppling inwards on top of each other. The noise in the room, with everyone crying out or screaming, added to the clamour of the ground juddering and the necromancer's chant that seemed to fill the cavernous room.

The remains of the statues were flung into the air. One piece hit Bree's shoulder as it went flying past. She wanted to call out to everyone to ascertain if they were unharmed but a moment later a darkness swirled up from the large hole that had been covered by the statues on their platform. The black mist whirled like a column of evil.

Bree's mouth fell open when the mist cleared, and a gigantic creature stood on the far side of the gaping abyss. Taller even than Cythala and with more brawn than Bran-dubh, the creature's skin gleamed the colour of burnished obsidian, two horns protruded from a bald scalp and its long nails curled like vicious claws. It wore loose trousers, but its muscular chest was bare and gleamed in the light from the oculus in the roof.

'Ahh!' Mór cried, stepping into the light and throwing back her head.

At first, Bree thought the woman wailed in agony. A moment later, Bree realised it was in exultation.

'My demon!' Mór exclaimed. 'What a creature.' Then she laughed, a wild sound that chilled Bree's blood.

The demon remained where it stood. Bree wondered if it was awaiting instructions.

'Another, another,' Mór shouted. She turned to the necromancer. 'I want another demon.'

Bree couldn't hear all the necromancer said in reply, but she caught the words... *another sacrifice*. So, demons were born through a blood sacrifice! And Mór wanted another one.

'Take me,' Bree called out. 'I will be your sacrifice, but you must let everyone else go.'

Mór swung around to her. The woman's glittering black eyes staring out of her white face beneath black arching brows looked menacing. 'Are you certain about that?'

'Yes,' Bree said, staring into Mór's eyes.

'No, Bree.'

'No!'

Bree recognised Lu's voice and that of her aunt.

Mór swung away. 'Very well. Why not? You will all die here today.' Then, she swung back and stared at Bree. She shouted at Brandubh, 'Release her hand. The one behind her back. Use my dagger.'

Again, her friends cried out. Bree didn't doubt their sincerity, but she wondered if they feared she was their only hope for survival. Without her, they would be dead, too.

Brandubh roughly untied Bree and brought her hand around to the front, the rope still tied around her wrist. He leaned over Bree's free hand and cut the cords with the dagger. Forged in black magic as it was, it appeared to be able to sever the ropes loaded with the glamour.

The instant—Bree knew it had to be at the exact second —the rope fell away from her hand she focused and brought the ancient fire to life in her palm. She blew on it and flames soared to encompass Brandubh. The man screamed. Bree grabbed the dagger in his hands before he spun away. Bree hated to submit anyone to the fate of being burned but she had her loved ones and friends to save. With the dagger, she cut through the rope that held fast her other hand.

Everything had erupted around her. Mór screeched and swung her cloak so that she became a flock of ravens that flew around the room. The banshees obviously saw this as their cue to join their evil mistress. They flew at Bree one after another, and Bree cut each one down with the powerful dagger.

The demon also raged around the room. It headed first to the necromancer who huddled and covered his head, as if afraid of the creature he'd brought forth from the depths.

Bree ran across to Lu and cut his bonds, the rope falling away under the evil dagger's blade. Lu grabbed her face between his hands and kissed her and then he turned to Diarmuid while Bree cut her aunt's ropes.

Mór metamorphosed to her female form and grabbed Bree's arm. 'Not so fast,' Mór said through clenched teeth.

Bree pulled away and slashed Mór's arm with the dagger.

Mór stared at Bree, shocked that the dagger could be turned on her.

'Be careful what you wish for,' Bree said and kicked Mór in the shins. The woman transformed into a raven and flew to the ceiling, where she hung on the cage that held Seraphina.

The demon continued to rage around the room, senselessly grabbing chunks of the broken statues and throwing them around, as if without any instructions, it didn't know what to do. It ran at the necromancer and lifted the undead man with one clawed hand, then charged at the huge doors, obviously wanting to run amok outside.

Lu and Bree freed the rest of their group, but Bree didn't know how to free Seraphina. Even Cythala couldn't reach her.

Through an entrance Bree hadn't noticed, other beings floated into the room and suddenly they were under attack by more of Mór's creatures. These individuals were ghost-like, a little transparent, their staring eyes not seeming to see anything, and with their long hair flying behind them. Bree recognised them from books she'd read. Sluagh—people who'd died and returned as malicious spirits. They sought the souls of living people.

While everyone else fought the sluagh, Bree knew they also had to stop the demon from escaping through the doors. He would be a danger to their world.

Bree wondered if a dagger forged by dark magic could kill a creature born of sacrifice and the same evil. Bree ran to the door.

Cythala reached it before Bree, but the demon swung around and hit the giant with his muscular arm, throwing him back into the room.

As the door shook under the demon's assault, so too did the ground shake. Bree ran up behind the demon and sliced above its ankle with the powerful dagger.

The demon cried out and turned on Bree. It dropped the necromancer as it did so. Even though she knew some of her comrades were running to her to help, Bree also knew the demon's hand would reach her first. She focused, the ancient fire warmed her palm and she blew it into the demon's face. It emitted a cry that curdled her blood. It flailed about, holding its face, charging into the walls of the room, nearly falling into the pit from which it came.

Mór flew down to Bree, transmuting into her female form. She staggered, blighted by the dark magic of the dagger. 'You will pay for this,' she told Bree.

When Mór lunged at her, Bree stabbed her again with the blade. It sliced through Mór's side. The Shadow Queen stumbled and fell, holding her wound. With what could have been the last of her energy, Mór transformed into a raven and flew up to the oculus.

Bree saw the black shape fly into the brightness.

When a falling piece of the roof just missed her, Bree realised that the room was crumbling. She had to free Seraphina. Then she saw Bearach climbing the wall, or at least using the crumbling chunks of stone as steps to aid him. By the time he reached the cage, Bree feared the ceiling was about to collapse.

One of the sluagh flew towards her and Bree stabbed it with the dagger. If Bearach was rescuing Seraphina, Bree would turn her attention back onto the demon, which was in danger of causing enough destruction to kill them all. She ran up behind it and stabbed the evil dagger into its calf. It cried out again and tried to slap her away, as if she were an annoying insect. They were close to the gaping hole in the floor. Bree summoned the ancient fire and blew the sacred flames at it. Shouting in agony, the demon stumbled into the abyss.

Bree looked around for the necromancer and found him injured and cowering on the floor near the door.

She ran to him and without hesitating she blew on the ancient flames. They engulfed the undead man. His body shrivelled and the fire extinguished itself. Bree found a piece of timber and used it to roll the man's burnt corpse to the hole. To be doubly certain, Bree stabbed the dagger into his chest and pushed him into the dark pit.

She summoned the fire into her palms and said, 'I am the Triple Goddess. I am maiden, mother, and crone. I am the poetess, the smith and the healer. I am creativity, inspiration and vision. *Bean an ti*, I am she who cares for everything. *Beatha*, I am the livelihood that sustains my people. I am *Comhluadr*, the harmony of being together. *Dochas*, I bring hope to the future. I am *Draiocht*, the magic that is unseen. I am *Fios*, knowledge and understanding. I was at the beginning of creation, in the middle of life and at the end of existence.' She gazed down into the chasm and added, 'By the holy fire, I cast you both into the depths from which you sprang, never to return to Tír na nÓg.' The ground shuddered even more as the floor sealed over.

Lu grabbed her hand. Bearach, holding Seraphina in his arms, was beside Lu. Áine and Niamh joined them. Bree gazed around. Everyone, except for Tiomoid who lay under the stone table, was there. The banshees must have followed their evil mistress. The sluagh were vanquished. Now they were in danger of being crushed as the room disintegrated around them.

Bree ran over to the entrance and placed her hands on the huge door. This time it responded to her touch. It shook and then opened.

They ran through, the door closed behind them, and the room imploded.

For a moment, Bree along with the others, stood panting, but if they thought it was over, they soon found it wasn't. The mountain next to the crumbling room collapsed and then, like those caused by a stone thrown in a pond, the ripples impacted the entire mountain range.

They ran to their mounts, pleased now that they'd saddled their horses. Bree jumped up onto Gealach's back. They'd never found Bearach's horse, but Heremon waved Bearach over and indicated he should jump on with Seraphina. Only Cythala would have to remain on foot.

The rock collapsing deafened them as they rode, the dust almost blinding them. They could only keep going until they rode into the forest with its dank and dark shadows. The dust and the noise followed them until Bree realised that the forest's silence was the only thing pressing in on her ears. She slowed down, as did Lu. They maintained their reticence until Lu called a halt.

'I think we can stop now and bunk down for the night.'

Bree gazed around. The area was flat and cleared and they would have decent visibility around the camp sight. It was as good a place as any.

Bearach slid down, lifted Seraphina from Heremon's back and embraced her. Bree hugged her too, but they were all too tired to talk, to process everything that had happened, to realise that one of their own lay beneath the rubble of the room.

After so many nights on the road, they fell to their tasks automatically. Bree lit the fire after kindling had been gathered. They ate… but very little and drank long of their water bags. Darkness settled early over the forest, and by the light of the fire, words started to flow.

They grieved Tiomoid's passing and the terrible manner of his death.

'Do you think Mór could still be alive?' Fionn asked.

'It's possible,' Lu replied. 'Even though Lady Bree stabbed her with the evil dagger, Mór might summon another necromancer to save her. I for one won't believe she'd dead until I see her body.'

'At least we know the necromancer met his just desserts,' Diarmuid said. 'Thanks to Lady Bree.'

'And the demon,' Lu added. 'Now that took some courage.'

They all gave a soft cheer.

Then, Áine told Seraphina the story of her birth—told everyone—and Áine's part in it. Silence was so thick a knife could have cut through it. Seraphina was astonished and initially disbelieving.

'It's true,' Bree said. 'Even though I didn't know before. That's why Mór kidnapped you. She knew that I would search for you. The trap was set to catch me.' Bree didn't think Seraphina took in the enormity of this news, but she stared with wonder at Bree.

'We're sisters, twins,' Bree reiterated.

Seraphina cried against Bearach's chest. Bree understood that the shock of everything was too great for her sister to focus on the tale. Once they were back in their realms, the story could be told again.

Lu took first watch. Bree joined him, sitting with him on a log. Kuon already snored happily now that master and hound were reunited. It made such a difference to have those whom one loved close by.

Bree stared at Lu's profile as he gazed into the forest, the flare of the flames showing his weariness. For a while he didn't speak. Bree saw a tension along his jawline.

Then Lu turned and took her hand. 'I thought I was going to lose you today.'

'I thought that I was going to lose you,' Bree replied.

Lu reached out and pulled her into him. 'You're not going to leave my side now.'

Bree smiled, feeling shy.

Lu glanced down at her, took her face between his hands and kissed her, a deep and true kiss.

Kuon groaned in his sleep and a paw came up onto Bree's lap, as if the hound approved.

CHAPTER TWENTY-FIVE

AT FIRST, when back at the palace, all Bree wanted to do was sleep, as did everyone else. Bearach had stayed with Seraphina in her village, but on the following day when Seraphina came to the palace with her new husband, Bree insisted they live at the palace.

'But my village, my lady…'

Bree took Seraphina's hands in hers. 'You must call me Bree now that we know we're sisters.'

'I can't come to terms with it yet,' Seraphina said, shaking her head. 'I mean, what is really going to happen?'

'You and Bearach can live at the palace. You must have the room next to mine. I know Bearach has chambers in Lu's tower but I'm sure he'll move so we can be close together. I understand your attachment to your village but there's no one there now for you. Your family is here. You can still visit Baile Meánach. It can be your task to oversee its growth and progress.'

'Oh, my la—' Seraphina broke off.

Bree hugged her. 'I'm so happy to have you as my sister.'

'I'm sorry that I didn't tell you the truth before this, Seraphina,' Áine said. 'I should have told both of you.'

Both Bree and Seraphina hugged Áine.

'We're together now,' Bree said. 'That's all the matters.'

'What about Mór?' Niamh asked.

'Let's hope we don't hear from her again,' Bree said.

A memorial was held for Tiomoid; a sad affair. Lu spoke about his young Immortal, who was brave and courageous, and who'd ultimately died to save all who were on the quest to rescue Seraphina. Bree lit a funeral pyre even though it was without a body, saying words as the flames rose that would take his soul to the Underworld where the Goddess Rhiannon would welcome him. Rhiannon added her own blessings.

Everyone gathered afterwards in the reception room and spoke of Tiomoid's deeds.

'This is how someone is remembered,' Lu told Bree. 'To speak of them.'

Bree nodded. 'Words hold great power.'

Bree was pleased to have her family with her. Áine, her aunt, Seraphina her sister and now Bearach, her honorary brother. Niamh sat on her shoulder. They were in Bree's parlour when pounding sounded on the door.

'Lu,' everyone said in unison and laughed.

Lu and Kuon joined them. Kuon jumped up on Bree as she sat on a divan and commenced drooling on her gown.

Bree laughed. 'Will you please get your hound off me.'

'He likes you,' Lu said. 'Kuon, down.' The dog sat at Bree's feet. 'I'm pleased to see you have moved in to your rooms here,' Lu said to Seraphina and Bearach.

'It's too much,' Seraphina said. 'I'm not used to such a life.'

'Me neither,' Bearach said.

'You great bear,' Lu said and lightly punched his Immortal in his shoulder.

Bree smiled indulgently.

Later, Lu asked if Bree wanted to walk in the garden.

'I'd love to.'

'And you can get that smirk off your face,' Lu told Bearach as he sat grinning at them.

The cherry blossom trees looked beautiful, as they always did. It was an excellent enchantment the Goddess Rhiannon had placed on the trees so that they would flower continuously.

As they reached the end of the garden and gazed over the waterfall dropping into the pool, the sound of the splashing water was soothing, but illogicality, Bree felt nervous. Lu hadn't spoken or smiled since they'd left the others. Bree knew it! He regretted kissing her. It had only been because they were caught up with their quest. Otherwise, he wouldn't have shown his affection. Bree felt her heart sink, as if it had plunged over the waterfall and was being battered by the intensity of the water. She stared ahead and waited.

She could say something, of course, declare her love for him… but she thought it unwise to do so. Lu was a man's man, strong and fearless; he loved being with his Immortals. He wasn't used to sitting down and chatting in a parlour or even a garden. She glanced sideways and was aware of the tension in him. No, he wouldn't be happy with her.

Then, Lu swung around. 'There's something I wanted to ask you.'

Bree's heart pounded. Was he going to ask her to marry him? After all, Seraphina married Bearach. Bree waited.

'I thought it might be a good idea…' He hesitated.

Bree waited yet again. Was this a proposal?

'I thought it would be a good idea to explore some other territories. We've sat in our realms, so complacent.'

'Oh,' Bree murmured, her heart heavy, disappointment surging through her body.

'There could even be other races in our land. The civilisation we discovered the remnants of must have been quite ancient. There might be other such societies of which we know nothing.' After a moment, when Bree didn't speak, he added, 'What do you think?'

'What you say makes sense.' Bree struggled to keep her voice from wavering. 'When do you intend to go?'

'Soon, if you agree.'

If she agreed, he would go away for… months, most likely. 'By all means, go.'

'I won't take Bearach with me, or Fionn.'

The married men. 'That's considerate of you.' Bree couldn't keep the irony out of her tone.

'We'll start making preparations, then, if you agree.' Lu turned her to face him.

'You have my permission to go, if that's what you wanted.'

'My Lady… Bree… I…'

'What?' Bree asked, feeling more and more annoyed with him. What did he expect from her? She thought, she knew, they had grown closer during their hazardous expedition to find Seraphina. But now… all that seemed not to matter… at least not to Lu.

Kuon, whom they both had forgotten about, pushed in between them.

'Sit there, Kuon,' Lu said and pointed at his side. Lu's jaw tightened but he didn't say anything else.

Bree walked away from him. 'I'm going back to the others.' With a broken heart, she felt like adding, but he wouldn't care. He was going away with his Immortals, without declaring his love for her. She wouldn't tell him now that she loved him. She'd been correct all along. Lu wouldn't be able to conform to a new life. He wouldn't be able to take second place to her.

Lu went back to his quarters, not joining the others. How could he now? He hadn't wanted to hurt Bree, but he saw the pain in her eyes. After becoming closer to her during their quest to find Seraphina, he understood that she must feel he'd let her down, abandoned her, but he had to do what he thought best. He'd decided previously that he wouldn't rush a relationship between them. He'd vowed to give her more time to settle into her role of Triple Goddess.

Perhaps he should have explained. He didn't because he feared she would persuade him to do otherwise. She might even want to get married, like Seraphina. No, he couldn't say he thought she needed more time. He knew she would gainsay him. This was the best way—go on a quest with some of the Immortals. By the time he returned, they both would have had time to think about what they really wanted of their lives.

The truth was he hadn't thought of getting married. His life was one of action and quests. He lived for his men. Lu witnessed the change in Bearach now he was married. The big bear had mellowed. Faced with that, Lu wondered if he wanted to mellow. He also had witnessed Fionn and Grainne's marriage. Sometimes, all was not well between them.

If he married Bree, what would his life be like? He had accepted her as Triple Goddess but... he was uncertain how marriage to her would work. Truth be told, he'd rather face that raging demon than decide what to do about a relationship between him and Bree. Truth be told, he was going away as much for this reason as any other. Truth be told, his thoughts scared him... he, who had never been frightened.

Before Lu took his Immortals on their quest, a wedding was held in the reception room. Bree insisted that Seraphina and Bearach have another ceremony, given that

Seraphina was kidnapped straight after they'd been bound.

It was a small wedding held in the courtyard so that Hilde and Heremon, and Cythala could attend. Niamh brought all the fairies with her. The fairies made Seraphina's gown of diaphanous blue and green—the way fairies would design a gown. Seraphina was overjoyed with it.

Bree wore a gown of green velvet—a simple gown that flowed snugly over her body. She wore her mother's emerald necklace and ring, along with the Claddagh ring that her aunt had given her, and the triskelion given to her by Lu sat on the front of the gown. She almost didn't wear it. She hadn't spoken to Lu since he told her he wanted to go away. She didn't even know if he'd attend this ceremony, even though she thought he would, given Bearach was one of his warriors—one that Bree knew he was not taking on his quest. Bree was thankful for that. How cruel Lu would be to take Bearach away from his new wife.

For the binding ceremony, Bree wore the *dath an óir draiochta* golden cloak.

Lu arrived, with Kuon, Corraidhin and Cadeyrn. The other two treasures of the Tuatha Dé Danann—the stone beneath Bree's throne and the cauldron had also been moved to the courtyard.

As Bree intoned the words to bind the couple, her thoughts kept slipping to *what if...* This could have been her and Lu marrying... a double wedding. Instead, she spoke the words she was happy to speak, and bind the sister she loved to the man she adored.

After the ceremony, the celebrations began. Banners

sown with the triquetra and triskele patterns entwined with runes, fluttered in the bailey, minstrels played the *cruit*, a small harp, and a *clairseach*, a bigger harp with thirty strings, along with a *feadan* or fife.

Bree danced with some of the Immortals—Fionn, Diarmuid and Bearach. She had learned a few dances now. For the most part she was content to watch the others dance. She chatted to Áine, Niamh, Rhiannon and Airmid.

Lu sat to the side speaking with Padraig and some of the other Immortals, not all of whom Bree knew well. She couldn't prevent her gaze from straying to Lu. She still felt angry with him, despairing that they would ever join together.

Bree didn't notice Lu move and sit down next to her. Her attention had been on Niamh, who was talking about the various properties of fairy dust. She sensed someone at her side and turned.

'Are we to part in anger?' Lu asked.

Bree stared at him, and couldn't define what she felt. 'Are you angry with me, Lu?'

'No, I'm not.' He sighed. 'Are you cross with me?'

'Why should I be?' She refused to tell him he'd broken her heart.

'I see you're wearing the triskelion I gave you.' Lu lowered his voice.

'I thought it would be nice to wear it for Seraphina's wedding. A *wedding* is special.'

'I know, it is.' Lu lowered his head.

'Do you want it back?' Bree asked.

'No, I do not.' Lu sighed again. 'I'm going away in the morning.'

Kuon put his head on Bree's lap.

'He'll miss you,' Lu murmured.

Bree gazed down at the enormous dog, and patted his head. 'I'll miss him too.'

Lu wanted to ask if she would miss him, but he didn't. 'We won't be gone long.'

'How long?'

'A few months.'

'I see.' Bree couldn't bear this any longer. She wished he would go now! Lu stared at her with those blue eyes that were hard to resist.

'Will you come and see us leave in the morning.'

'I don't think so,' Bree murmured. 'I'll wish you well now.' She patted Kuon. 'You too, you hairy hound.'

Lu rose and moved away. He left the celebrations, with Kuon following him. Kuon gazed back and barked. Lu kept his gaze forward.

That night, sleep didn't come easily to Bree. After staring at the ceiling for hours, she threw back the bed cover, trying not to disturb Niamh on the pillow next to hers, and walked to the window. She pulled the drape aside and stared out into the night. A gibbous moon shone, casting some silvery light on the trees, but Bree couldn't see anything else.

Her thoughts claimed her concentration. Anger... no, not anger, annoyance still charged through her body when she thought of Lu. She loved him, but she had to come to accept the fact they would never be together. He would always have some task to do, or quest to go on with his men. Bree felt no rancour to the Immortals, but they would always come before her.

In any case, she was young. She had years to decide if she wanted to marry him, or marry anyone. She huffed out a breath. Of course, she wanted to marry Lu, but it probably would never happen. She wasn't too young. Seraphina had married Bearach. Seraphina was her twin.

But would a marriage between herself and Lu work? She wasn't going to find out any time soon.

Bree jumped, startled, when Niamh flew over to her.

'Are you all right, my lady?' Niamh asked, her circlet askew on her short blonde hair.

'Yes, and no. I can't sleep.'

'Should I wake Sorcha? She could fetch you a drink?'

'No, I can get myself a drink.'

'I could sprinkle some fairy dust… some sleep dust.'

Bree smiled. 'Perhaps.'

This time, both Bree and Niamh were startled when something flew at the window and hit it. In that second, when she stared at the glass panelled window, Bree caught a glimpse of a large black bird. Mór's raven!

As they watched, the raven disintegrated, and a ghoulish white face appeared.

'Mór…' Bree said on a breath. 'A thought projection.'

Niamh gasped, and when she spoke her words trembled. 'What does it mean, my lady?'

'It means she's still alive.'

The evil face dissolved, but not before it laughed, a

manical sound that sent a shiver through Bree's body. Mór was alive and Bree would have to confront her another day.

Find out what happens next in *Beneath The Mist*, book 2 in The Triple Goddess series.
Buy Now

Also by Ellen Read

The Triple Goddess

The Ancient Fire

Beneath The Mist

MORE FROM SERENADE PUBLISHING

Songbird

By Sarah Williams

The Outback Governess

By Sarah Williams

Brigadier Station Series

By Sarah Williams:

The Brothers of Brigadier Station

The Sky over Brigadier Station

The Legacies of Brigadier Station

Christmas at Brigadier Station

Heart of the Hinterland Series

By Sarah Williams:

The Dairy Farmer's Daughter

Their Perfect Blend

Beyond the Barre

The Spring of Love Series

By Virginia Taylor

Forever Delighted

Forever Amused

Forever Heartfelt

The Tooth Fairy Chronicles

By Victoria Rocus

Tooth Decay With A Side Of Fae

Toothaches And Wedding Cakes

Baby Tooth And Tangled Roots

Wisdom Tooth And The Awful Truth

A New Page

by Aimee MacRae

It Happened in Paris

by Michelle Beesley

The Bondi Bubble

by Megan Krolik

The Love Healer

By A.K. Leigh

For more information visit:

www.serenadepublishing.com

About the Author

Multi Award Winning author, Ellen Read, is the author of The Thornton Mysteries – cosy murder mysteries set in Australia. Ellen also writes ghost stories and thrillers. Her latest book is a fantasy, based on the Triple Goddess of Celtic mythology.

When she's not writing, she's reading, painting or taking photographs.

Ellen loves to read fiction, non-fiction, and poetry. She particularly loves history and stories of ancient myths and legends. Authors such as Robert Graves, Mary Stewart, Edgar Allan Poe, Agatha Christie, and Victoria Holt have influenced her work.

www.ellenread.com

ACKNOWLEDGMENTS

My special thanks go to my husband, Eric Read, for his constant support, proof-reading and for listening to me regale him with my stories.

My heartfelt thanks go to ARC readers.

I'd like to thank my wonderful friends and supporters on Instagram and Facebook.